THE GLITTERING WORLD

Alora's Tear, Volume V

NATHAN BARHAM

BARHAM INK
MOSCOW IDAHO USA

Edited by Zoë Markham
markhamcorrect.com

Cover illustration, layout, and map by Isis Sousa
www.artstation.com/isissousa

All characters and events in this book are fictitious.

All resemblance to persons living or dead is coincidental.

ISBN-13: 979-8-218-82565-2

Published by Barham Ink: barhamink.com

Ordering Information:

Quantity sales. Special discounts are available on quantity purchases by corporations, associations, and others. For details, contact the publisher at the address above.

Orders by U.S. trade bookstores and wholesalers, please contact In-gramsSpark: www.ingramspark.com.

Table of Contents

For Dad,
because we fathers know that we must
never stop trying,
no matter what.

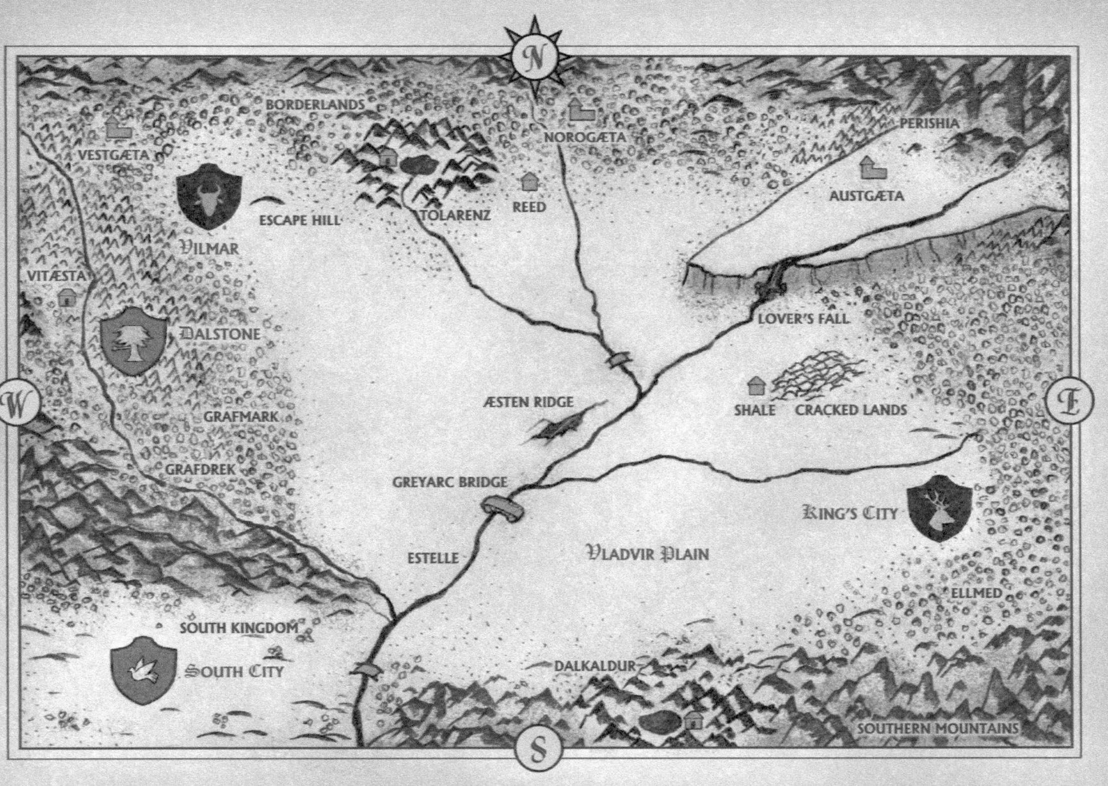

N
W
E
S
BORDERLANDS
VESTGÆTA
NOROGÆTA
PERISHIA
ESCAPE HILL
TOLARENZ
REED
AUSTGÆTA
VILMAR
VITÆSTA
LOVER'S FALL
DALSTONE
ÆSTEN RIDGE
SHALE
CRACKED LANDS
GRAFMARK
GREYARC BRIDGE
KING'S CITY
GRAFDREK
ESTELLE
VLADVIR PLAIN
SOUTH KINGDOM
ELLMED
SOUTH CITY
DALKALDUR
SOUTHERN MOUNTAINS

THE GLITTERING WORLD

CHAPTER ONE
Restless

The moon scowled purple through thick gouts of smoke. Into the sky they poured their choking fumes, smothering the hillside, the trees, the mountain itself. Beneath it all—flames—a sullen orange line that deepened into a pulsing smolder of crimson. An animal shriek lanced through the night, for a moment clear and present, racing ahead in terrorized flight. It echoed ever fainter, swallowed by the haze, and fell silent. The great blackened lunar eye glared on, over river and grass and all of the wide plateau.

Askon walked the familiar ribbon of river, its waters rippling, twisting—for once not silver in the night's light but smudged sanguine and ochre, obscene shapes roiling and lurid on its surface. He checked his stride, almost turned to meet the suffocating malice of the moon. Almost.

Instead, he blinked hard and felt the cold sharp edges of the thing he carried, felt its facets, imperfect as they were and perfect as they were. The space of a breath had him squeezing through pain until, fingers lined with blood, he tucked it back inside his cloak; a tattered wrapping for a broken thing. Behind him the fire raged, for a moment dimming the moonlight and washing the clouds in yellow-gray and veiny black.

Askon felt the wind's hot breath against his face, heard it rush over his ears and howl down the river. He took a step, felt his back grow warm, took another, the blaze so bright it seemed to set the stream itself aflame.

Now he was running. Panting against the wind, pelting over stony bank and sparkling grass. His cloak whipped behind him, hands red with blood, lungs burning; he ran though he had nothing and no one, only the moon, and the fire, and the river unending.

A loose stone turned underfoot and his legs gave way. He was crawling now, scrabbling, clawing wildly as the smoke engulfed him. The wind roared, the flames lapped like waves, like tide.

Then the world grew still. A silence fell upon him, all the deeper for its contrast to the inferno. He stood, his last breath searing his insides like light and flame and fear. Had he not felt smooth stone under his feet, he'd have been certain of his own death, certain the fire had taken him. Instead, he stepped forward, slow and silent. He dared not look back, walking on and on, the world turning, rolling, spinning beneath him. He traveled a thousand miles in a step, a thousand thousand in ten, and finally stood at the edge of it all, where the water leapt into the sky and fell uncountable miles more.

There, far below the pool of stars and glittering mist, was Thomas. He lay empty-eyed and dead. Broken and pleading.

Bound and struggling. Beating the doors of his cell. Cast there, neither furious nor stoic, staring up through the ceiling into watchful half-elven eyes—one green and one brilliant blue.

Askon flung himself over the edge into darkness.

They were both awake already, his sister and the shell that had once been Thomas's wife. And now so was he. He shook the dream fog away, trying to forget his friend's face. But whether he closed his eyes or opened them, it stared back in all its forms at once.

"A dream?" asked Líana quietly.

Askon nodded and turned his gaze on Elise. She hunkered, rocking forward and back, arms encircling her knees, staring through her curtain of black hair down at the lights spread across the caldera.

"We'll find him," Askon said.

The rocking stopped. She rose, made a determined effort forward, lost her footing, fell.

"She won't rest," Líana said, her eyes sad. "She wakes as soon as sleep dares to take her. I can't help."

Askon rubbed his face with his hands, another effort to clear the dream. Far below, the lights dimmed as the horizon grew gray in advance of the sunrise. They'd stumbled down the slope as far as they could, toward Dalkaldur. At the summit, the sea of lights on every side had been overwhelming. He couldn't decide where to go or how to get there. The lighted spike in the distance, a tower of some sort, almost certainly the High Spire Thomas had seen in his last vision, was too far. So they had turned instead to the caldera where the lights were fewer, reachable in a matter of hours.

But Elise couldn't see in the night over the pathless stones, couldn't navigate trackless forest. And though there were many lights, they were far away and often obscured by the susurrating trees. They'd slept in turns, Askon and Líana, waiting out the morning. Elise had barely spoken.

Now she lay against a fallen log, eyelids aquiver, squirming fitfully. She murmured something that sounded nothing like her husband's name—though Askon knew it was. With a final pained clenching, her limbs hung limp, and a shallow shuddering breath carried her into restless sleep.

Askon opened his mouth to speak, saw the glare in his sister's eyes—one blue and one green, the opposite of his own—and chose instead to keep his thoughts to himself. As Líana watched Elise, Askon wondered if she too was thinking of the man she'd left behind: of Edward.

The stifled words careened through his mind while he waited. Where would they go? How would they even begin to search for Thomas if he could be anywhere in the sea of lights they had seen from the summit? The Spire made the most sense, but it was so distant, so tall besides, and likely guarded as heavily as he dared imagine. He thought of Brâghda and the words Elise was always repeating: "The world is how it is."

And true as that might have been, as Askon watched the sun rising on the Glittering World, the home of the Elves, of his people, he faced the maddening incompleteness of the Norill belief. "The world is how it is," he muttered to himself, "but which world? And which how?"

By the time Elise gasped awake, eyes red-rimmed and wild, arms flailing over leaves and fern and soft earth, daylight had come. Before them, at the edge of the densely clustered firs, Dalkaldur revealed itself. The ancient keep hunkered in the east, entangled in fingers of cloud which spread out over a village of rooftops poking adventurously above the fog. All the way down to the lakeside the fingers stretched until the clouds unfurled over the water, leaving the shimmering surface free to mirror a yawning silver sky.

But it was the western shore that stole his breath.

Thrust up against the water's edge stood a domed structure that glowed blue all along the roofline of its outermost ring. Sheer walls, smooth and somehow soft, wrapped its sides—though from this distance Askon could not tell what material might have been used in their construction. He was reminded briefly of the polished bar at the Bones n' Stones in Finnestre, and imagined an edifice molded from a single unbreaking piece of dark hardwood. Scattered around the building were smaller structures that marched off toward the edge of the caldera. From the rim of that high ridge, a pair of snaking lines twisted their way down, here and there sparking with bright flashes that disappeared behind the dome.

The eerie circular glow had held steady for the better part of the night but from time to time faded and pulsed on an interval

Askon was unable to determine. At one point during his watch, he'd thought the light altogether extinguished. It went dark for a quarter of an hour before flickering weakly to life, faltering, and failing again, only to repeat a similar pattern several times before it stabilized. Now it simply glowed, constant and ethereal as the sunrise overtaking the valley.

Líana had made her way to Elise. She knelt, lifting her friend's head from the damp ground and letting it rest in her lap. She stroked the straight black hair away from a forehead beaded with sweat.

"These furs are too much here," Líana said softly, releasing the toggles on her coat, careful not to disturb their sleeping friend. "We might have to leave them behind. Something tells me it's going to be much warmer than we expected in the Cold Valley."

Askon stared over the foothills of Dalkaldur and across the water at the dim blue of the dome. "Heavy furs would certainly draw attention. There's no snow, no frost even. It's as though we opened a winter door and stepped directly into spring."

"And that's the most familiar difference."

Hours later, with the sun nearing the center of a wide sky, the three of them slipped into a flimsy outbuilding a few hundred feet from the glowing dome. With a last wary glance, Líana snapped the door shut, stirring a cloud of cobwebbed dust that filtered through thin slices of daylight.

Askon disentangled himself from the assemblage of arms and legs that had of late been Elise. After she'd awoken on the hillside, stumbled half the distance to the lake, and fallen—wordless and murmuring—to her knees, they'd taken it in uneven turns to carry her more than a mile to the weatherworn shed where they now rested. For the moment, Elise slept soundly against a stack of small earthenware pots lining the far wall's wooden slats.

"Can we leave the furs now?" Líana asked, her voice practically pleading—becoming for a moment the girl of eleven that she ought to have been if not for the tragedy in Tolarenz. "I know you hate suffering the heat. Back home you'd have left them at the roadside by now."

He smiled. "And thinking all the while of Mother's disapproval."

Líana lifted her head, arranging her face in an exaggerated frown. "What can be worn has no right to be wasted."

Askon mirrored the frown. "So you keep that skirt clean, young lady," he said, a grin forcing the feigned expression away.

With a muffled laugh Líana pulled her long blond braid over one shoulder, running her hands slowly down, squeezing the midpoint for a moment before letting her hands fall into her lap. "I hated when she called me that: young lady. And now what am I but that? Exactly that."

Askon tried to interrupt, to stop her, to remind her of where they'd been, what they'd seen since she and Edward had set out from King's City, of all she had become, but she was already talking.

"I arrive at the scheduled time. I entertain their insipid conversations. I hunt, when they let me. I sit in a chair next to Edward—

for hours sometimes." She stared into the dusty corner, an amused smirk flickering over her lips. "He tries. He tells them I can do as I will. And still they whisper, about the 'elf-wife' and their secret plans to undo the marriage when 'the young king tires of his little exotic.' They have a list… Of suitable replacements." She gripped the braid again, and the smirk soured. "I hear them, because when I stay, I've nothing better to do than listen. Perhaps I should have listened to *her* more often, been more of a lady." She thumped a fist against the wall. "Perhaps then I could—"

She tilted her head and put out the other hand, the braid falling loosely to her side. "Did you hear that?" she mouthed, pointing at the door.

Askon kept perfectly still, holding his breath. Heavy footfalls sounded outside. Líana spun and pressed her face against the boards. As she peered through the gap, she waved him over.

Along the path in the grass, a huge Norill lumbered toward the shed. Over one rag-wrapped shoulder it carried a pickaxe while the other hand dragged a second weapon through the dirt by a long wooden haft.

Askon drew his sword. Líana's already glimmered in the slanting light.

CHAPTER TWO
Dalkaldur Park

Líana had fallen back to the rear of the shed where Elise lay. The curved blade of her sword shimmered as she crouched, waiting. Askon positioned himself at the opposite end, next to the door, ready to slam it shut after the Norill entered. A dull scrape sounded, and a *thunk* as the long haft contacted the outer wall. Askon raised his weapon until it stood vertical, only inches from his face.

The door creaked open.

Líana recoiled, momentarily blinded by the morning light reflecting off the lake. She shielded her eyes with her right hand, sword level in her left. The Norill retrieved its second weapon and stumped through.

After a few shuffling steps, the door closed behind the creature with a brittle *clack*. Askon stood ready to block the exit should the Norill attempt an escape. When no reaction came, Líana rose, wary and slow. "We mean you no harm," said the voice like water.

The Norill, easily six feet tall, enormous for its kind, slapped its meaty lips together and snuffed a long breath. It dropped the pickaxe, letting the handle come to rest against a table on one side of the shed. The second weapon arced across the dirt floor and clattered against the axe.

"A shovel?" Askon said, bewildered.

But the huge creature didn't respond. It simply stretched its long limbs as far as the little building would allow and stepped forward. Líana lowered herself again, ready to strike, but the Norill pawed her out of its way as one might slide a jar to one side of a cupboard when another needs retrieving further back. Líana lost her footing and stumbled into the stack of pots. Askon stepped forward, but the creature showed no sign of further attack. It moved forward again—and in the same curiously gentle motion— pushed Elise out of its way. At least it attempted to do so, but she was wedged against the pots and only now rousing from sleep. The Norill grunted, snuffling again. Líana scrambled to her feet, and both she and Askon drew back their blades, readying for a lunge.

With a last rumbling sound deep in its chest, the Norill scooped up Elise, slinging her over its shoulder like so many potatoes in a sack, and flopped her onto the table where it had stowed the pickaxe and shovel.

"Stop!" Askon shouted.

"Do you understand us?" Líana said slowly. "Stop."

But the Norill did not stop. It rummaged past the pots into one corner, lifted a bag, sniffed it, seemed pleased with whatever it found, then turned to face them both.

"Please listen," Askon said levelly. "We don't mean you any harm."

He barely had the chance to finish the last word before he ducked to one side, the burlap bag sailing over his head and colliding with the wall near the door. Askon's sword flashed down as the Norill scooped up its own weapons, but it was too big and slow; Askon's stroke would take its right hand. He braced for the impact, and met cold steel instead.

Effortlessly, Líana spun Askon's sword aside and gripped his forearm.

"Wait," she breathed.

Flicking its wrist, the Norill thumped the pickaxe hard into the dirt. A garden spider the size of a small rodent skittered over the floor and up the wall where the broad-bladed shovel ended its flight, shaking the whole structure and sending a shower of dust down upon them. With a satisfied snort, the Norill shouldered both axe and shovel, snatched up the bag, and lumbered out into the brilliant daylight. There, it followed the path to a fork that led off toward the other outbuildings that surrounded the huge dome with its sheer walls and glowing outer ring.

"There are more gentle ways to wake someone," Elise rasped, sitting up on the rickety table. "You might have used one before letting a stranger manhandle me." She rubbed her forehead and eyes with her fingertips, blinking a bit in the settling dust before flicking the toggles free on her furs. "It's hot. Damned hot. What the hell was that all about?"

Askon shook his head. "I don't know."

"You don't know," Elise repeated. "That's quite the ride for a girl to have taken, and all the great protector can say is 'I don't know.'" She slipped the furs off one shoulder, then the other, tossed them onto the table, and duplicated the process with the heavy leggings. Beneath it all, her clothes were damp with sweat. "You could have gotten me out of those sooner."

Líana grinned, nodding in Askon's direction. "He wouldn't hear of it. Said we needed to keep moving, that we'd find a place to stow them, that we might need them again." A moment later, she had wriggled free of her own furs and leaned against the table next to Elise, the two of them billowing the collars of their shirts to circulate the heat away.

"Has he gone dense?" Elise asked. "Why are you just standing there? At least get out of your own furs so we can decide what to do next."

Askon looked again at the door where the Norill had marched off out of sight, then to Elise who had begun unabashedly adjusting the rest of her clothing, and abruptly turned away.

"Not this again," Elise said with an exasperated sigh. "Would you hide your face in the corner if I were John or Edward? There are still two layers between your gentlemanly honor and my comfort."

Askon stayed where he was. He pulled off the leggings, hung his cloak on a peg near the door, and said, "How is it that you go from unconscious to lecturing me in the space of a breath?"

Elise shrugged, her mouth pressing into a thin line. "Apparently being slapped onto a table by a six-and-a-half foot Norill will do that to a person. Why didn't you stop her?"

"Her?" Líana asked.

Nodding, Elise waved a hand loosely in the direction of the door. "Yes, her. It's not always simple to say with them, especially considering what she was wearing, but I've a fair enough idea to make a reasonable guess."

"Either way, she wouldn't respond," Askon said, turning back to them. "We spoke clearly, shouted, drew weapons, and—"

"Nothing," Líana finished. "Not even a sideward glance. Askon would have severed one of her hands over a spider had I not stopped him. Even the clash of our weapons didn't distract her at all. It was as if we didn't exist."

Elise grabbed one of the little pots from its place on the stack and whipped it across the room. "Catch!" she shouted.

Askon's attempt was earnest if not successful. He managed to get a finger on the rim of the pot as it whisked by, spinning it dizzily before it struck the wall and shattered.

"Broken pot says we exist. So that rules that out." Elise dusted off her hands, crossed her arms, and waited. When nothing more than a giggle from Líana was forthcoming, she grabbed another pot. "Do you think a second one might rouse him?"

"Alright, stop!" Askon said, more forcefully than he had intended. But, before he could apologize, the second pot struck him square in the chest.

"Don't tell me to stop," Elise snapped, her voice a wolfish growl. "You are the one who brought us here. You are the one who had the grand realization in the snow. You sent away John and Edward. You dragged us to the middle of a wasteland only to let Thomas be taken!" By the last, she was shouting, her pale complexion red. She slid from her seat on the table's edge, took a step toward him, and raised her wrist. "Remember that I carry the —"

She stopped. And any thoughts the others might have had stopped as well. The gem in the bracelet was black save for a tiny sliver of crimson glowing weakly as if from far away. The Death fragment was not a roaring flame as they all expected but a spent ember.

Líana leapt to her side, placing a hand on Elise's shoulder. For a moment Elise allowed it, then brushed it away and took a few unsteady breaths. As she relaxed, the Death fragment's light grew until the entire surface of the gem pulsed its usual heartbeat rhythm.

"They don't work the same here," Askon said when Elise seemed to have regained what limited composure she might. "Or they don't work at all. I can't be sure."

"We're also carrying all of them now," Líana added. "Back in Vladvir we had our own fragments. They had power, and that power shifted and changed depending upon whether they were together or apart." She held out Space and Life and gestured not only to Elise's red-gemmed bracelet, but its counterpart on the opposite wrist with its curious mechanical enclosure.

Askon stared at his hands, rubbing them together slowly, stretching the fingers one by one. "You're right. They work differently—or not at all—in combination. But it's not *just* that. On our way down from the ridge, while the two of you were sleeping, I tested the Time fragment—alone. It doesn't behave the same way here. Something's wrong."

Elise had retreated back to the table. She sat cross-legged, rotating the clicking clasp on Thomas's bracelet back and forth. "They weren't behaving properly, even in Vladvir." She didn't look up. "They aided us in traveling here at least. We'll have to get along with them in whatever capacity they'll present to us for now."

A gust of wind whistled through the shed, stirring the dust again. Askon covered his face against the grit and peered through the slats. Outside, the sun was high and warm—much warmer than it would have been in Tolarenz at that time of year. Another curious detail had occurred to him as well: since they had first arrived, the weather had cycled quickly, clouds blowing in and out with the fickle wind. Though they had seen no rain as of yet, within an hour they might see warm sun, chilly wind, and thick blankets of cloud cover. Squinting through the gap in the boards, Askon watched a pale shadow spread over the lakeside and climb the wall of the domed building.

"Why are we hiding?" he asked, turning from the wall to face them. "If we've truly come to the Glittering World, wouldn't we be best served to simply ask for help? Isn't that exactly what Caled and Morrowmen did all those years ago?"

Líana billowed the neck of her shirt again and smiled to herself. "He told the story so powerfully, like he'd only just seen it happen." She made a fist, tilting the Life fragment's purple stone through the thin bands of light. "I miss him. He wasn't always kind, but he always meant to help."

Askon imagined the old man's walking stick whistling through the air, ready to strike him for some perceived foolishness, but of course, it never came. "If he were here, I wonder what he would tell us to do."

With a frown, Elise reached back to scratch between her shoulder blades then down to her knee, where she readjusted the stiff leggings she'd worn beneath the furs. "Well, Morrowmen wasn't in the Glittering World when they called for help," she said. "The Elves came to Vladvir for their own reasons—reasons we may never know. Now we've come to them." She gestured to herself. "And we certainly don't look the part of emissaries or respectable representatives of any kind. Who would listen to us looking like this?"

"She has a point, Askon," Líana said. "We're days out from Finnestre, through a fight, and hours carrying Elise through a much warmer day than any of us expected. We need a chance to refresh. The lake is right there, and there's plenty of daylight to dry our things. We'll wash, get some of the road's grime off ourselves and our clothes. At the least, it will give us time to plan our next move."

Askon felt himself forming an argument, would have spoken it, but Líana cut him off.

"Elise could use the rest anyway," she said. "We've only just gotten her back."

"One way or another," Elise added, "I'm here to find Thomas. To do that we'll have to find people who will talk to us. Three sweat-stained, weather-beaten vagrants are likely to draw more attention than if we clean up a bit."

"Let's go," Líana said, "while the sun is out."

Askon floated on his back, staring into the sky. The lapping water at the lake's edge gently disturbed the silence, lulling him into a sort of half sleep in which he felt every ripple over his arms and legs while his mind wandered somewhere above, somewhere in that sky, those clouds. He remembered what it had been like to float down through them; to see her face—Alora's face—fearful as she ran; to see her fall after turning her ankle; to see her body go rigid as the strange weapon from this world struck her, just as it had struck Líana on the Greyarc bridge.

He stood, the water line level with his chest, and shook the thought away. A spray of droplets sparkled through the air and scattered over the surface. Wading back to the shore, he wrung a few more drops from his hair, much as he had earlier wrung out his clothes before setting them to dry upon the rocks. Now he climbed the same rocks and lay himself out to dry in the sun. After a moment he reached for his trousers, found them still damp, turned them over, and tried to remember the sky.

A dozen long, slow breaths later, with the sun's rays warm on his body, he heard Líana and Elise talking and laughing through their own bath on the other side of the rocky outcropping. He chuckled to himself, recalling their time in South City: the practical joke the women had played, and Edward's unfailing confidence, even in the face of striding stark naked through an unfamiliar palace. Askon sighed, feeling the sharp absence where, in the same memory, a nervous Thomas had stood, resolved to follow the then prince of Vladvir in this strange, new—and entirely invented—custom.

Under the midmorning sun of the Glittering World, Elise had been against separating, had given another lecture on Norill culture and their lack of taboos regarding nakedness. But Askon wouldn't hear of it; Elise was his friend's wife, and Líana not only that but his sister. He found the whole premise preposterous, but there was no use in arguing. When they'd spied the rock formation and found it suitable for quickly drying their clothes, he'd marched directly to the opposite side the instant Elise began to unlace her boots.

After another few moments of muffled chatter, he heard the slap and patter of them climbing out of the lake and onto the warm flat stones. Then came a gasp followed by the noisy splash of one of them falling back into the water. He grumbled to himself. There wasn't time for this. Elise of all people should know better.

"Stop right there!" a man's voice shouted.

Askon sat up, made a vain attempt to cover himself, looked around for the source of the command, and saw no one.

"I said, stay where you are," came the voice again, stern and gruff, a voice accustomed to authority. "This is public property. You can't do that here."

The echoing stones had confused him at first, but now Askon was sure the sound had come from Elise and Líana's side. He grabbed his not-entirely-dry trousers, struggling to tug them over his not-entirely-dry feet. He didn't bother with shirt or boots but snatched his long hunting knife from its sheath and climbed ledge after ledge, his chest low to the ground.

"It's two girls," said a second voice, softer, a woman's. "Don't give me that look. I should have you reported for that look."

Askon made his way to the top of the formation and peered over the edge. Just up from the shore stood two figures in dark uniforms with the familiar glass visors they'd seen on the Greyarc bridge, at the Bones n' Stones, and in the vision of Dalkaldur. The smaller of the two put out a hand, palm first, to the other.

"You stay up here," said the woman's voice. "Probably just a bit of youthful adventure. I'll handle it."

She turned away, heading toward the water's edge. The other figure stepped forward. He cleared his throat. "What if it's—"

"You're not following me down there to lecture two women who decided to go for a naked swim in the lake." She pulled off her helm and set it on the ground, revealing dark skin, close-cropped hair, and pointed ears overset by a dull metallic circlet. "They'll be embarrassed as it is, I'm sure. And you've seen enough." At her hip, Askon saw a black shape, the same weapon the soldiers had used on Alora.

The man turned away, crossing his arms in the process. The woman headed down to the water where Askon could see Líana waiting in the shoulder-deep lake water. Elise, he could not see, save for a soft shadow spread out over the rocks. It shifted slightly, but made no other move. The dark-skinned woman put her hand out in the same gesture she'd given her partner, the other hand dropped to the weapon at her side. Askon tensed for a spring. If he could get behind her, he might use her to shield himself from any attack by the man in the visored helm.

"Ladies," the woman said gently. "Now just stay calm and—"

"Don't come any closer," Elise snapped, her voice low. Askon couldn't tell whether she meant it to sound threatened or threatening.

The woman popped open the buckle on her weapon's sheath. "Careful. That kind of talk won't get you anywhere." She stopped her advance. "Now I'm sure you two thought this would be all manner of fun and excitement to try. And I certainly won't be making any comments on who you spend those exciting times with, so long as you spend them in a private residence and not in broad daylight in Dalkaldur Park. The law doesn't make exceptions for anyone in this respect, regardless of how pretty they might find each other."

"Oh!" said Líana, sinking a bit further into the water. "We aren't, we weren't—"

"Doesn't matter," the woman said with a wave of her free hand. "Can't have the two of you out here like this, in nothing more than your skins."

Elise's shadow shifted, lowering itself slowly, reaching out for something.

"Now hold on there," the woman said firmly, her voice growing tense and strained. She drew her weapon. "I didn't have you raise your hands before, to save you the embarrassment, but I'm not above asking if the situation calls for it." She leveled the weapon. "Do not reach for anything just yet."

The man in the helm turned his head at the change in his partner's tone. Askon rocked forward, gripping the long knife so tightly its leather-wrapped handle creaked against his fingers.

"Stand back up," said the woman. "And it's alright to cover up. Just no sudden movements."

Elise's shadow rose and moved forward; one step, then another. Her head and bare shoulders emerged from where she had been obscured from Askon's view by the rock. And there she stopped. To her right, he saw the gleam of her sword, hidden in the shadow of the stony step, next to her drying clothes. She put her hands on her hips as the woman's searching gaze darted from the clothes to Líana to Elise and around the triangle again. The dull metal circlet glinted in the sun.

"Wow," the woman said, shaking her head and lowering the weapon. "Not a speck of modesty at all." She scanned the area once more. "I see that maybe this started innocently enough. Looks like one probably pushed the other in, considering the state of these clothes. Then the second jumped in after. Is that about right?"

Elise shrugged.

The woman glanced back at Líana—who had now sunk all the way to her chin—and affixed the clasp on her weapon again. "Alright. Dry off, even if it takes a little time, but then get those clothes back on. And keep them on. I don't want to see you two down here again. Or anywhere else! You hear me?"

Elise neither moved nor spoke.

"Yes. Yes we do!" Líana called. "We hear you."

"You won't see us again," Elise said.

At that, the woman seemed pleased. She took a backward step or two. "We'll come through here again a bit later, my partner and I. My advice? Be somewhere else."

Turning on her heel, the woman walked back up to the other soldier, gathered her helm, and slung it under one arm. She mumbled something to him, and he glanced down at the water where Líana and Elise had disappeared from view. The woman gave him a disgusted shove up the hill. Askon breathed a relieved sigh, watching them go before he scrambled over the rock formation to collect his own clothes and the rest of his gear.

CHAPTER THREE

Unfamiliar Territory

"We can't afford any more encounters like that," Askon was saying. They'd retreated to a shady place once their clothes were dry and before the afternoon heat had a chance to undo the efforts of their bathing. "Those guards might have known to be looking for us. They could be working for the group who took Thomas—for Sehlín."

"Or they could be no one," Elise responded curtly. "If we're in the Glittering World, it stands to reason that there'd be any number of powerful people who could employ guardsmen."

"And women," Líana added. She'd been quiet since they'd regrouped.

"And women, it would seem," Elise said, nodding. "Apparently, here, one needn't be a man to be a guard. Perhaps the Norill and the Elves have more in common than I thought."

Askon's clothes were stiff and uncomfortable. He adjusted the shirt and began the process of attaching the leather pieces that completed his armor. "It was probably for the best that they only saw the two of you."

"Easy enough for you to say," Líana said, her cheeks reddening a bit. "Even in the water, I felt so exposed. So vulnerable." She shared a look with Elise, who gave a small understanding nod.

Askon's eyes narrowed. "If anything had happened, I would have—"

"Leaped down from the battlements to save us," Elise scoffed. "We know. You'd have fought them both off, barefoot and shirtless, I'm sure."

With a deepening frown, Askon pulled a leather strap tight and hooked it into place. "I've done it before," he said, with more certainty than he felt. "But I suppose you're right, considering their weapons and the fact that the Time fragment isn't responding."

"And even if it were," said Líana, "remember how unpredictable the fragments had become before we arrived here. We could hardly make use of them without exhausting ourselves."

"Or falling unconscious," Elise added.

"Regardless, we can't be so careless again," Askon said, lacing the final strap through its loop. "We'll have to find someone who will talk to us. Perhaps there's an inn or a tavern where we can coax some clues from the locals."

Elise pointed at the huge domed structure to the north. "That's as likely a place as any. A building of that size is bound to have plenty of people to talk to. Let's hope we're presentable enough that they'll listen, and reply, without us stirring up any suspicion."

"What do you think it is?" Líana asked. "It doesn't look like a keep or citadel, though it's certainly large enough to be one."

Askon traced the edges of the building with his eyes, followed its impossibly smooth outer surface, the ridges along the round sloping roof. "The guards called this place Dalkaldur Park. What do you think that means? Is that just what they call the area by the lakeside, or does it name a larger part of the valley?"

Elise rubbed her hands together, looking up the grassy rise toward the dome. "Maybe we can get someone to tell us. Though we'd probably do well to use the name to our advantage. At this point we know at least a few new things about this place: the Norill here treat us as if we're invisible; elves apparently *always* carry water to their private residences to bathe—waste of time in this heat if you ask me; and Askon still thinks he can single-handedly save us all, but I suppose that's the same as it is in Vladvir." She waved them forward.

"Let's find out if they watch the doors to that place as closely as they watch the shoreline."

An hour later, with a markedly cooler sun preparing its descent toward the crest of the caldera's ridge, they approached the path which led to a pair of tall wooden double doors on the domed structure's western side. The carefully swept cobblestones meandered between neatly clipped rows of roses sectioned by lines of silver-barked aspen on either side of the path. Askon could see two other such paths on his left and right with the same rows: roses and aspen, roses and aspen, until the paths passed into shadowed entryways where he presumed he'd find identical sets of wooden double doors. Between the paths, wide patches of clover unfurled like lush green carpet. The pattern appeared to repeat all the way around the western wall and was eventually eclipsed by the building itself.

Along the outer edges, the walls alternated from an opaque material, which Askon still could not identify, to clear frameless glass. With no border or seam of any kind, he wondered what Thomas might have said if he could have seen it, what the young father's analytical mind would have guessed about its construction. He wondered, too, if on the other side of those smooth walls Thomas waited in a cell like the one where they'd kept Alora—the white room and the dark—and he wondered if Sehlín would speak as kindly to this new captive or if they would proceed immediately to more violent means.

Askon tried to cast away the feeling and turned instead to Líana and Elise. Though he had tired of watching it some time earlier, their gazes were still transfixed by what was likely the greatest wonder of them all: the carriage system. On a regular interval they hummed along the lines, up or down the slope, crackling with energy as they went. They were roughly rectangular with metallic piping attached on either side of the thick cables that dangled from the ridgeline, high and distant, to a platform near one of the dome's entrance paths.

Once, a handful of passengers had stepped out from the carriage's sliding panel door, rising casually from upholstered seats, making their way out and onto the cobblestones. On the other occasions, however, the carriages had arrived, waited at the platform, and continued on until they were obscured by the tall smooth walls. Askon guessed that they made a circuit before returning to the platform, waiting, and fast as a falcon in flight, traveling back up the slope to the ridgetop. From there, he could only assume that they hummed along, over the ridge and down the other side to some faraway destination amid the Glittering World's unending sea of lights.

Líana tugged at Askon's cloak. "We've come this far. It's time to try for some answers." She pulled him along the pathway stones toward the massive double doors beyond.

"And what if we're not welcome?" he asked.

"Oh, you know perfectly well how you'll handle that," Elise said.

Halfway down the path, she halted, holding out a hand. "Over there," she whispered with a jerk of her head.

Kneeling at one of the many silver trunks was another large Norill. Nearly motionless and altogether silent, it might as well have been invisible, until now. With long slender fingers, it reached into a burlap bag and scattered a soil mixture around the base of the tree. Two more handfuls came from the bag in this fashion before the Norill gently pressed the newly laid soil flat and rocked back on its heels. A bee, which had hovered around the nearby roses, alighted on the creature's shoulder, broad and bare and gray in the westering sun. The cords of muscle twitched at the touch, but the insect didn't move. Without looking, the Norill lifted its hand above the bee and waited. After a long, slow breath, the hand lowered, allowing the insect time to climb the fingers and toward the wrist. Rotating in its crouch, the Norill lifted its hand high. The bee took flight. The Norill watched it go and turned its gaze on Askon.

At first Askon was unsure how to react. In Vladvir, the Norill they'd encountered from the Glittering World had acted very strangely; calm at first, almost expressionless. Then they began chanting that single word, *sors*, again and again until they became viciously, mercilessly hostile. However, with the eyes of this apparent gardener upon him, Askon remembered the eyes of another Norill: the one that had turned its own knife on itself at the top of the Æsten Ridge. With that silent, pained struggle in mind, Askon stepped forward with his hands held low, palms forward.

"Hello," Askon called.

The Norill stared past them.

"Un daiwan thén ten ahten," Elise said, her voice raspy and low, almost a growl.

Still staring as though it could see right through them, the Norill snuffed, breathed deeply, and returned to the burlap bag which it shouldered in a long swooping arc before lumbering through the roses and across the grass between the paths. It looked up and down the next row, settled on another aspen and turned its face to the western sky. A moment later, it knelt by the tree, scooping handfuls of dark earth and patting them firmly around the base of the trunk.

"What was that?" Líana asked, when it was clear the Norill would continue on as though they didn't exist.

"It's Norillésse: Norill language," Elise said. "But that's its name in our language. In theirs, it's called Obra'Ghân."

Askon sighed. "We assumed as much, that it was the Norill language. But what did you say to it?"

"Her," Elise replied with an arched eyebrow. "What did I say to *her?*"

"Fine. *Her.* I clearly can't tell," Askon said, crossing his arms.

Elise arched an eyebrow. "Honestly, for the Grafmark Norill, labeling gender isn't of all that much importance. In fact, one has to go out of one's way to identify it at all. There's just something about the way you say *it*, like she's not even a person."

"I'm sorry," Askon said. "A lifetime of training to the contrary, I suppose."

Elise placed a hand on his shoulder. "You must've had terrible teachers."

"But what *did* you say?" Líana asked.

"Good evening," Elise replied with a shrug. "Or a version of it, anyway. Roughly, 'May the dark times be good.'"

"And still we get no response," said Askon. He watched the Norill finish with the tree, rise, shoulder the bag, and move down the row. "Do you think they see us at all? Even if their language isn't the same as Brâghda's people, I would expect that they would attempt to reply in their own tongue."

"So would I," said Líana. "That's two of them now that wouldn't respond. I wonder…"

"If they can't?" Elise offered. Her expression dimmed, the hard line of her lips turning downward. Askon considered suggesting more, pursuing the mystery of these silently oblivious creatures, only to hold back. He could guess what had brought on that look. It was akin to the emotion he felt, though for her it was surely sharper, far more painful. Thomas would not only have had a suggestion, he would have had the answer.

Behind them, the smooth scrape and accompanying buzz of another carriage sounded. They turned to watch it glide along the thick metal cords which arced down from the ridgetop, blue sparks flashing as it went. In a moment it had whisked behind the building where it would pause to release its passengers and travel on to wherever its next destination might be. When their eyes returned to the path, the Norill was gone. They stood, the three of them, alone with the frisking leaves above and silent roses below.

Dry gravel popped under their feet as they stepped from cobblestone to smooth slate and shadow. The air in the archway felt unnaturally cold, as did the handles to the large double doors. Askon gripped the shiny brass levers and flung the doors wide— as if they weighed nothing at all. He stumbled backward and would have fallen, if not for Líana and Elise who propped him up just before his balance failed. Together, they gazed inside with wide eyes.

CHAPTER FOUR

Little Bird

Dansil busied himself with polishing the bar. How many times was it today? He dared not count. He'd spent enough time counting already. How many days had it been since they'd come through, upending his business and his life? He would have said it didn't matter, that they were long gone. But it *did* matter. Folk had died, a safe place had filled with vicious creatures without warning. People were afraid, and small towns—even if you can get them to forgive—never forget.

Of course, Finnestre likely wouldn't ever get the chance for the former. John of Dalstone, his half-elven friends, and all the rest had probably frozen to death looking for that godforsaken valley by now. Enough others had. He'd seen them pass through, not hundreds or even dozens, but every couple of seasons since the Bones n' Stones had gotten its footing, a handful of intrepid explorers would march into town asking questions, demanding supplies, hiking off into the mountains, never to be seen nor heard from again.

"Thinkin' about him again?" Flarah asked, emerging from the pantry with a crate of vegetables. She'd handled the minor repairs after the wreckage of the battle as efficiently as she handled anything, but he couldn't help but notice her looking over her shoulder more often. Too often.

Dansil faked a smile. "As the sun rises."

His hands came together, the fingers of his left twisting the ring on his right, feeling the grooves where the etchings crisscrossed and intertwined. He let them fall, grabbed the towel, snapped it out. At the end of the long wooden bar, a patron looked up dizzily from his glass. After a moment his eyes focused on Dansil.

"Feelin' alright there, my boy?" the man asked, scratching under his thick gray beard.

"Oh, and that beard!" Dansil muttered under his breath.

The old man lifted a hand to his ear. "Say again?"

Dansil snapped the towel out a second time, deftly catching either end in either hand and spinning its middle before setting it back on the bar. "I said," he spoke much louder now, "that storm's about here!"

The old man nodded sagely. "It'll be a barn-rattler, sure as sure," he said, and returned to his drink.

"You hated the beard," Flarah said with a chuckle.

"I hated the beard," said Dansil. He picked up the towel again.

Flarah, now finished with both crate and vegetables, snatched it away from him. "You keep scrubbing this bar, thinking of that great oaf of a man, and we'll have two problems: one, there won't be any bar left when you're done; and two, we'll have to start sell-ing seats for the nightly revival of the Tragedy of Dansil's Lament." She snapped the towel at his flank.

He jumped and sidled down the bar. "Alright, you win!" He put his hands up. "And anyway, that was a one-night performance. I'd had enough to drink that I'd be lucky to remember half the lyrics."

"Good," Flarah said. "Why don't you get outside and breathe a bit o' fresh air?" A sly half-smile inched its way across her face. "Varlen's daughter's been pacing up and down past the front porch all day, pretendin' she's got business at every building in town 'cept this one. Though, you'd never know it, the number o' times she goes by peering through the windows. Might do you good to have a little distract—"

"Tilda? I don't think that a girl—"

Flarah clacked a mug onto the bar. "I didn't say you had to carry her off to the hay bales. Just that it'd do you good to have a conversation with someone other than me, a third-cup customer, or your own imagination." She closed the gap between them and shooed him toward the outlet behind the bar, then with a resolute shove, to the doors beyond. "It'll be gettin' dark soon. If ya don't hurry, she'll give up an' go home."

Dansil rolled his eyes, took a breath, and transformed his face —starting with the brilliant smile and nonchalant eyes he knew had drawn Tilda to the Bones n' Stones in the first place. He turned back to Flarah.

"That's a terrible name, by the way: The Tragedy of whatever you said."

"Is it, now?"

He pushed open the door. The hinges creaked. "It is. I certainly don't *lament*. I'm going, but I expect a much better title when I get back."

"Whatever it takes to get you outta this tavern."

With a wink and a wave, he slipped out into the sunlight.

On the narrow porch, long shadows stretched out to his left, leading a slow glow of warmth that pressed itself against his right. He turned toward it, ran a hand through his sandy shock of hair and, squinting in the orange light, allowed the heat to sink through his shirt, down to the tight wrappings around his chest, and into his skin. He raised his arms, elongating himself, not unlike the shadows, and felt the sun seep through the fabric of his leggings into the joints and muscles. Arms aloft, he breathed deep, turned, leaned with his elbows against the railing, and let the sun warm the other side.

"Dansil?" chirped a reedy voice.

With rehearsed languorousness, he rotated his head this way and that, stretching the neck muscles, allowing the weight of his back and shoulders to rest a little more heavily on his arms.

"*Ahem*," coughed the little bird, regaining a bit of its composure. "Dansil? I—what a—I was just..."

"On an errand?" Dansil said, looking up from one side, not even really seeing her yet, but knowing that she was seeing him.

"Oh!" she said, as if so surprised she might have just startled herself. "How did you—"

He shifted to one elbow now and turned subtly toward her. When she came into focus, her tidy blue dress twitching lightly back and forth at her ankles, the dark careful curls—and where they carefully fell as she held her hands clasped low behind her back—he allowed a smile to sidle over his face and settle around his eyes like a slowly warming sun.

"A little bird told you?" she asked, with a smile to match his own.

Dansil laughed and there was no artifice in it, but still, a great deal of art. "Something along those lines," he said, standing and vaulting lightly over the rail to land only a short step away. At first she leaned back, as he expected she might, but after a half-caught breath she swayed toward him.

Smiling again, she looked up with eyes transfixed, her breathing rapid, though he was sure she didn't know it. A hesitation. "I was hoping, now that you're here, you might..."

But Dansil didn't hear the rest. He'd allowed his eyes to wander from hers to those dark curls, to her ear, then along the curve of her exposed collarbone, where his gaze halted.

Beyond the shifting slope of her shoulder, a much more literal bird alighted on the building across the way. Its blue-gray wings shouldn't even have caught his attention, indeed wouldn't have— nor any man's who could appreciate Tilda's gently bridling outline. But this wasn't the first time he'd seen this bird. Nor the second. He'd seen it first when John had arrived in town. They'd taken

Askon from the tavern to Flarah's after the fight was finished and the half-elf had blacked out.

"Where'd they come from, John?" Dansil asked as they carried Askon, unconscious, out of the Bones n' Stones. "And what's wrong with him?"

It was dark, and the moon cast the big man in a flattering light. His muscles flexed against Askon's weight but his face showed no strain. The marks of battle were still upon him. "Can't rightly say," he mumbled through that cursed snarl of beard. "Even if I could say for certain, it's all twisted up in a powerful-important secret."

"I know a thing or two about those," Dansil replied with eyes that whispered of a lakeside long ago. John looked away at that, as Dansil thought he might. "You can tell me. You know you can."

But he didn't. Instead, as they reached the house, John busied himself with the door, though Flarah was already waiting for them on the other side. With a sigh, Dansil tried to let it go…

…and had watched that bird flutter down to perch on the fencepost nearest the door.

"I mean, I'd be lying," Tilda was saying, "if I didn't tell you I've been a little curious…"

Dansil took a step forward, meaning to cross the street, and found the young woman much closer to him than she had been a moment before—found it by brushing his bicep over the sweep of her chest. She recoiled coyly, her lips parting in mock alarm. He hardly took notice at all, maintaining instead his focus on the bird. Tilda murmured something behind him then snapped to his side and laced her arm through his.

The second time he'd seen it had been the morning after the attack on the tavern.

"Oh, a great number o' things been troublin' the countryside these days." Without knowing it, John had let the spread of breakfast lull him into a general sense of comfort. And when John was comfortable, he talked.

"You've got yer ordinary bandits, o' course, a damned sight more Norill crawlin' here and there—though, if I get the time, I'll tell ya 'bout a turn I had in that particular corner of knowin'. Not all bad, the Norill, that is. Not all bad after all."

Askon still hadn't awoken. And, while they'd waited, Flarah had let her face communicate all the tender-hearted feelings she'd had for John's initially sulky but now predictably performative return. The woman's constant grimace had been ten shades of stay-away-from-him.

"And you'd think that'd be enough," John continued, "two battles, a third if ya count the attempted ambush in Grafmark, skirmishes up an' down the known corners of the world, thinkin' we'd lost people that we later found, and —"

"Maybe you should stop there," said one of the others. Dansil couldn't remember which, maybe the pretty half-elf sister?

"I'd like to know," Dansil said.

"I told you," John barked. "It's secret!" He rose, pushing his chair back, indeed nearly toppling it, before storming out onto the front porch. The others exchanged apologetic looks but did nothing to explain any further details. Flarah went on glaring as she had done since they arrived.

After an awkward moment that shifted the conversation to more mundane matters, Dansil slipped outside. When he opened the front door, John stood arms crossed, glaring into the sunrise as if he might intimidate it back below the horizon. Beyond him, either unmoving or recently returned, the bird perched, still as a stone, right where it had landed the night before.

"…and I thought we might make our way out to one of the trails that go up the hillside. Maybe bring something to eat, something to drink?" The request itself seemed half-hearted now, as if it knew it wouldn't receive even a remotely desirable reply.

"Dansil?"

She was still clinging to his arm, pawing at it almost. He turned to her, put his hands on either shoulder, squeezed gently. "I'm sorry," he said, consciously taking the time to wrest his eyes from the bird—and the memories—to make her feel noticed, if only for a small moment. "Another time, maybe. It was good to see you."

Tilda's face revealed her disappointment for no longer than it took Dansil to release her shoulders. "Oh, alright," she said, smoothing the expression away with a brush at one side of her curls, "I suppose… I'll just head home then."

"Didn't you have an errand here in town?" Dansil asked, immediately knowing the answer, but not knowing what else he might have said.

She looked back over her shoulder. "I did. But it'll keep."

He watched her walk away, fast enough not to linger, slow enough for him to know she would rather have stayed. When she'd rounded a corner and passed out of sight, he allowed his mind to return to the thoughts that had been calling to him all along.

On the peak of a neighboring building, the bird perched, staring down at him, its intelligent eyes fixed, as if considering whether it approved of how things had gone with Tilda, or if it could feasibly carry Dansil off. A chill rippled over him, afternoon sun or no, and it was then that he stopped thinking of it as a bird. Though it was small, this was a falcon, a predator, which made that unflinching gaze all the more unsettling. Dansil drew closer, admiring the creature for a moment. Sure enough, it was the same falcon that had accompanied John and his friends.

It took flight, like an arrow from a bowstring held taught for too long. Dansil did his best to follow. He watched it circle overhead, beat its wings once, twice, then dive into the fields behind the tavern, rising again in a flash with something in its talons. It alighted on the corner of the tavern roof, holding its catch, and once again stared down at him.

Dansil took a step toward it, then another. The falcon began to tear into its meal. When Dansil stopped, the bird stopped. When Dansil walked, the bird feasted. So Dansil kept walking until he stood almost directly beneath it. By that time, whatever the falcon had been ripping apart was all but entirely consumed. It took flight again, circled, and landed another couple of buildings to the north. Dansil followed it, trying his best to look like anything other than a person chasing a falcon through town. He assumed that those efforts weren't very effective.

They carried on in this fashion, predator and prey, until they reached the northern edge of Finnestre. Landing at last on a bent fencepost, the falcon stared coldly back at him, as it had for the entirety of their small journey, like a tiny feathered statue.

Dansil drew closer, within a few feet of the creature. It stared back. Now only a foot. It stared back. Now a few inches. An inch.

His fingers made contact, and the bird stared back. Half a heartbeat passed. Then the falcon took flight, circled once, and sped north on rapidly beating wings.

CHAPTER FIVE

On the Inside

No one spoke. Not Elise, not Líana, not Askon. They gaped.

The outside of the domed building had been a curious sight with its glowing ring and sheer, smooth walls of glass and stone, but what lay on the other side of the wide doors, Askon lacked the words to describe.

They entered on a balcony with curved staircases descending from either side. There was no ground floor, aside from several similar balconies all around the building's outermost circle, only a vast subfloor and the ceiling high above. Brass railing lined the stairs, and a thick stone ledge protected observers from a fall more than twice Askon's height. The tops of the ledges had been hewn with indentations deep enough to plant dark-leafed ivy that cascaded over the edge like a thick green waterfall.

Beyond the guardrail, the enormity and wonder of the hall revealed itself. Rising up from the floor below was a maze of shelving arranged in concentric circles. In Vilmar, the region of Vladvir that had been home to Iramov's family line for generations before the last of that name had burned his way from Tolarenz to South City with the Death fragment, wealthy landowners grew mazes like these out of hedgerows and held competitions wherein the victors were awarded prizes, entry to exclusive gatherings, or highly compensated positions within the household. Here though, the maze was made not of boxwood hedge but shelves, heavy hardwood of rich red-brown, filled with hundreds upon countless hundreds of books.

There were libraries in Vladvir, of course, but nothing like this, not even in the lavish palace of South City where resources abounded and Lord Apopsé had no reservations in displaying his wealth at every opportunity. Most were stuffy, dusty affairs where books moldered as often as were read, or where old men searched for accounts of stories many times told, only to find the truth less interesting than the embellished fictions they'd learned from their grandfathers—and further embellished on their own.

But this library was immense, easily larger than any collection he'd ever heard of by double, maybe even a factor of ten. He didn't bother to count the books, though he made an attempt at counting shelves before switching to whole bookcases. He'd reached fifty or so when movement tugged at the edge of his vision, a glimmer of brass, like the railing and the carriages outside. Almost silently it rose between the landings of two staircases, flashing reflected light from the dome above as it went. Askon followed it with his eyes until it disappeared into the dome itself. No, he realized. Not the dome, a floor, the first of another set of concentric circles that widened toward the center as they climbed.

The brass cage was another sort of carriage, a lift to the next story. Askon looked across to the lip of the first level. Upon it were more bookcases, more shelves, more books. Below, reaching down from each of the floors, cylindrical pillars of stone upheld the inner rings, three sets of them, rising higher the closer they came to the center. There, encircled by walls and dome and maze and pillars, sat the largest desk Askon had ever seen—indeed larger than the bar at any number of taverns in Vladvir. And it was then that he knew where they were.

"This must be where she found *The Book of the Tear*," Askon said, his voice loud and uncouth in the quiet hall.

Elise rolled her eyes. "Well that seems obvious enough," she scoffed.

Líana put both hands on the stone ledge and leaned over, looking down upon the shelves below. "And that," she pointed, almost giddily, beyond the pillars to the desk, "is where we find her friend Maerin—or was it Aeron?"

"Daeron," Elise corrected. "With any luck he'll know where they're keeping Thomas."

Askon approached the ledge, placing his hands on the cool stone. "It's a start, at least. The first step—"

"—always comes before the second," Líana finished, smiling. "Like Father used to say."

Askon smiled too. "Yes."

Elise already stood on the second step below them. She turned back, her dark eyes level, determined. "And the Norill say that caution is not the same as to refuse the beginning."

They followed her down the stairs.

By Askon's estimation, a quarter of an hour had passed before they reached the center of the main floor. At first, he'd been entranced by the rows upon rows of books, even taking a moment to remove a title or two from the shelves, to little benefit. Though gorgeously bound and meticulously maintained, he could make almost no sense of the words within. Written in letters that he knew, and generally with words he recognized, every paragraph, indeed every line, contained some smattering of terms he'd never encountered or phrases that simply meant nothing to him. This, and Elise's impatience to make their way through the shelves, kept him from any further efforts.

They emerged at the center, impatient, and somewhat disoriented. The symmetry of the dome's interior—the landings and stairways all around, the circles within circles, the precisely arranged support pillars—made it difficult to discern whether they had exited the maze in the direction they had intended or if the circuitous paths had led them further around to the rear of the building as they had perceived it upon entering. The nature of the light beneath the dome compounded the problem. All the shadows, what shadows there were, traveled outward from the center. Some trick of the building's construction concentrated all light so as to create the sense of perpetual midday, even though Askon knew the sun would be setting before long. He wondered what the cavernous room would look like then.

The only useful reference point lay at the very center of the huge room. Wrapping two-thirds of a circle, with openings on either side, and backed by a substantial set of its own shelves, the desk showed them the way.

Líana gestured to the back side of the shelving. "The aisles must have led us nearly halfway around."

Elise's brows knit together. "I tried to keep the straightest path possible, but between the turns, the long stretches, the endless books, it all just started to look the same."

Askon laughed, short and soft. The sound reverberated through the open air above them. "Always go left," he said to himself.

They made their way around the center of the main floor. Having exhausted her patience, Elise stepped toward the long mahogany surface, but Askon extended his arm, holding her back. She glared at him.

"Have you noticed," he said quietly, "anything unusual about this place?"

She pushed his hand away. "You mean, aside from Norill who act as though we don't exist, the floating carriages, and enormous glowing buildings?"

Líana laughed. As the sound escaped into the echoing hall, she lifted her hands to her mouth.

Askon remained serious. "No. Well, yes. But in addition to that?"

Líana lowered her hands. "There's no one here."

Indeed, all around them from the center of the floor to the stairs to the carriages to the tiers above them, not a single sign of another person could be seen. At first Askon had assumed the building was simply large enough that chance had kept them from encountering anyone else. Then he'd looked more closely at the silently rising lifts and noted no passengers there either. Lastly had been the inner circle where they now stood. The place was simply empty.

Undeterred, Elise approached the long wooden surface. "We'll see about that," she said. "Hello?!" The word echoed around the building, a half dozen crystal clear repetitions that faded into nothing.

Askon moved to stand next to her, looking, listening for any evidence that her voice had roused someone from their duties amid the stacks. No sign presented itself.

"How about this?" Líana said after a long quiet moment. She was pointing at a gleaming object on the other end of the desk. Brass, like so much of the metalwork they'd seen thus far in the home of the Elves, it sat lonely and out of place on the wide surface, a round little dome to match the ceiling high above with a tiny nubbin on the top. Next to the object lay an artfully etched sign that read 'Ring for attendant.'

Líana reached out and touched the top of the object. It moved downward imperceptibly and emitted a muted *chuck* sound. She pressed it again, with a bit more confidence this time, producing a long clear *ping*.

They waited. When no one appeared, Elise stormed over to Líana, cocked back her hand and slapped the object with the full weight of her arm and shoulder. It *chucked* quietly again, her hand producing more sound against the wood of the desk. An exasperated growl exploded from her mouth, through clenched teeth.

Líana put out both hands. "Here," she said soothingly, "let me try it one more time." She lifted her hand, and instead of slapping down onto the little brass dome as if to put it through the solid wood, she brought it down swiftly and let it bounce off the nubbin at the top of the metal hemisphere.

This time the *ping* rang out loud and clear, as it had before, but something was different. The sound traveled up and around them, as expected, but it also traveled *down* as if the floor itself had become one with the bell's resonance. It echoed above them, and Askon felt the sound move through his feet, into his bones, and come to rest with a steady pulsing vibration in his chest. He watched the same feeling travel over Líana and Elise's faces. They all three steadied themselves against the desk.

"Well, if they didn't hear that…" Líana began.

A low grinding sound grumbled behind the long wooden bar, the scraping of stone on stone. Askon's hand dropped to the hilt of his sword. Líana looked around warily. Elise continued to seethe, unsurprised by the sound. It scratched along for another moment before coming to rest with a deep, resonant boom somewhere far below.

Then they heard footsteps, light and dry. They started quickly, *tap-tapping* against the stone underfoot, then slowed, and slowed again. From beneath the bar, a brass circlet rose atop a head of tight black curls, followed by arms with skin nearly as black wrapped around a decidedly precarious tower of books.

"I'll be just a moment," called a voice from behind the stack. "I thought I might have heard something, but it gets so quiet down there when the stairwell is sealed that I wasn't quite sure. And I *was* a bit engrossed. Did you know that surveyors have actually found layers of shell beneath the topsoil in the Perishia Heights? There might actually be something to the myth that all of Basin City was under water at one point."

Askon couldn't be sure whether the voice was talking to them or itself as the stack of books made its way to the desk.

"Either way," the voice went on, "there's a lot to be said for things in the archive that I'd written off. That a lot of people have."

The books dropped heavily onto the desk's surface, a cloud of dust erupting all around them. "However," said the voice, still hidden behind the stack, "the shells they've found could easily have been a collection some ancient person squirreled away in their hovel after traveling to the sea. They were likely considered valuable, I'm sure, or even…" the voice chuckled to itself, "medicinal."

The laughter continued for a moment or two longer than was comfortable, and the dark hands came to rest on either side of the books. "Oh!" the voice said, sliding the tower to one side, "I might've gotten carried away there. My name's Daeron. How can I…"

It was him. Just as Thomas had described him. They'd seen the hair and deep brown skin, but now they saw the kind face, pointed ears, wide eyes, and mouth that for the moment could do little more than hang half-open in confused surprise.

Elise had no time for the inane babble nor the wordless expression. "You can begin by telling us where Thomas is being held."

Daeron's face quirked into half a grin. "Oh, I see what this is." With an exaggerated raise of one eyebrow, he cleared his throat and began again. "I see ye come to me thus and verily of good cause and..."

A laugh spluttered from his pursed lips. "I'm sorry, I just can't—" he said, interrupting himself with another laugh.

"What an odd reply," Líana said.

Askon nodded.

Daeron laughed harder, bracing himself against the desk with one hand and holding the other to his chest. Tears began to form at the corners of his eyes. "Oh wow!" he said between gasps. "You three are good." He chuckled again. "Very convincing."

Elise's eyes narrowed. Her hand lowered to the weapon at her side.

Daeron didn't see it. "Alora?!" he shouted, brushing the tears aside.

Elise retracted her hand. But no response came.

Daeron puffed up a bit. "Alora!" he called again. "I know you're out there!" He returned his attention to them with a wry smile. "No one else would think this was even funny. I mean, the detail is incredible. Just, wow."

"We have not come here for your entertainment," Elise growled. She drew her sword and clacked it down on the desktop.

"We're here for Thomas of Dalstone, my husband, who we believe may have been taken to the High Spire."

Daeron flattened the grin, an attempt to take her seriously, but it lasted only the space of a breath before returning. He stifled a giggle. "Oh, certainly my lady fair. Sir Thomas of Dalstone, author of *The Book of the Tear*. Thine quest lieth north a journey of less than a fortnight afoot-eth." He shook his head. "Or a stop west on Line Five, two on Line G, and then east on Line One." He grabbed the stack of books again.

"What does any of that even mean?" Elise asked. "Are you working for Sehlín? Did she, or her agents, reach you before us? What are these *lines* you speak of?"

Daeron rolled his eyes. "Sehlín eh? Don't we all?" He looked at the sword. "Well, that's a fantastic piece of craft there. The story… Your whole outfit… It's all truly on another level. I commend you for that. But I have work to do. Alora!" he called again. "Alright. You won't come out. Just—you're going to have to call them off!"

"She's not here," Askon said. "We think she might have been captured as well. Held in the same place: the High Spire."

Daeron's face shifted from humor to anger. "Alright, enough. That's not funny." His expression slowly shifted to fear. "Who— who are you? No. Just get out."

"Excuse me?" Elise growled again.

"I said, go," Daeron snapped back, "and I won't send a report to security." He turned and marched back down the stone steps. "Thomas of Dalstone," he grumbled incredulously to himself.

"Go! Before I change my mind and contact the guards right now. I don't know who sent you—and it's one thing to tell your tale about a long-dead historian—but to suggest that a real person, my friend, Alora, of all people, would talk so lightly about *that* place is just too much. There are jests and there are fantasies, and then there's just utter disrespect for those whose families have suffered. I've had enough."

As if he might shove the tower over the edge, he pushed the stack of books toward them and turned away. His head of curly hair disappeared below the line of the floor. The grinding sound began again, and in a moment the staircase too had vanished, leaving only a smooth seam and silence.

Hidden

Elise stomped a tuft of grass flat in the darkening twilight. "We're never going to find it this way!" she hissed.

Askon put the heel of his boot on a large stone, tipping it backward and sending a handful of crawling creatures scurrying for cover. "You sound like John." He rolled another rock onto its side.

A line of nearby bushes rustled, softly at first, then more vigorously as Líana burst through. She disentangled herself from a stubborn vine, dusting off leaves and spiderwebs as she went. "Nothing back there. But I did climb the ridge to get a better view. We're in the right place. We just need to keep turning stones and parting grass. From up there it looks a bit like traveling down from the sky, like when we saw this place in the fragments. You see those trees?" She pointed west at a clump of sumac. "It's no farther than those. And the rocks down by the water?" She pointed east. "That's the other border for our search."

They'd been searching for half an hour already, looking for the chest that had contained the fragments in the vision of Dalkaldur. Askon wasn't sure what they'd find; their information about the Glittering World was so limited. When Daeron had disappeared into the library's basement, they thought they could wait him out. At one of the short arcing tables that made up the library's innermost circle, their impatience had gotten the better of them. Daeron simply never re-emerged, and no other attendants were present. Whether he had escaped through another exit or stayed in the sealed lower level, they couldn't be sure.

From there, they'd made their way back through the shelves, up the stairs, and out into the rows of aspen and rose surrounding the dome. With the sun already beneath the faraway line of the caldera, the yellow brass of the carriages shifted toward gray as they had approached. Eerily empty, like everything seemed to be in the Glittering World, they'd stepped onto one of the cars, timid at first, feeling their weight press the floor ever so slightly lower, as it might on a river raft.

Then with no more than a blue spark and a low hum, it had carried them swiftly along the northern side of the lake toward the small village on the eastern side. They rode in awe of its speed and quiet, watching the lake waters slip by through the glass. Every few minutes, only a few dozen yards away, the returning line whipped another identical carriage past them. Soon they had found themselves feeling the floor rise gently as each of them stepped off onto an identical platform. Behind them, the carriage sparked, hummed, and sped away into a tunnel, only to return moments later headed in the opposite direction on the other line.

Elise's frustrations mounted by the minute. Despite their collective amazement with the carriage, her anger had won out. They picked a way along the lakeside, deliberately avoiding the village, while she shouted about how Askon should have stopped Daeron from retreating down the stairs, railed about the latter's flippant mockery of their every question, and finally took to brooding over their lack of information. Now, they were all tired. And though Askon and Líana could see as easily as if it had been midday, in the gathering darkness Elise began to stumble and curse as her eyes failed her.

"Ow!" she shouted. "Blackened hell!"

Askon crouched and brushed his hands through a shock of sharp grass, finding nothing. "Perhaps we should stop. Or maybe now would be a good time for you to sit and rest."

"I'll rest when I'm dead! And I'll sit just as soon as we uncover this cursed box," Elise snapped. "There's no way of knowing anything in this place. We see Norill who won't speak; we encounter two guards while in no position to leverage them; and we meet a librarian so cowardly as to flee a simple conversation. Any of them could tell us what I—what *we* need to know."

"Maybe Askon has a point," said Líana. "We still haven't fully recovered from the trek through the snow, or the fight with Sehlín."

"Don't talk about it," Elise said.

Líana kicked over a dry log that tumbled a few feet before teetering to rest near the water. "We're going to find it. Maybe if you just slow down a bit. Give yourself the chance to breathe while we keep looking."

Elise did not slow down. With a vengeance, she tore through the grassy mound near the stone that had only recently stopped her foot. "I told you," she said, her breathing ragged. "I'm not going to stop…" She parted two bushes. "Until…" She rolled a heavy stone aside with a grunt. "I find…" She rose, took two steps. "What we're look—" And fell into the rocks.

"Ah!" she yelped, then hissed through clenched teeth. "Krahte süldur níhl!"

Líana rushed to her side, kneeling. "Are you alright?"

"Yes," Elise said, squeezing her foot. "I can barely see my own boots at this point. Maybe Askon was—"

"Wrong?" Askon finished.

Elise sat up. At her feet, the lid of Alora's hiding place lay ajar, the sod skewed aside during her fall. Together, they peered inside.

Askon didn't know what they expected to find. They were already carrying the five fragments, so he wasn't surprised when the multicolored light they'd seen in the vision didn't appear. The *Book of the Tear* perhaps? Inside, the chest was all but empty, save for a small square of paper. Askon didn't have the words for the image he saw there. Neither drawing nor painting, the best he could later describe it was as if a person's reflection on a moving pool had been frozen onto the page. A woman with dark almond eyes and tightly spiraling curls that overflowed a circlet of gleaming silver stared up from the image. Her skin—like Daeron and the officer they'd encountered at the lake—was deep brown. Folk like this Askon had heard tales of, from time to time in his days with Codard's army, but here in the Glittering World, dark skin seemed as commonplace as light, if not more so.

"Her mother?" Líana guessed. "Thomas told us she'd lost her mother."

The mother, whom Alora so often thought about. One of any number of exhaustive details Thomas had explained while recounting the Sight fragment's visions. One more clue that brought them no closer to helping either of them.

Elise leaned in further. "What is it? I still can't see."

"Here," said Askon, as he threaded the silver chain from beneath his tunic. The Time fragment spilled light across the paper, revealing the image in slow green waves. "I think it's a keepsake. A way to remember."

Elise pushed her hair back, grimacing in the verdant glow. "What else is in here?" she asked no one, rifling through the interior of the box. A moment later she retracted her hand. In it she held a thin volume that read, *The Idols of Myth: Stories of Forgotten Treasure*. She flipped through the pages which were mostly covered in tiny, precise lettering. Every several sheets, she came upon an image like that of Alora's mother. Each was clear and flat, richly colored, and ringed with a gauzy halo that faded to nothing at the edges. No evidence of paint or ink remained on the page. She snapped it shut.

"This isn't it," she said. "It's not *The Book of the Tear*. There are no fragments here. There's nothing."

Líana placed a hand on Elise's shoulder. "It's *not* nothing. We'll find him."

"How can you be so sure?" Elise said, dropping the volume limply back into the chest.

"I have to be. Otherwise, we've left it all behind for no reason: Edward, Tolarenz, John, your son—"

"Don't you mention him!" Elise cried. "Don't you remind me!" She tugged her shoulder away. And then she did cry. The tears came like a flood, pausing only for thick, heaving sobs. Her pale fist beat the ground near the open chest while Líana held her until she could do little more than whimper, and finally weep silently.

Then she rose.

"Thank you," she said to Líana, clearing the tears with her fingers. "And you too," she added without looking in Askon's direction. Instead, she stared back at the blue ring of the dome in the distance. Askon didn't need to see a glowing red fragment to know what she would do next, what she was planning.

"We're going to find out where this Alora lives. We're going to find out how to get to the High Spire. And we're going to find Thomas." She kicked the chest shut. "We'll start with the librarian. If I have to strangle it out of him, I will. And if he's not there, we'll be waiting when he returns."

Beneath the dome, all was ghostly blue. The ring they'd seen from outside cast its rays down through the intricate reflecting system in the library's main chamber, a cold, haunting replacement for the sun. And still it was enough light for a person to read by if they cared to.

They'd first heard the voices while deep in the book maze and far from the balcony. Low and muffled, neither voice seemed likely to belong to Daeron. As they came closer to the center, the conversation grew clearer.

A mumble, difficult to understand. A man's voice. "—requests today?"

Then Daeron. "Not really, but I did see…"

Askon lost the words of it. Though they all understood the laugh that ended it. Rounding the corner at the final stretch of bookcases, they found themselves looking across the desk at Daeron and two guards in profile. A large book lay behind several stacks like those he had brought out at their first meeting.

"That's it!" Líana whispered. "That's *The Book of the Tear.*"

One of the guards turned a pale ear in their direction. When he didn't attempt to get his partner's attention or further pursue the sound, Askon assumed it was nothing more than a reflex.

Daeron seemed to shrink under the glaring eyes. He said nothing.

"We're not here to listen to stories about how boring your daily work is in this dried-up husk," said the guard furthest from them. "Who even comes here anymore? Gods know why they don't just shut the whole place down and convert it into an arena."

The second guard went on undeterred. "What about old volumes? Something long out of circulation." He leaned forward against the desk, forearm flexing as he clenched his hand into a tight fist. Between the thumb and first knuckle, Askon saw a dark spot, a teardrop.

Daeron's eyes widened as he shrunk back again shaking his head.

The pair of guards shared a sly sidelong look. "Listen to me, you little book weasel!" shouted the man leaning on the desk. "We can tell you know something." He nodded at the other guard.

With a rush, the second man shoved two stacks of books off the polished wooden surface. They fluttered to the floor along the desk's inner arc. *The Book of the Tear*, still unnoticed by the interrogators, went with them. Daeron jumped back. They laughed.

The larger of the two stopped, slapped a heavy hand onto the desk, and the laughter ceased. "A person could lose their employment in a place like this with so many books coming to harm on their watch. I'd be more careful if I were you. I hear some of these things are pretty valuable. Mistakes like that get hard labor most times."

"Or removal from the work lists altogether," added the second guard.

They laughed again, making their way out into the book maze.

Daeron dropped beneath the surface of the desk and scrambled to retrieve the fallen volumes. One by one they reappeared on the desktop—stacked, as far as Askon could tell—in exactly the same order as they had been before.

"Neeman's Heredity," he mumbled to himself. His breathing rapid, eyes still wild and darting as he placed another book carefully on the stack. *"Mucosal Suspensions."* Another book. *"The Backwater Alchemist."* Another.

He went on in this fashion for a minute or so. Askon stepped forward, but Elise grabbed his cloak and yanked him back into the narrow hall between shelves. "We wait," she said, almost so softly that Askon could have mistaken it for a breath. Líana lifted a hand, and with the other pointed to the same area where Askon had seen the tattoo on the guard. He nodded. She made the same gesture to Elise, who seemed not to understand.

"Teardrop tattoo," Líana mouthed.

Meanwhile Daeron mumbled the names of a few more books, which in turn appeared atop the reassembled towers. Then he gasped. *"The Book of the Tear!"* he said in a whisper, and a bone-dry echo rebounded through the chamber. He winced at the sound. A terrified question washed over his face, clear as if he had screamed it into the dome above: had they heard him?

For a moment all was still. The blue light overhead faded, faltered, went out. Askon could hear Daeron's breathing in the well of pitch dark. Elise, still clutching Askon's cloak, held him firmly in place until the light flickered weakly back to life, slowly, tentatively, as if it too feared the unknown repercussions if the guards were to find what they were looking for.

But Daeron no longer stood at the desk. Askon cast his gaze about the wide room, searching. The lights dimmed and died again. He strained to see, but the darkness was complete. Only the ghostly forms of Líana and Elise wavered at the edges of his sight. He closed his eyes and listened, following the sound of shuffling cloth and scuffling feet. The light returned.

Askon opened his eyes. With a satchel over his shoulder, and *The Book of the Tear* absent from its place behind the stacks, Daeron stood on the opposite side of the circle. He paused, listening perhaps for the guards' return. When no sound came, he disappeared into the maze.

A heartbeat later, Elise had crossed to the desk. In two, she had disappeared into the hallway after him. Then it was dark again, and Askon and Líana found themselves following the sounds of their friend, feeling their way along row after row of books, hoping they would remain undiscovered when the lights returned.

They'd been lost twice, once as a pair, before they could catch up with Elise, and once as a trio after Daeron had exited and they were unable to follow the sound of his footsteps. Most of the chase had happened in the pale blue of the dome's huge ring light. But on a number of occasions, they'd been forced to fumble through darkness so deep that even half-elven sight made little difference. Now, on the other side of the wide glass doors, the moonlight seemed bright as midday to all three.

"Where is he?" Elise whispered, the sound unsettlingly flat outside of the echoing chamber. "He can't have gotten far!"

"Shh!" Askon hissed. "Keep listening." He closed his eyes.

"There!" Líana said, pulling him by the arm. "I see him."

In the pale silver and blue, Daeron's silhouette scurried furtive-ly through the gardens. The satchel flopped awkwardly as he half walked, half ran toward the carriage platform. The guards were nowhere to be seen.

Elise pointed along the edge of the library's rounded wall. There, moving quickly, a carriage appeared, sparking intermittently as it went. "We have to hurry," she said, looking back at Askon.

"He'll hear us if we run."

The carriage drew closer to the platform, slowed, stopped. Daeron picked up his own pace, his footsteps clear in the open air.

Elise's face turned from plaintive to frustrated to resentful.

"And we'll lose him if that thing leaves before we get there," Líana pleaded.

Askon stepped forward, determination cast in fluttering shad-ow across his face. Lifting the glowing green Time fragment on its chain and closing it tightly in his fist, he breathed deeply. The world began to slow around him, and all grew brighter, clearer: the carriage, the dome, the gardens.

"No!" Elise cried. "Not that!" She watched him for what seemed to Askon like a long moment. Then she turned, and start-ed to run.

Suddenly a ring of darkness pressed in upon his vision. It re-minded him of the Norill at Austgæta, of the endless army of dead faces brought back to fight again. It reminded him of the moment just before Elise's sword had pierced Iramov's chest. The moment when he thought he would die. So he redoubled his ef-forts, drawing on the memories of Brâghda and the arrow and

Elise's fall from the South City wall. For an instant he pushed the darkness away, steadying the world around him.

Then he saw Líana, looking back and forth across the gardens as the darkness pressed in again. Now she had him by the shoulders. Was she shouting? Shaking him? She looked north, toward the platform. When she turned back, her mouth was moving, slowly, so slowly. She grabbed his collar. Shook him again. Turned. And sprinted off through the gardens.

As he fell, the darkness closed in all around him. He watched her gain on Elise and nearly overtake her. She looked back one more time. The carriage began to move. They lowered their heads, feet peppering over the pathway in silence, and leapt for the railing on the outside of the carriage.

Elise fell short, but Líana caught her—one hand clinging to brass and the other to her friend's wrist. As the carriage sped away, she wrenched Elise up, and the two climbed to the roof, keeping their bodies low.

And then there was nothing.

CHAPTER SEVEN

Lights and Shadows

Líana's fingers ached as the wind howled over her ears. What had seemed wonderfully swift on the inside of the carriage was frighteningly so on the outside. She clung to the railing and pressed herself flat against the cold metal. In the intermittent flashes, she saw Elise, face tight with force of will, gripping the rail as though she might crumple it in her fists.

The air grew warmer, and the light shifted from blasts of blue to a cascade of color: red, green, orange, purple—and others too numerous to count and too subtly different to name. Tall buildings raced past above them, each with windows upon windows reflecting their own reflections. The lights grew brighter, though she hardly thought it possible, and the buildings climbed higher.

The wind's howling softened as the carriage slowed to a stop. Elise pulled herself into a crouch, her joints clearly stiff and aching as well.

"No!" Líana called and dragged Elise back down against the roof. She gave a sideward nod, indicating that they wait for Daeron to exit. He didn't.

"We can't be seen," she whispered.

A crowd of people shuffled from the platform to the interior of the carriage. Liana watched them as they went. These were talking animatedly, and those were holding hands. One was reading a long scroll with the same tiny lettering they'd seen in the books back at the library. Several others simply did nothing, said nothing, and stepped through the doors.

Above, the colored lights shone on. Most were simple glowing orbs that illuminated lampposts or hung from ropes strung between the sheer walls. Others, attached to the walls themselves, cast light in only one direction. Groups of these had been arranged to form simple shapes: an arrow, a circle, triangles, squares. As her attention flitted from light to light, the carriage sparked to life and glided slowly away from the platform. Before long the wind was howling again as she pressed herself ever flatter, feeling the air tug at her tired arms and hands. Líana watched Elise for a moment—her pale face pink against the cold, her eyes and jaw clenched. Líana closed her own eyes and waited for the next stop.

It arrived sooner than she expected, maybe a quarter the travel time of the ride from the library to the city, maybe less. Stiff and cold, the aches long replaced with throbbing numbness, she forced her fingers apart. They responded sluggishly, coming free of the rail and tucking instinctively under her arms as she rolled onto her back.

Elise, still on her stomach, sidled to the edge of the smooth carriage roof. "Half the passengers," she said. "Many with skin like his, all with pointed ears. No Norill."

"And Daeron?" asked Líana.

"No Daeron."

A flash of blue lit the line between them and they were tugged again into motion. Líana stayed on her back, reaching above her head for the rail as the speed and wind grew in force. She dug her heels against the slim footholds and hoped the ride would be short.

It was. Four more times. And every time, Elise catalogued the departing riders. And every time, Daeron was not among them. Líana began to wonder if Elise had simply missed him in the passing of a large group at another stop.

Lying on her back had been a foolish experiment. It was harder to hold on and colder. On her stomach, she could shelter her face with her hood, keeping off some of the wind. However, her legs needed the change of position, growing painful and weak after the third and fourth stops.

As the carriage hummed into motion again, she wondered how many passengers remained on board. It couldn't be many. She curled up and placed both feet, knees to chest, on a bracket that fastened the rail to the outer edge of the roof. The stretch in her legs felt good after being extended and tight for so long. She loosened her grip and flexed again to reset it. The warm stretch began to burn. She tried to shift her position, but the burn lanced into sharp pain as her left leg cramped and spasmed. The overburdened right leg held briefly before buckling under the pressure.

Against her full body weight, her cold, tired fingers slipped from the rail, not one by one, but all at once. Then she was sliding, scrabbling for purchase, her numb hands thumping uselessly over polished brass. She struck the rail at the back of the carriage and felt her weight tip over the edge. Closing her eyes and clenching everything there was to clench, she braced for impact.

The momentum of the carriage shifted, and she came to rest on the rooftop's flat surface. Her muscles relaxed as she lay on her back, arms splayed out beside her. Above, the lights were fewer and less vibrant. A skyful of stars peeked down, pale and faint.

Elise's face appeared between Líana and the stars, hovering for a worried moment before dragging her to the safety of the rooftop's center. Liana sat up, allowing herself a pair of deep shuddering breaths. They peered over the rail at the platform. There, unmistakable with his clumsily swinging satchel, Daeron crept down the steps, head swiveling from side to side in ungainly wariness. They leaned out, risking a better look over the edge and, finding the interior otherwise empty, slipped down the way they had come, obscured by the carriage and the platform itself.

Thwack!

A pause.

Thwack!

"He's not going to find them," Elise muttered.

Líana wrenched the blade free of a wooden bench. The strokes left an 'x' identical to a dozen others she'd cut along the way: platform steps, signposts, windowsills, other benches. The sounds were a risk, but after the first attempt, she'd found Daeron to be remarkably oblivious despite his furtive movements and wary glances. As for Askon, she'd had the same doubts as Elise, of course: that her brother would never even find the right platform, let alone the small markings she'd left behind to guide him. Then an old voice had swept the doubts aside.

"Slim chances are infinitely better than none at all," it cawed. *"You and I, South City, Vladvir, all of it… The world itself exists upon an unknowable count of slim chances."*

The street glowed silvery blue under a string of glowing orbs. Not lamps, like those hung in the Tolarenz town hall gardens with their tallow candles and oil reservoirs, but spheres of light that seemed almost to have no container at all. She followed the lines down the glimmering street, the ever-narrowing path showing far fewer signs of life than the first or second stops. No people had crossed their path, though the buildings all around looked capable of housing thousands. Once or twice Líana had heard muffled voices arguing behind window glass, or doors opening and closing on squeaky hinges. Down one fork, she'd heard the telltale hum of a carriage line and watched its brassy underbelly rush north, high overhead, toward its destination.

No wind blew here, and city smells arose as Líana had ever known them to, without warning and lingering long. There *was* a howling, though, constant in its way and cacophonous at the same time. The cats.

"Damn it!" Elise snapped as the chorus began anew. "How does anyone live here with that sound all the time?"

Líana shrugged. "I suppose one would just grow accustomed to it." She turned a corner where they'd last seen Daeron. Pointing down the alleyway, she watched as he slowed to a stop. "At least it's kept him distracted."

He looked in all directions, including above and, curiously, below. Then, flustered by his own foolishness, he made the cycle again, muttering something before ducking into an even narrower alley to his left. The cats wailed once more, and Líana thought of wolves, one triggering the others deep in the forest, or of dogs back home, barking in endless circles in the middle of the night. Elise followed Daeron.

"Have you ever heard cats do that?" Líana asked after hurrying to catch up. "Call to each other that way?"

Elise shook her head as they approached the intersection where Daeron had disappeared. Slowly, she peered around, knees bent, head down, fingers gently resting on her sword hilt. Líana allowed herself a small smile, remembering the clumsy, infuriated strokes her friend had taken under the sparse trees of the South Kingdom when they'd first agreed to trade the ways of a lady for the way of the blade. It seemed a long time ago. She wondered if Elise ever watched her the same way and wished that she had taken so easily to the propriety of a courteous address or an evening of poetry recitation.

Líana laughed at that. No, surely not.

And then the moment and the memory were gone. Elise slipped around the corner, still crouching, motioning for Líana to follow. The alleyway dead-ended a hundred yards from where they stood. Near its full depth, Daeron approached a low stoop, three steps high. He put his foot on the first, leaned forward, and turned away. His hand rose to his face as he shook his head, talking to himself all the while. He circled the alleyway a time or two, now pulling out the book and holding it in his hands as if to proffer it to someone, now putting it back in the bag. Lifting the flap, he displayed it to the door as if it were a golden idol stolen from some faraway ruin. He seemed to think better of that and pulled the book out again. Then he stopped, took a deep breath, and approached the stoop once more.

This time, he made it as far as the top step, right hand balled into a tight fist. He cocked it back, and all the air rushed out of him, his arms falling limp at his sides, his head hanging loosely.

Líana tensed.

Daeron hung there like a stringless puppet for a brief moment until, from the crook of his arm, the book toppled out. He flailed to catch it, slapping it once with his opposite hand before mashing both together in the empty air. *The Book of the Tear* fell face down in a flutter of crumpled pages.

They sidled along the wall behind a stack of crates that smelled as if they'd come from a fish market. Elise made a face. "What is he doing?"

Daeron straightened like a startled deer. Líana pushed Elise back and pressed herself against the boxes. They waited with hearts hammering. The cats yowled. She heard Daeron sigh. And still they waited.

Bang, bang, bang!

Out of sight, they listened for a response. None came.

Bang, bang, bang!

When no one answered, Líana ventured a peek into the dead end. Under the pale blue glow of one of the circular lights, Daeron stood with his fist raised to the door. He knocked again.

Bang, bang, bang!

Líana felt Elise rise up beside her to peer over the crates. Daeron backed down the steps, clutching the book tightly to his chest, staring at the motionless slab of metal. Back and forth he paced at the foot of the stoop, murmuring to himself, debating whether to knock again. He tucked his chin against the book's thick cover, moving it up and down, up and down.

Elise kicked one of the crates with a boom like a broken drum. Líana turned an astonished glare on her.

Daeron made a small, frightened noise and leapt from the street to the top step. Losing his balance, he swayed, almost steadied himself, and toppled into the wall. He stuffed the book back into the bag, pushed himself upright, and pounded on the door.

Bang—

Líana heard a thin *click*.

A tall man with a wild tangle of gray hair appeared in the frame. He held a weapon aloft. Daeron backed away and nearly tumbled down the stairs. He clutched his fist as if the last knock had injured it. For too long they stood frozen there, until Daeron put out both hands and glanced down at the satchel. The figure in the doorframe lifted his weapon higher. As it rotated, the shadows shifted, and Líana saw it for what it was: a simple carpentry hammer. Not a proper weapon at all, though she didn't doubt it could accomplish its task if called upon to do so.

Daeron twisted his hip toward the figure, lifting his hands to protect his face. The figure's head tilted slightly before menacing Daeron with the hammer again. They did this several times.

Next to her, Elise sighed. Líana watched her draw her leg back to kick the crate again.

"Oh, stop it!" a woman's voice called. The shock of it set the cats wailing anew. "Daeron, my father is not going to bludgeon you to death."

Líana turned back just in time to see three forms at the door. "Get in here!" the exasperated voice snapped.

And the door swung shut.

Elise grabbed Líana's shoulder. "That's her!" she said. "That last voice. It's Alora. I know it."

Staying low, they crossed the alleyway and sidled along the wall toward the stoop. As they drew near the door, Líana heard muffled voices from the other side.

"I've told you about him, remember?" said the woman's voice. The conversation continued, but the words were obscured. Líana guessed that they had moved deeper into the room. She strained to listen.

"Just don't call the authorities." A man's voice, not Daeron, followed by an awkward laugh.

Líana slipped up onto the stoop, gently resting her ear against the door. The metal was cold, its edges orange with rust. Elise did the same across from her.

"—you couldn't take this from the library," the woman's voice was saying. A few muffled words and, "—wouldn't get to read it."

Across from Líana, Elise's brows knitted together. They pressed their heads tighter against the door.

"I knew it!" The man's voice.

Elise mouthed, "Her father."

The voice was still talking. "Are you working for them?!"

Líana pulled her ear from the door. Elise followed.

"Is this—"

Elise nodded and tapped each wrist where the Death and Sight fragments sat in their bracelets, pointed to the two rings on Líana's fingers, Space and Life. Then she straightened, eyes wide, and jabbed Líana in the chest.

There, the Time fragment glowed green on its silver chain.

"You stole it!" Elise whispered.

With thumb and forefinger, Líana rubbed her temples. She shrugged and lowered the hand. "He dragged himself under trying to use it! I couldn't just leave it there…" The words caught in her throat. "The way I just left him." She stared down the glimmering street.

Elise grabbed Líana with both hands and shook her. "No." Another shake. "There's no time for that." A third shake. "How many assignments did he take with King Codard's army? He'll be fine. Confused, but fine."

He *had* been on so many missions. She'd watched him go, followed him along the stream all the way to the gap in the little mountain range that ringed Tolarenz. When he'd passed out of sight, she'd worried, waited, swinging stick swords and training against trees. He'd be gone for weeks—months sometimes—and still she waited.

But he always came back.

She pressed her ear to the door again. Elise was already listening.

On the other side, Daeron was talking about the patrol that had arrived to question him at the library. "One of them grabbed the edge of the desk," he said, and then his words were muffled as Líana adjusted her footing. She closed her eyes.

"Did you tell them?" The father's voice. "Alora, if he told them, we have to go. Now."

"I didn't!" Daeron. "Not after what I saw."

"What did you see?"

Daeron spoke again but the words were masked by a scraping sound. A stool scooting over the floor? A stiff cabinet hinge? Líana shifted again, straining to listen.

"Between the thumb and first finger, there was a teardrop-shaped mark."

The sound came again, and Líana opened her eyes. Elise had turned the handle, bit by bit, until it wouldn't turn anymore. Inside the metal slab, an internal mechanism clicked. Líana reached out to stop her.

The door swung open.

CHAPTER EIGHT

On the Wing

Dansil cinched the final strap and patted the mare's neck, pausing to run his fingers through its coarse black mane and over its gray shoulder. The animal nuzzled him with a noisy breath then plunged its nose into the trough at the edge of the tavern's porch. He counted the packs and recounted what he'd stored inside each one. On either side of the horse's flank, his crossbow and bolts hung tight, just in case, and alongside the bolts, a knife.

There was one thing he'd yet to pack.

With absent fingers he brushed his hand over a fine paper envelope. The blue sealing wax had long since flaked away from the flap, but below, half of a stag rampant remained, the king's seal. For what must have been the dozenth time, he slid the letter out and unfolded it. There, in print as fine as the paper, their handsome king, Edward son of Codard, had written a message.

Dansil,

As I find myself busy with the work at hand, marshaling forces, investigating the Norill threat you saw for yourself at the Bones and Stones, offering my assurance to Vladvir's various settlements and their respective leadership, and so on, I find too a message that must be delivered on behalf of a dear friend.

Alongside myself and my queen, John of Dalstone ventured into the Southern mountains, as did the rest of our party as you met them in Finnestre. We left in search of Dalkaldur and the secrets there kept, which are of greatest import to Vladvir, its people, and the aforementioned Norill disturbances. I cannot tell you what we found there, but I do find a responsibility, a duty, to inform you concerning John of Dalstone.

The first time he'd read the letter, Dansil's breath had caught in his chest, hung there frozen, as if he might not breathe again. He'd torn his gaze away from the paper, crumpling it a bit at the corner. The creases he'd made still showed now, reading it once more. This time the breath did not catch, but it did shudder and slow. He'd lived a life of certainty for so long. Certain that he'd become a brewer, certain that he'd own a tavern, certain that he'd be free of Isilda, that he'd make it so. Even small things: a table's order, the right drink for the woman who'd never had a drink, the crowd that needed a song to lift the spirits, and the one that would respond better if he tugged their heartstrings.

As he had done the first time, he forced himself to read what came next.

And to that end, I must inform you that my friend—and yours—is alive and well.

Dansil sighed, his eyes leaving the page for a moment as he failed to shake the feelings that had come when he'd first read the king's news. Dread. Relief. Confusion. Longing. But nowhere did he find the familiar certainty.

I've thought long about this letter, of the danger into which I might be sending you, but circumstances have taught me what it means to be a world away from one who carries the better measure of my heart.

John of Dalstone resides for now in Tolarenz, just west of the Estelle and a few days ride north of the Æsten Ridge. I tell you this knowing that not everyone will be as understanding as his closest friends. I tell you this knowing that in all of Vladvir there are none more accepting than the half-elves of that place. And I tell you this knowing that I might be wrong about all of it. However, with the information laid before you, you may do what you will.

But you can now do so knowing that he is alive and safe, for the time being. I cannot say for sure what will come of these Norill incursions. And of what we found in Dalkaldur, I dare not write, only that we did find it and that safety is not indefinite for any of us. I wish you happiness and to return your kindness by giving you the knowledge you need to make your own decision.

From one who'd rather see hearts made whole,
Edward, King of Vladvir

Dansil stared at the last line. "King of Vladvir" it said. Never in his life had he expected to receive a missive directly from a king. He smiled, shook his head, and patted the horse again. It lifted its own head from a bag of oats, pausing its soft crunching for a moment before going back for more. Across the street, a familiar blue-gray shape alighted on a rooftop peak. It circled down to the porch rail and waited a moment before burying its beak in its feathers. Satisfied, it cocked its head and waited. Dansil folded the letter and slid the closed envelope into one of the packs. Then, looking up at the tavern's porch, its door, its sign, he ducked inside.

Flarah had kept the note from him at first. Of course she had. Early on, he'd discovered that those who'd come to accept the truth—that he'd *never* been Isilda—those who'd known he was Dansil all along, before he'd ever even said the name, they were the ones who'd hold the grudge closest, who'd sharpen their knives for the next person to speak up when the wrappings around his chest worked loose, or when a patron deep in his cups went on about what makes a man a man and a woman something else. It was then that Flarah sprang into action.

Dansil, on the other hand, had been forced to learn to forgive. Not everyone, of course. But many more than he'd expected to forgive at first. Most people, with whom he cared to have the conversation, took it in with a series of halting hesitations and a familiar circle of questions. Almost everyone, even those with the best intentions, gave themselves away through the eyes: a twitch of the lids, a single line between the brows, a quirk of the mouth, a tilt of the head. He'd learned to forgive those too, for they often came and went without another word or deed. And the ones who did hang on—to the looks, to the questions? Even they usually meant no harm. Though, often the harm was done anyway. So, to avoid endlessly recounting the entirety of his life, and all its many complications, he'd simply learned to forgive a thousand nicks and pinpricks. Survival was made of them.

But when the wound went deep, friends like Flarah were there, ready to retaliate, to slice to the bone if the need came, without hesitation. And for that, he could not have been more grateful. After all, there was no wound of its kind older than John of Dalstone—and no wound deeper than the day at the lake. The day he'd cast aside the costume of Isilda and arrived, as ever he had done on the inside, as Dansil.

"Never should'a let ya have that letter," Flarah said over the bar, her hands full of a dusty bottle and the knotted rag with which she'd been polishing it. "Never should'a let 'em in in the first place. There's taverns to spare, but he shows up at this one." She set the bottle down. A thin wedge of dust-smeared glass still marked its surface. "Trouble. That's all he's ever good for."

"Well," Dansil began. "Not only—"

"Oh, I'm sure he's brought plenty else. I see it on your face when you're readin' that letter." She grabbed another bottle. "But ya know what's tied to every little smile an' flush? Trouble."

She was right, of course. Though, Dansil thought back to the times that Flarah had even come into contact with John of Dalstone: the number was small, hardly enough points of reference to make such a determination. Dansil shook it off. He'd made up his mind already. He wondered if Flarah's need to play the argument out again was meant to change it or simply to speak the words, move through the motions that would ease her mind after he'd gone.

"Oh, don't let *me* keep you," she said. "Don't let a life ya built with yer own two hands, and sweat, and sufferin', don't let that keep ya another moment." The bottle rang dully as she thumped it down against the bar. "Don't let all of us who've helped and protected ya, who've got the heart to accept what others don't, who've hurt when you've hurt…" Her voice trailed off.

"Flarah, I—"

"No!" she said, and her voice cracked with the sound. "Don't let an old lady whose hands have spent more time dusting these bottles than holding onto a man stop ya from walking right into the kind of pain that breaks a person."

Dansil crossed the floor of the Bones n' Stones, making his way through the tables and upturned chairs, around the bar to where his friend stood. This time, she didn't even let him get out the first word.

"Ya know they kill people like you? You know that, right?" She rubbed the bottle in her hand, but it was already clean. "Folk can't even recognize the bodies when they're done."

The bottle tipped out of her hand and rolled along the bar. Dansil reached out to catch it, would have caught it, but he caught Flarah instead. Or she caught him, wrapping her arms tightly around his chest, squeezing as if she might crush him into staying.

When the bottle shattered against the floor, he could feel her sobbing. He encircled her head and shoulders with his arms and hands, and sobbed along with her.

Full morning had settled over Finnestre. Away in the distance the Southern Mountains glowered beneath a plume of purple clouds. In other parts of Vladvir, a storm for certain, but here at the edge of the kingdom, the edge of the world, they were just as likely to blow away west or hover in the foothills until they exhausted themselves with flurries of snow that wouldn't last. Sharp shadows stood in stark relief to trees and heavy stones, homes and storefronts, and the tavern itself, even the barkeep and the wiry woman at his side served now a place to hide from brittle sunlight that threatened the fierce midday to come.

On the afternoon when he'd first followed the falcon to the edge of town, he'd noticed the shadows too, long and languorous, as if tired out by a hard day's work. But the morning's shadows were not these, and the sun was not that sun. They reached now, tight and intense, for something unknowable way off to the west. He closed his eyes, and could almost feel himself slipping away. He hugged her again. No tears this time. Both had cried the last of them out. For today.

And then he was astride the mare, at a gallop that put his fears behind a wall of pounding hooves and rushing wind. Sage and dry grass replaced the weatherworn wood of Finnestre, a dusty place that only hinted of the rolling golden fields to come. Fanning out before him lay the horizon, and sable gray falcon wings.

CHAPTER NINE

Unexpected Guests

Alora listened intently, coaxing the story out of Daeron with now and then a calming expression or gentle gesture. He clearly still hadn't overcome his fear of her father. The thought of it made her laugh. Daeron didn't know it, of course, but he was more likely to have been struck by lightning on the way over than he was to be bashed by the hammer her father had brandished at him. The weapon in question now lay on the worktable, where she'd placed it after the two had come to a comical stalemate in the doorway.

"Between the thumb and first finger," Daeron was saying, "there was a teardrop-shaped mark." A nervous smirk appeared on his face, and a short half-hearted laugh leapt from his lips. "After the actors you sent, in those costumes…"

Alora's encouraging expression dropped away, leaving only confusion. "What are you talking about?" she asked. "I didn't send anyone."

Across the room, the door sprang open. Daeron twisted to look over his shoulder, falling from his stool and landing on the floor with a dull thump. Her father leapt up, toppling his own seat in an effort to reach the worktable and the only weapon ready to hand.

In the doorway crouched two women, one of them pale as death with black hair, the other with a long blond braid and striking eyes, one blue and one green. Both women were dressed in leather suited more to a historical battle reenactment than to any current fashion, but it was the dark-haired one who had managed to open the door. Now she gripped the hilt of a sword, Alora's father's hammer made all the more ridiculous by comparison. The one with the braid carried a sword of her own, which hung at her hip, though her face said more of surprise than any will to attack.

Daeron scooted backwards across the floor toward her father. "Them!" he squeaked, pointing toward the two women in the doorway. "They're the ones that came before. Them and one other. A man with eyes like hers." He turned to Alora. "You didn't send them?"

"Of course not," Alora said, trying her best not to make any sudden movements.

Wolfish and seething, the black-haired woman rose and stalked across the room. She leveled the sword at Daeron. "You have something we need," she growled, her voice cold and commanding.

"Don't," the second woman said, and the tension in the room seemed to lessen at the sound. "They're not a threat. Look at them." She closed the door. Alora eyed her father, Daeron, her own square-cut cotton nightclothes—an unimposing trio if ever there had been one.

The dark-haired woman's resolve flickered momentarily. Alora's father took a step forward. In a blink the resolve returned, the woman's pale face and gleaming blade standing between him and the worktable.

Moving away from the door, the second woman came into clear view. Her clothing could only be accurately described as armor, dyed deep purple, with a soft hood that cast shadows over her features. She pulled it back, revealing a face to turn heads anywhere across the city. With hands spread wide, she spoke again.

"There's no need for anyone to be harmed. My name is Líana. This is Elise. We've come a long way, and we need your help, or you need ours." She took a step toward them. "We know Daeron already."

Alora's thoughts spun as she tried to speak. They looked as though they had stepped directly off the pages of *The Maidenknights of the Mark*. Leather armor with hand-wrought clasps, hoods and cloaks, swords. Eyeing the two again, Alora caught a glint of green and silver at the neck of the woman who'd called herself Líana. She glanced at the second woman and saw similar flashes of red at her wrist.

"I knew we wouldn't be safe here anymore," her father was saying. "I should have packed us up days ago." He turned away from the worktable. "And I never should have let you keep visiting the library."

"And how, exactly, would you have stopped me?" Alora asked.

"Enough!" shouted the dark-haired woman, the one called Elise. Her eyes seemed to grow even darker.

"Yes, that's enough of that," said Líana. She lowered her hands and reached out to Daeron. "What about a peaceful agreement? My friend will lower her weapon. All we ask for now is that you continue the story you were telling." She pulled him up from the floor. "We need to know about the man with the teardrop tattoo and *The Book of the Tear.*"

Daeron stared at Líana. Whether in fear, awe, or simply confusion, Alora could not say. He glanced back at Alora and shakily resumed his seat. "I—"

"Now wait just a moment," her father said in an equally shaky voice that he'd surely meant to sound firm. "This is my house. You've broken in and demanded information from us. What makes you think we won't just call the authorities?"

"I thought we were just supposed to call you 'Corwin'?" Elise said dryly, lowering the blade and sliding it back into its sheath. She and Líana shared a look that was almost a laugh. When Alora found herself smiling along, she felt herself relax.

"Go on," she said to Daeron. "If they meant to harm us, I have a feeling we'd be sure of it by now."

Daeron rubbed his hands together, his deep brown fingers hissing against pale palms. "It was just the usual Guardian routine," he began. "They wanted information. They made some threats, knocked some books over, generally disrespected the sanctity of one of Basin City's remaining edification centers in order to get what they wanted."

He rested his hands in his lap and looked to Alora. *That* look. She met it, hoped it would pass, coaxed him onward. "And then?"

"And that's it. They wanted *The Book of the Tear*," he said, still looking at her, into her eyes, past them into places she didn't want him to see because she wasn't looking back, not like that.

Alora sighed. "And I was the last person to borrow it." He was protecting her.

"I was protecting you!" Daeron's wide dark eyes followed her face, her reaction, her every movement. She turned away. "You know how they are, the ones with the teardrops. They don't care about protocol or process. They just—"

"Make people disappear," her father interrupted.

"And now you've brought the book here," Alora said, equal parts grateful, embarrassed, and afraid. "What if those men waited to follow you? What if they're here right now?"

"They're not," said Elise. "This clumsy halfwit wouldn't know he was being tracked if his pursuers beat a broken box like a drum in the street behind him. I have no doubt if you were to ask him, he'd say he wasn't followed. But here we are."

"And what about you?" Daeron asked, a flicker of his argumentative self reappearing momentarily.

"I have enough sense to know when I'm being followed. And my friend here? I'd expect her to know well before I did. Besides, had we been pursued, they'd be upon us already."

Alora's father failed to stifle a laugh of his own. "You can't be serious. You break into our home, threaten us with barbaric weapons, and expect us to take you at your word, to trust you?"

He laughed again. Elise did not.

"Tell me more about these tattooed guards," she said.

Daeron's eyes pleaded with his interrogator. "I told you. I don't—"

"Not you," snapped Elise. "Our laughing host, Corwin. He seems to think he knows a great deal about all manner of officers lurking around this city's darkened corners." She picked up the hammer. "Well?"

Alora's father took an unconscious step backwards and straightened his glasses. "I'll not be taunted about a subject that's touched my life as closely as this one. Our old friends might not believe me. They might make fun at their gatherings and their dinners and their wine circles. But I know the truth. Even my own daughter mocks me when she thinks I don't notice." He paused, turning to her. "Aren't I right?"

A flush of warmth rose to Alora's cheeks, and she turned away. He was right. About her. About all of it. At first, it was why she had thought they had begun moving so often; the real reason. He'd become so unstable, going on about *them* and *they* and so many other shady people who were certain to be after him, after her, after her mother. She had humored him, of course, especially after her mother's death, but Alora never took him seriously, not fully.

Líana took a step forward, somehow both graceful and dangerous all at once. "We just want the truth. If you give us that, we'll be grateful."

Alora held her father's hand, squeezing it gently. "I'm sorry," she said. "It's alright. We're all listening now."

His eyes reddened a bit at the edges, and he drew a long shuddering breath. "It may sound hard to believe, but our officers, a profession easy enough to obtain after proper, publicly supported training, are actually two separate forces. The first simply do as their employment requires. They see to it that laws are enforced, criminals are apprehended, and chiefly that no violent outburst occurs amongst the citizenry."

Elise scoffed. "Would that more guardsmen could follow such a stringent code. Seems every other one, back where we come from, would as likely add to the violence as stop it."

"Indeed, indeed," he went on. "And so it is here as well, though I'd expect far fewer than one in two. But so it is anywhere, I assume, where those who'd promote safety carry weapons that imply danger. However, that is not the second faction. The second faction has only the tips of its tentacles amongst the officers. Zealots, the lot of them! A cult, even."

"And they all have teardrop tattoos," Líana said.

Alora's father smiled. It was a joyless smile. "And they all have teardrop tattoos."

"Their leader is called Sehlín." Elise growled the name.

The smile vanished. "Sehlín is the maddest zealot of them all."

Líana rested her hands on the table. "They're hunting us. And we know why. What are they doing here, in the Glittering World?"

"The Glittering what?" her father laughed. "You're in Basin City. Where did you say you were from?"

"We ask the questions," Elise growled. "Now, what purpose do these tattooed guards have here?"

"Power," her father said simply. "Like anyone else, they want power, control. They work in secret, and they've managed to make themselves seem a joke. Ah, but some of us, some of us know better."

"Who knows?" Elise asked.

"I do, and…others. I won't give up my contacts."

"You will if I tell you to," Elise threatened. "But that can wait. Show us the book."

Alora did as she was told, sliding the thick book across the discolored metal table. Daeron scooted his stool to one side to make way for Líana and Elise. The lamps flickered, dimming slightly before going dark. A moment later they glowed again, bathing the room in light. Both women had their hands at their weapons, their eyes wary and alert.

"A common occurrence these days, I'm afraid," her father said. "Time was, not too long ago, a person could go for weeks without seeing the lamps falter. Not anymore, though. Now we're lucky to get a couple of hours' worth of uninterrupted light. And the city's other systems are worse yet, the water—"

Elise held up a hand. "*The Book of the Tear*," she read, lowering her head over the embossed leather cover, "by Thomas of Dalstone." Carefully, slowly, she leafed back and forth through the first few pages. "A history culminating in the Battle for the Tear and the various conflicts that came before." She turned another page and ran her fingers along a line of gently looping script. "It's written in his hand."

Alora watched the hard face soften and the black eyes well with emotion. After a breath, Elise wiped away the tears with her sleeve.

"Be careful!" Daeron said, reaching for the book. "That's a one-of-a-kind volume. In a properer time, under better leadership, it would be a museum piece. It must be hundreds of years old. It's a wonder the thing even holds together at this point."

"I beg your pardon," Líana interjected. "Are you saying that *this* book is hundreds of years old? Surely, you jest."

"I most certainly do not," Daeron said, sitting a bit straighter. "Why would I? I'm one of the few people left who genuinely cares about such things, the books themselves, I mean. This particular volume is remarkably old. And the events it discusses are so distant as to be unrecognizable in any factual historical record. They're myths, this Knight of Vladvir, the Great Darkness, and all the rest. Even the author refers to them as a long-forgotten and little-known past, when he himself and his time are just as long forgotten to any ordinary citizen of Basin City—myself and Alora here being two exceptions, obviously."

The two women stared at him, their armor creaking softly in the silence. "That can't be..." Líana said.

Elise underlined the text on the book's cover with a pale finger. "Thomas of Dalstone is my husband."

Outside, the cats yowled. Everyone froze. Alora watched as Líana cocked an ear toward the door. When nothing came of it, she turned back to her task, the same task with which all their hands had been busy for the last hour. The room that had once been home was stripped almost entirely bare of any evidence that Alora and her father had ever set foot there, let alone lived there. Along one side of the room, her father had pulled back the layers of a false wall, and as they had packed each of the cases with his tools, their clothes, blankets, and other various bits of a lived life, the room's remaining personality evaporated. Like so many rooms had done so many times before.

The questions had run out in the first few minutes. Either that, or the answers had. She'd gleaned all she could from Elise and Líana, about their pursuit of a man who by anyone's reckoning but theirs had been dead for a dozen generations. Daeron had argued with them, blamed it on coincidence. After all, Alora's name appeared in the tales as well, of course. Líana had refused his theory, but when he had pressed for more information, she would only say that they had come from far away.

At the heart of it—what the two strange women would willingly share anyway—lay two things, both of them men who needed rescuing. The first was Thomas of Dalstone, Elise's husband, whom they expected was being held captive in the High Spire. The second was the other companion in their search, Líana's brother Askon. They had left him behind in their rush to pursue Daeron.

"I'll need time to speak with my contacts," her father said as he slid another case into the hidden niche. "We can take you to the station platform and give you directions back to the library, but from there you're on your own."

"And what about this High Spire?" Elise asked. "How do we get there?"

Daeron stuffed an armload of items, wrapped in the blanket from her father's bed, into a box and forced the lid down. "I told you before, it's not somewhere you want to go."

Elise glared back at him. "And I told *you* that if Thomas is there, we're going anyway."

Alora's father waved them on. "Just hurry up with that. I'll give you directions for both. But I'll warn you, getting into the High Spire is not as simple as following a librarian to my door and picking the lock."

"We'll take our chances," Elise replied, handing him the final box. "Now close that thing up so we can get out of here."

CHAPTER TEN

Better Left Alone

Askon?

Yes, Liana.

When do you leave?

In a few days' time, like I told you before.

And after you're gone, you know you have to come back, right?

I know.

B—but you know you have to.

I know I have to.

Because I'll still be here.

Don't worry.

Don't die.

He heard his own pulse first, throbbing in his ears. But there was nothing else. For a long time, only the swish and thump of his heartbeat existed in a veil of infinite black. Calling out was useless, he could tell. Moving seemed pointless; where would he go? What had come before the darkness, before the nothing, before the beating of his own heart? He thought for a long time about that.

And then, he released it. He imagined fingers that he'd once had and relaxed their grip, knuckles not white but warm red. Fingers. He imagined bones stacked one atop the next in a fragile column from hip to neck. And beneath them, legs and knees, calves and ankles, and feet with toes. Toes. A chest he envisioned, with which to breathe, with which to protect that beating heart. And shoulders so he could carry burdens.

For a moment the darkness hung there, compressing him, enshrouding him, toying with its meal. He thought it might laugh, which reminded him that he should have thoughts. He rose to one knee, and the darkness retreated in faint tatters, as though it were nothing. He opened his eyes—yes, he had eyes—and the darkness fled. For miles and miles, tendrils of black smoke coiled and uncoiled, snaking their way back, receding to where they belonged, at the edge of his half-elven sight. There they lingered, rank on rank, joining one another, waiting, longing, salivating for the moment they might again stretch out toward their prey.

All around Askon, the Glittering World came back into focus. Deep night had fallen and the garden had grown still. Even so, the barest shift in the night air set the trees around him whispering, silver pillars gossiping of his folly. He looked for the moon but could not find it, the cold echo of his boots crunching in a thousand iterations down the empty path. Further on, the dim blue dome of the library glimmered to life. He turned in place—remembering what had transpired before he blacked out—and looked for their trail. In the opposite direction lay the platform, empty, save for the carriages that came and went, where he last recalled seeing them running, leaping, being carried away.

He put a hand on his chest, patted it, moved, patted again. A third time. He lifted the neck of his shirt. The Time fragment was gone.

A wind whipped down the path, and the whisper of leaves became a cackle. He snapped his hood over his head and gathered the rest of his cloak tightly around his shoulders. His sister was gone. Elise was gone. Thomas was gone. The fragments were gone. And without them…

It didn't matter. Whatever he was without it all, whatever his purpose, there was little he could do now. He watched as another carriage buzzed along the line, stopping at the platform and speeding away moments later. If he tried to follow, he risked being lost in the endless sea of lights that he had seen on the lip of the caldera when they'd first arrived. If he didn't follow, he risked losing Elise and Líana, and their only promising lead, in that same sea.

The wind blew hard again, and Askon turned to face the library's dim glow. As the leaves rattled alongside him, he walked down the path toward the heavy wooden doors. At least there he knew of one person with whom he could speak, from whom there were answers to pry. Daeron would be back eventually, and if nothing else, Askon could fulfill Elise's promise.

Alora watched them move: wary, graceful, almost predatory in the lamplight. From time to time the power had faltered, casting them all in darkness, and each time she expected them to disappear, to vanish like smoke or a half-remembered dream. But they didn't. The light would pulse back to life and there they'd be, deep purple and shadowy gray, stalking the lane as though some hideous monster lurked around every corner. They'd taken her father at his word. It was, if she had to put it into words, an unusual occurrence.

She walked side-by-side with Daeron, who had seemed to relax a great deal since the women had barged through her door with drawn swords. His panic and confusion had settled into something between apprehension and awe. For no less than the fifth time, his hand brushed hers. The first time she'd willed herself into considering it accidental. The second, she managed only incidental. By the third, intentional. The fourth time, she'd gently nudged his hand out of the way, but now she was certain the contact had only encouraged him.

Between them and the two strangers, her father scuttled along, muttering to himself, eyeing the windows and doorways as they passed. Where the oddly dressed women seemed competent and calculating, to describe Corwin as fretful seemed generous. Whatever Líana and Elise were watching for, their manner of watching convinced Alora the threat could be real. Her father, well, his worries were always difficult to take seriously.

Daeron reached for her hand again. *Again.* She pulled away, aiming an irritated backhand in the direction from which his had come. But this time, he didn't relent. His hand gripped hers tightly and tugged it toward him, causing her next step to stump awkwardly against the sleek pavement stones.

"We could run," he whispered, slowing slightly, putting distance between them and the rest of the group.

She tried to pull her hand free, but he only squeezed tighter.

"There," he said, flicking his hand in the tiniest of indications off to their right. "That alley. We'll lose them. They don't know the city."

She tried to retract her hand. The grip tightened until pain blossomed around the press of his fingertips.

His eyes grew frantic, pleading. "Let's go, now!" he breathed. "We'll run. We'll d—"

"Disappear?"

The word fell like a heavy stone on fine sand.

Her hand came free.

"You won't." Elise's eyes bored into him. If it wasn't impossible, Alora would have sworn that their dark depths had grown darker.

"And this," she hissed, jabbing a pale finger at the reddening circles on Alora's hand, "where I come from, the Norill call this 'krínen thüldun.'" Her eyes narrowed. "An act more cowardly even than deserting the lines of battle."

She turned her gaze on Alora. "And you. My advice to you? Tell him. Say the words. The sooner, the better." Then with a swift jab of her elbow, she moved Daeron down the street.

"Walk with Corwin," she said and resumed her careful watch, now in step with Alora at the rear of the group.

A number of tense moments passed. What couldn't have been the span of an hour felt long enough that she kept expecting to see the sunrise. With Elise padding along beside her, Alora followed the woman with the blond braid, her father, and Daeron through the empty nighttime streets until they came within sight of the nearest platform.

She remembered a rainy day not so far in the past when she had walked this same stretch of city, taking in the sights, the sounds, the smells of a busy market, sheltering under the awnings, hopping from one stall to the next before riding the carriage to the library. There, she'd read page after page of magical tales in which the heroes brandished swords and wore armor, warded off the strokes of their enemies' blades and dealt deadly strokes of their own. A small smile found its way onto her face.

As the platform came into view, the group came to a halt. Elise, who hadn't spoken a word since Daeron had tried to convince Alora to escape, stepped between the two men and leaned in close to Líana. Alora noticed, for the first time, that the pale woman's ears were unusually round. She had heard of such people elsewhere in the world, but not in Basin City. Low points, like Líana's, she'd seen frequently. The elongated tips of the city's highborn even, which they never allowed anyone to forget, could not be considered rare. But not round, not here. It was another in a growing list of curiosities about them.

Elise pulled away and turned her attention to the distant platform. Líana set her two-colored eyes and striking features upon the remainder of the group. Alora felt like a mouse under a hawk's shadow.

"And now," she said, her voice nothing like the hunter, instead pure and clear, "we must ask you for help. We're here to find Elise's husband, the three of us."

"Three?" Alora's father asked, his eyes darting from one side of the street to the other. "What do you mean, three? Where is this third person, and why haven't they shown themselves?!"

"It's the brother," Alora said gently, "the one they left behind."

He ran his hand through his hair. "Oh! Yes, right. All this talk of the High Spire and teardrop tattoos must have taken up residence in that part of my mind." He stopped. "But why would we help?"

Elise breathed deep. She still wasn't facing them, but Alora saw it, a long slow breath, full of threat. Líana reached out and placed a hand on the flat of her friend's back, between the shoulder blades.

"The story is long," said that smooth, calming voice, "and we will tell it to you when my brother is with us again. For now, you'll have to trust that we mean well. You seem to know that Sehlín, and whoever else hails from the High Spire, mean nothing but ill toward my friend's husband. And we will tell you what we know of her, of her plans, of what we've seen. She seems no ally of yours—"

"She most certainly is not!" Alora's father's voice rebounded off the walls and windows all around. A curious look came into his eyes. He had surprised himself. "And, if your information is good, if it can help my daughter and I…stay safe…" he paused and tilted his head, listening for something that wasn't there, "then I will help you in return. But I'll not be staying here a moment longer than I must. And neither will Alora."

"Fine," Elise said, still refusing to turn and face them. "I'm in no mood to wait, either."

"Alright," her father said. "You want information about the city, and I want information about Sehlín's dealings. So here is what I propose. Not far from here," he gestured west, along the carriage line, "I have a place where we can stay, assuming that it hasn't been discovered. Alora and I will make our way there. I'll give you," and at this he pointed to Daeron, "the directions to our location. Tell them only if this brother doesn't seem to pose a threat. I expect they'll all play nice because they want to know what I know." He redoubled the gesture at Daeron. "But if *you* get *any* sense that they mean harm to Alora or myself…"

Elise scoffed. A brittle, humorless sound. "We don't." She turned to face him and, despite her words, the threat of death seemed to float all around her. "But if we did, what's to stop us from just torturing your location out of him?"

Now her father took a turn in laughter. "Daeron won't tell you," he said easily, "not if it means putting my daughter in danger."

"Father!" Alora hissed, surprised that he'd picked up on it so quickly. Perhaps it was luck. But she knew he was right. And the look on Daeron's face confirmed it.

Elise shrugged. "Everyone talks at some point."

Bristling a bit, a spark of Daeron's usual self lit up behind his eyes. "Actually, it would seem that some might die before talking, others might give false information, while another fraction might —"

"Would you like me to test your theory?" Elise offered, her bone-white hand gripping her sword hilt.

Daeron's eyes grew wide.

"Let's just hope it doesn't come to that," said Líana levelly. And something beyond that steady, calming voice told Alora that she'd just as readily wield the sword herself if it meant achieving their goal.

They waited there in the shadows for some time while her father scribbled out the directions and coaxed Daeron through memorizing them, all the while carefully making certain that neither Líana nor Elise would overhear. And, though Alora could tell that Elise desperately wanted to simply take the directions for herself, Líana showed no sign of breaking their deal. Then, the first carriage arrived. A half-dozen noisy young men stumbled out. They laughed and shouted, pushing each other and otherwise carrying on about whatever watering hole had aided in their intoxication. Before long, their hoarse voices faded into the night.

In the span between carriages, she'd seen her father's face change. He always appeared harried, disheveled, on edge, but this was something else. He looked exhausted. Were his wrinkles deeper, his hair grayer?

"Are you alright?" she asked.

"Fine," he said with a sigh and a smile that crinkled around his eyes. "Just old."

She sat down next to him, leaning her head on his shoulder like she had when she was young. It always seemed to calm him. "Where are we going? Do I know the place?"

He rested his chin on her head. "You do. We're going to Jhed's. He owes me at least one more favor."

The second car carried two fully uniformed Guardians who held up the line for several minutes, during which Daeron tried to make a break for them, only to be stopped cold by Alora's father. While he might not like the idea of being surprised in the night by two well-meaning strangers dressed like assassins, he would be loath to actually alert a patrol. He trusted no one, but he trusted the Guardians even less. Fortunately, the scuffle with Daeron didn't draw any attention, as the two officers seemed focused on other matters. Soon, they stepped back onto the carriage and headed onward.

The third car was empty.

As it glided up to the platform, its power cables arcing blue-white sparks, her father went over the directions one last time with Daeron. And though she hadn't heard them before, she now stood close enough to catch the final series of steps.

"And once you're off platform two, head south and take the next right."

Daeron nodded, his eyes a little sleepy, a little glassy, but confident in knowing the way. He gave Alora a last look and backed onto the carriage. Líana followed.

Elise glared at Alora's father. She seemed always to be glaring at someone, or something.

"When I get back, I want answers. Everything you know," the pale woman said, and ducked onto the car.

Her father let a short laugh escape. "You'll know what you need to," he muttered as they each took seats inside: Líana looking impatient, Elise looking angry, and Daeron mouthing the list of directions. With a hum and a hiss the doors began to draw together. Her father breathed a heavy sigh.

And Alora bolted for the gap.

CHAPTER ELEVEN

A Rash Decision

Energy thrummed above Alora as the windows flickered from light to darkness. They were miles from her father now, somewhere ascending the mountain slope toward the library in Dalka-ldur Park. She hadn't said a word. Not to him, not to them, not to Daeron who had tried to stop her as she'd slipped through the doors with no more than a fingersbreadth to spare before they'd snapped shut. The *click* of the locking mechanism had resounded in her head—a tiny sound loud enough to nearly drown his protests and frantic prying at the seamless seal.

"What are you doing?!" he'd shouted, pounding his fists as the carriage whirred into motion. He'd said something else, but even now she couldn't remember it, and wasn't sure she cared to.

Alora did remember the look on her father's face, his outstretched hand, his heavy breaths, how brittle he had looked as he shrank into the growing distance until she could no longer make out his shape against the blurring lights. Minutes went by before she felt any kind of surety about her choice—and even then, her surety wasn't sure. It had been the right thing to do, to go with them, but had it been the right thing to do, to leave him there without as much as an explanation? She didn't know, and it was too late now.

Then the lights had shifted, different colors, different shapes. People had climbed aboard, looking curiously at the four of them sitting together, two dressed like ordinary people in close-fitting brightweave of single solid colors, hers blue, his burnt red, their circlets gleaming bronze and brass. And the other two, dressed as if they'd just come directly from a stage performance of *The Fel Knives of King Beregan*. After another wordless stop, a few more passengers had entered, but their expressions read only fear and an anxious need to remove themselves at the next available station. By the time they'd cleared the last lines in the city proper, only the four of them remained. And so it was that they crested Dalkaldur's rim in darkness and dipped down the slope toward the library's dim blue glow.

"He gave you the wrong directions," Alora said to the window, her face a bare inch from the glass. In the reflection she saw Elise allow herself a thin smirk.

Daeron attempted to stand, but the pale woman's outstretched arm and fist met his abdomen, driving him back into the seat. A rush of air escaped. "Wh—what do you mean he gave me the wrong directions?! You mean h—he *lied* to me?"

"Of course he did," Elise said flatly. "He wanted us," she gestured to herself and Líana, "out of there, one way or another. If that meant sending you with us, possibly to die? So be it, I suppose."

"Jhed's," Líana said in that smooth voice of hers. "That's where you're really supposed to go, isn't it?"

Alora turned away from the window and leaned back against the railing. "How did you hear—"

"Practice," Líana replied with a smile. Her eyes pierced deep, almost past Alora, through her somehow. "When you have an older brother with a habit of being sent on secretive military assignments, you learn a thing or two about eavesdropping." She ran her fingers down the length of her long braid. "Then when your mother wants you to learn needlepoint, and you disappear into the woods, you learn to listen for sounds that don't want to be heard."

As they swooped down the darkest side of Dalkaldur Park toward the platform, Alora wondered if her father had gone on to his intended destination or if he'd hopped the next carriage and followed them. Their own carriage glided to a stop, the lock clicking before the doors retracted. A gentle hand fell upon her shoulder. She turned her head, expecting Daeron, ready to swipe away another unwanted show of affection.

"We'll get you back to him," Líana said, and gave her shoulder a squeeze. "You did the right thing. So will we, just as soon as we retrieve my brother."

They stepped off the platform, the four of them, together. Before their feet had a chance to hit the loose stones of the Dalkaldur Park pathway, Elise motioned for them all to stop. "Do you think he followed us?" she said to Líana, almost as though she had forgotten that Alora and Daeron existed.

"It seems likely," Líana replied. "Wait, do you mean Askon? Or Corwin?"

Elise laughed dryly. "Both, now that you mention it. But I was referring to Corwin."

Alora watched them think it over for a moment or two, watched them considering, calculating, deciding. Something about them made her want to share, to help.

"He won't," she said, interrupting the silence. "He's solitary by nature, and he'd run into a burning building to save me, but not if he thought fire services would have a better chance without him getting in the way."

Líana and Elise shared a strange look that Alora couldn't easily read. It might have been confusion.

"Fire services," she repeated, "they're employees of the city whose task it is to put out fires?"

"Where did you two say you were from?" Daeron asked, marshaling the courage for the first time since Elise had thumped him back into his seat on the carriage.

"Never mind that," Elise said. "We might tell you. But not until we've found Líana's brother and gotten ourselves somewhere safe."

Alora shot Daeron a glare. "Point being, I don't think my father will try to pursue us without help, and—"

"And Jhed still owes him a favor." Líana finished the thought for her. "Should we be concerned?"

"Don't tell them any—ugh!" Daeron coughed, Elise's elbow reteaching the lesson his courage had forgotten.

Alora turned her eyes to the pathway. "Honestly, I don't really know. I know who Jhed is. I know where my father means when he says 'Jhed's place.' But I don't know what sort of help they'd offer. If we can find your brother and get back to him before he tries anything too rash, I think I can reason with my father. Get him to help you, honestly, this time."

Elise yanked Daeron upright again. "You'll be alright," she said dryly, and gave him a shove forward. "Just don't get in my way. And as for Corwin and his friends, we'll have to keep our eyes open. If he's our only way to get the information we need about the High Spire, then we have to make sure he doesn't become an enemy."

"Well, kidnapping his daughter might have been a mistake," Daeron muttered.

"If anything," said Alora, "I kidnapped myself."

Despite the strange evening, Alora managed to enjoy the walk through the library gardens, quiet and peaceful as ever. Perhaps more than ever. The swish and rustle of slender trees mingled with the sounds of crickets, frogs, and the owls that hunted said frogs. The same air carried with it the faintest hint of roses in bloom, and she wondered if the thorny flowers pulled their petals close at night like those her mother had kept in wire baskets when Alora was only a child.

"If you keep picking those blooms, there won't be any left for us to enjoy."

"I like wearing them in my hair, though."

"Well, so do I. So do I."

Alora ran a hand over her right ear, remembering the feel of the fragile stem, the petals soft against her temple. She remembered the color of the same flowers against her mother's rich dark face, white as a smile with a center of deep blue. They'd made circlets of them, once, or had it been many times?

And then the memory was gone.

They stood now in the deep shadow of the southwest library doors. Elise had been talking, directing Daeron as they approached. He reached for the handles, pulling them taut with a brittle *clank*, looking to Líana first, then Elise, before pulling again.

"Don't you have a key?" Elise asked with an arched eyebrow.

Daeron fumbled through his pockets. "Well, I do, but it's not usually necessary since this is my assigned place of work." He fumbled some more, and when he came up with nothing, checked the satchel which still held *The Book of the Tear*. "There!" he said, almost as if he'd been surprised to find it, and held up a circular metal disk slightly smaller than a person's palm. "Just a moment."

He held the key to the door, pressing it flat to the center, sliding it upwards, rotating the disk as he went, sliding it to the right, rotating it the other way, and returning in a careful diagonal to where he had begun. A dull sound clunked inside the door. Líana gaped.

"Elaborate," said Elise, her brow furrowing. "Thomas would like that. He'd ask you how it works."

"Actually, the design is quite clever, it—" Daeron began.

"No," snapped Elise. "Save it, and maybe you'll get the chance to explain it to him yourself."

Alora didn't think she sounded very confident.

Daeron pulled the doors back, and the four of them stepped inside, onto one of the landings with their waterfalls of ivy and carefully polished stairways. The great dome of the Dalkaldur Library spread out all around them. It always felt like home.

"Get down!" Elise whispered.

Reflexively, they all lowered their bodies and pressed themselves up against the ledge, following her lead. Alora watched as Elise slowly lifted her head above the ivy. "Below us."

Daeron lifted his head next. Peering over the edge to the shelves below. After a tense breath, his face relaxed and he stood. "Nighttime custodial," he said, and the sound carried across the open circle of the building, dissolving eventually into the surrounding pillars.

"Quiet!" Elise hissed. "They'll hear us. We don't want to draw any more attention."

Daeron smiled. "Unlikely," he said, his voice unchanged. "Those things don't respond to people."

Elise's eyes narrowed. She took a seething breath.

Something in the air shifted behind them and a long shadow stretched over the floor. Alora stifled a cry.

"The Norill *are* people," said the voice of the shape.

Alora expected Líana and Elise to whirl into action, to draw their swords, to do something, anything. But Elise went on glaring and Líana only smiled. Daeron took a startled step, nearly tumbling down the stairs. Alora rushed over to grab him, but Elise was already there, holding him by the shirt as a mother wolf holds her pups by the scruff of the neck.

"You found the librarian, I see," the shadow said. "But who's the other—"

Alora turned to face him, placing herself between the voice and her friend. She held out her hand, as if it would have stopped anyone from doing anything, and looked up.

Under the dim blue of the dome, the shadow became a person, a man. He wore armor of brown leather, similar to Líana, thick boots to match, with a long knife and sword at either hip. Over all lay a deep green cloak with leaves and vines embroidered at the edges, the hood of which he pulled back slowly, revealing brown curls that fell to his angular jawline, ears with low points, and piercing eyes, one green and one brilliant blue.

The eyes searched hers, just as his sister's had, but then they went blank, as if seeing a long-lost friend after many years gone. When they snapped again into sharp focus, the figure fell to one knee.

"Alora, of the Glittering World?" he asked, waiting.

She didn't know what to say, how to respond. What was "the glittering world" anyway? Líana answered for her.

"It is."

He bowed his head, and his shoulders rose, as if the weight of a heavy burden had suddenly been lifted.

"My name is Askon of Tolarenz. I offer you my sword."

CHAPTER TWELVE

Off Guard

Alora wasn't quite certain what, if anything, she was supposed to do now as he knelt there before her, head bowed, deep green cloak pooling widely around him. Was she supposed to say something? Accept…his sword? As many times as she'd imagined scenes like this, all she could think to do in that moment was laugh.

So she laughed.

It was a solitary sound; sharp, hurtful, she realized after it had already escaped. The library's blue glow swelled and then faded around them. The lighting engineers would have to sort out that problem sooner or later. When she was younger, she remembered, they'd go weeks without any interruptions like these. Now, such outages had become a constant, and all the more irritating when one was trying to read, or address a person who was solemnly attempting to offer you their service.

The laugh finished rebounding somewhere far off in the stacks, but the man before her remained motionless, almost statuesque. Daeron looked from the kneeling stranger to Alora and back down again, his mouth open slightly, as if a thousand questions, battling to escape, had lodged themselves between his teeth. Líana seemed unperturbed, gazing around the library as if nothing at all were out of the ordinary. Elise rolled her eyes and, after a moment, gave Alora a look that might have said, "Could you please do something about this?"

At any rate, laughter had certainly not been the appropriate response. Embarrassed, Alora thought back to the countless tales she'd read, the stories that mixed incredible adventures with historical events and customs. In her search she found knights and princesses, assassins and thieves, kings who ought to have been peasants and peasants who ought to have been kings. She knew the words that one of these characters might say, knew them by heart. No, not words. Not a specific quotation to recall but a manner, a method, a proper way to approach, to address. A deep breath filled her lungs and her posture straightened.

"Hello?" is what she said.

It wasn't right at all, of course. "A pleased—pleasure to meet you?" she added awkwardly, certain that *that* wasn't right either. The words themselves were bad enough, but the questioning tone with which she'd ended—twice? That was definitely worse.

"I beg your pardon," the stranger said, and his was no question, even though she was sure Daeron would have made a strident case that there existed no instance in which that sentence could be a question. The cloaked man cleared his throat. "I am Askon of Tolarenz," he repeated. "I've come here from farther than might seem possible to believe. I'm here to offer my sword, my assistance, in whatever way I can."

"Assistance?" Alora asked. She didn't need help, that she knew of. Until the bizarre events that had begun with Elise and Líana at her door in the middle of the night, she would have described her life as almost perfectly boring. Sure, her father was a little eccentric, but whose parents didn't seem strange to their children? As for any aid that she might need which required traveling from wherever these three had actually come from, Alora found herself at a complete loss for words. "You seem very…" she managed, searching for the right word, "honorable, but I don't think I require any assistance."

When he didn't respond, Líana crouched beside him, whispering into his ear.

"What?" Alora heard him whisper back. "That's—that's…a stroke of luck!"

Then he lifted his head, his two-colored eyes once again wistful, as if seeing someone again after a long absence. And she recognized the look. Why? Because she'd seen it in herself, through streaks of tears in the mirror's reflection on days when her mother's features appeared in her own face. She'd seen it in her father some days when he looked at her, and some days staring at one of the captures they'd made before her mother's illness. Before…

A smile turned up at one corner of Askon's serious mouth, jarring her from the recollection. "Well," he said, "I offer my sword nevertheless, at the time when you find that you need it."

Daeron stepped up beside her. Close. Closer than would ordinarily be comfortable but that under the stranger's gaze was just close enough to put her at ease. Then she felt his hand on her shoulder and fought the urge to pull away. So much for the ease of the familiar.

"So," Daeron said calmly, "should she carry it in hand? Or…" He drew the last word out. "Is there a sheath or shoulder harness of some kind?"

Elise cracked her knuckles and Alora felt Daeron's hand—and presence—draw back, almost to vanish.

"Now ordinarily," Elise said, "I would relish any sarcastic comment toward my well-intentioned but often altogether too-self-serious friend. However, from you, I've already had enough."

She turned from Daeron to Alora. "Just accept his help, so he'll stand up. My husband, the father of my child, whom Askon has, thanks to your admittedly quite pretty elvish face, apparently forgotten—"

"I haven't forgotten!" Askon said loudly, his voice filling the cavernous library chamber. "Believe me," he added, with so little sound that she almost didn't hear it over the echoes, "I have not forgotten him."

He rose, looking down at his own hands, resting one lightly on the pommel of his sword. Then his eyes met hers a third time, but something in them had changed. They didn't pierce or hold fast, they came up and, almost shyly, turned away toward the featureless stone floor at their feet. The space of a breath passed.

"I set out hoping to find you," he began without looking up. "My friends, five of them, agreed to follow me. Two chose to stay behind, their responsibilities too great. But one, the one you already seem to know—Thomas—was taken. Before that, I had my reasons for coming here, the most important of which was to rescue you, to retrieve you, from the High Spire, but—"

"Retrieve me?!" Alora said, the words bursting out before he had a chance to continue. "From the High Spire?" Another laugh leapt from her lips. "I've never been within an hour's walk of that place. And if my father knew, he'd be beside himself that I'd come *that* close." She shook her head. "No. If it has anything to do with the High Spire, it couldn't have been me."

"But it was," Líana said gently.

Askon leaned forward, and his hand came away from the sword. "This is going to sound strange. Perhaps even frightening. Just please listen. You are in danger. I don't know when it will come, but it will."

"And how can you be so sure?"

Líana smiled. "There's a lot that we already know. And we'll readily tell you. We just need you to trust us, for now. And then, when we're safe with your father, when he tells us how to locate our friend, we'll answer every question we can."

"Tell us now," Alora said. "How are you so certain it's me you're looking for?"

"Your name is Alora," Askon said, "after the woman who was lifted from the mortal world to live amongst the gods."

"Líana could have told you my name just now," Alora said. "And though I've read about Alora and Heraphus, the Breaker and the Mender, I don't think that's what my mother had in mind when she chose my name."

Daeron scoffed. "And it's etched onto her circlet." He lifted his own from his head and rotated it, first toward himself and then toward Askon. "Oh, look! I have mysterious knowledge of…" he ran his finger along the underside of the lettering, "Daeron," he said very slowly. Too slowly. It was like he couldn't help himself.

"Fine," Askon said, nodding, his eyes briefly leaping up to hers. "You come here, to the library all the time. You borrow books with stories where the people look like me and Líana and Elise; where there is magic, adventure, secret powers."

Daeron stepped up, shoulder to shoulder with her again. He shook his head. "No. No, you could have easily asked any of the caretakers here to get that information. They know me well enough, and they could have checked the ledgers for her name."

Askon's eyes narrowed. "I don't see anyone doing your job now," he said.

"That's because it's the middle of the night!" Daeron snapped back.

"Enough," Alora said firmly. "I agree with Daeron. There's nothing you've said so far that a passing knowledge of my comings and goings here wouldn't tell you." There was more. She could see it written plainly on Askon's face.

"And have you listened to yourself?" Daeron asked. "Knowing this much about a stranger doesn't sound the least bit unsettling to you?"

Askon took a deep breath. "It does. I know. It is as my sister said. You'll just have to trust us for now. When we first saw you, it was on the eastern shore of Dalkaldur, near the village."

How could they possibly know that? No one had followed her there, not ever. She'd checked, been certain, always so careful.

"There's a section of turf," he continued. "It looks to all the world like just another clump of wild grass. Underneath is a keepsake box of some kind. You pulled away the grass and earth, opened the box, and inside was *The Book of the Tear*."

"I've never taken that book there," she said reflexively, immediately wishing she could take it back.

"But you admit the box is there, that it's yours?" Elise said.

There was no retracting it now. Alora nodded. "So, you've been spying on me?"

"No," said Askon earnestly.

"Then how?" she asked.

Askon shook his head. "I'm not certain you would believe us if we told you."

Elise elbowed him, much the same way she had elbowed Daeron. "And I don't think we should share it until we know we'll get the help we need," she said.

Daeron put himself between Alora and the others. "I think I've had just about enough of this." He crossed his arms. "No more dictating terms, telling us what to do and what not to do. I should alert the Guardians and have you all hauled away. If it wasn't for Alora and her father, and those two officers with the tattoos, I would have done it already."

He puffed up his chest. "I'm asking the questions now. First of all, where did you say you came from?"

"Far away," the three of them said together.

Daeron laughed. "That's what I thought. Now, what does that mean?"

They looked from one to the other, as if trying to decide if they wanted to make this piece of information known. If Alora had been forced to guess, she would have said that Líana and definitely Elise wanted it to stay secret. For some reason, though, Askon was desperate to tell. He really had come here with a purpose.

"Vladvir," he said, and the other two gaped at him. "My home, Tolarenz, is a village in the kingdom of Vladvir."

It was then that she knew they were telling the truth, at least what part of it they were willing to tell for the moment. In *The Book of the Tear*, Vladvir was a mythical realm existing some unspecified count of years before what was now called Basin City. One would have had to read the book to know. She'd not seen or heard that name used anywhere else. Scanning their clothing and other gear, she finally saw it, finally let it in. These were no mere costumes; the fabric was all wrong, even for the high quality designs she'd seen on stage. It was coarse and worn, clearly used and reused on the road and in battle. The weapons she'd never assumed were fake, but now she could see they showed signs of careful hand-craftsmanship, the work of hammers and chisels and tongs, not the faultless lines of machines. If they weren't standing so close, she never would have been able to tell. It all fit. They didn't just look like they'd stepped out of a storybook-world long forgotten. Somehow, they actually had.

A *clunk* sounded behind them. Metal softly grinding against metal. Then another *clunk*. A slow slide followed, and a soft *click*. She watched Askon's eyes turn wary. He, Elise, and Líana receded into the shadows where he'd hidden when they'd first arrived. Alora simply stood there staring at the door as it swung open with a rush of night air.

"Oh ho," said a voice.

Two silhouettes appeared in the doorway. Behind them on the pathway, Alora saw another half dozen, their spotlights posted amongst the garden trees, facing the entrance, backlighting the two who had led the way.

She heard a low laugh. "Well, if it isn't our little book weasel. We told you. There's ways of making sure you lose your precious post."

"But you didn't listen. Had to go running off with what we wanted."

The larger of the two gave the other a hard slap on the shoulder. "And then he's got the lack of sense to come back here."

"On the same night!"

They laughed together.

"Pretty stupid for someone who likes books so much."

The men advanced. Alora watched as the smaller of the two drew a baton, a white flash sparking at its tip. They ignored her for the moment and sauntered over to Daeron who, for all she could tell, had nearly leapt over the ivy wall to the hard stone floor ten feet below. His eyes darted. His mouth opened.

Behind them, the doors slammed shut.

A hooded figure appeared behind the larger officer. A pair of two-colored eyes gleamed. On the other side, a smaller figure appeared. Alora expected to hear the sound of cold metal, feared the bloody outcome if their blades were put to use. She glanced again at Daeron, his back against the railing as the two officers approached. His eyes flicked over the shoulder of the large man. The officer spun, faster than she would have thought possible, to face the hood and glittering eyes behind him.

But Askon wasn't ready, he'd been prepared to restrain or subdue from behind. The Guardian dropped his shoulder, thrusting it forward to create distance. Askon's blade glimmered blue in the half-light. Too late. From a hip holster, the large officer had already drawn the pulse cartridge, unseen by the two-colored eyes.

A flash rippled over the blade, and the cartridge struck Askon in the chest. He stumbled back, his head twisting downward with sudden pain. For a moment she thought he might not fall, but a tremor spiked through the officer's weapon, reaching the muscles of Askon's legs. He fell to the stone floor in a heap, then quivered, helpless, as the secondary charges surged through him.

A dull thud sounded behind the fighting. The other officers were trying to break through the door, but for the moment, Líana had braced herself against their efforts. The door remained shut.

The second Guardian had been slower to turn. Elise drove her foot into his knee, and he fell to the ground. With a sound like dry grass, her blade arced overhead toward the officer's collarbone. A *clang* rang out cold and clear through the chamber. He'd lifted his baton only just before she would have taken his head. With a flick of his wrist, he spun the weapon aside and drove the baton's tip into her stomach.

The air rushed out in a gust. Her eyes opened wide and began to water. The baton flashed white. And then, the white turned red. Deep red, like painted lips, like wine.

Elise's eyes closed, and the baton crackled. The red deepened, like searing coals, like blood. A wicked smile appeared in the glow.

The next sword stroke destroyed the baton, its broken pieces shattering like so many shards of glass. Elise rounded with a fist, and the bracelet on her arm shone with red light before smashing into the Guardian's jaw. He sprawled over the floor, and the point of Elise's sword lanced down, once, twice, coming up slick and red.

A whimper escaped Alora's mouth, and Elise looked up, just in time for the larger guard to fire upon her. The cartridge hissed through the air and struck her in the back. She stood straight, out of reflex or maybe surprise, and the prongs crackled, sending their debilitating pulse into her flesh.

The bracelet deepened, redder and redder, darker and darker, until crimson became black, not the absence of light, but the presence of dark.

Elise laughed. A hollow, giddy, chilling laugh.

She pulled the cartridge from where it had stuck, the darkness swirling around her all the while, and stepped slowly toward the larger officer.

A boom sounded, and Líana's boots skidded over the floor. Driving in her heels, she slammed the door back again.

The second officer had fallen to a knee now, choking, gasping, the heavy shadows pressing down on his hunched shoulders. Eyes wild, Elise spiked the cartridge into his neck, staring down as the pulses sparked through his nervous system. He fell to the floor, and the shadows retreated. At her wrist, the gem in the bracelet glimmered dimly.

She slid to her knees next to Askon and removed the cartridge, slapping him hard across the face in an effort to rouse him. He mumbled something, tried to rise, and faltered before managing to stand with her help on the second attempt.

A third boom sounded, and Líana redoubled her efforts one last time. "We have to go!" she shouted. "The next one will break through."

Alora stumbled toward Daeron, his dark eyes fixed on the slowly forming pool of blood beneath the first Guardian. She grabbed him by the shoulders and forced him to face her.

"How do we get out?" she said, frantic. "Did you…tell them? Did you call the Guardians?"

He glanced back at the blood, then again to Alora. "No!" he said, his voice cracking. "They must have known I used the key. It's why we couldn't get in without it."

"The way out!" Elise shouted.

Daeron flinched. And waved them down the stairs.

CHAPTER THIRTEEN

Shadows and Screams

When the battering ram sounded for the final time, the thin chirp of boot soles over polished stone followed, then footsteps, the rustle of ivy leaves, and silence for a moment as Alora watched a silhouette with a long braid vault over the ledge and land with no more than a gentle *tap* ten feet from where she had leapt. With face and chest low to the ground, knees and arms bent to absorb the shock of the fall, Líana took a deep breath and rose, sprinting toward them, telling them to run.

Above, the rest of the Guardian forces poured noisily inside, fanning out over the balcony. Had they been spotted? Did the officers know where they'd gone? Would the bodies slow them down? Alora hadn't seen for herself before slipping into the twisting paths of the bookshelves.

Daeron took the lead, goaded on by Elise's threats. After seeing her in action on the balcony, Alora doubted that her meek librarian friend, argumentative nature or no, would ever challenge the pale woman again. For now at least, the threats were theoretical as Askon leaned heavily on Elise, not yet fully recovered from the pain and paralysis of the cartridge. Elise supported his weight, entirely unfazed by the same weapon's effects. And though it had been a marvel of resilience, her utter disregard for a charge that Alora had seen fell men twice her size made her all the more terrifying.

Turn on turn, row on row, they dashed through the stacks. Under the low light, the narrow aisles felt like tunnels in a great cavern. Alora knew her way to the main desk, of course, the path being far simpler than the offset rings of bookshelves made it seem. Rounding another corner, she'd become certain; their path would not lead directly to the center of the chamber. At her best guess, they had traveled around the circle rather than through it. They moved quickly now, with quiet footfalls, listening for sounds beyond their own breathing.

Somewhere behind them, the Guardians had quieted their pursuit as well. A scuffle, a boot clomping heavily, a murmur, a question, a response; they were still out there, still following, but she couldn't tell if they were far or near or both.

Daeron slipped through another set of shelves, darting down the aisle. He waved Elise and Líana forward. Alora watched as Askon steadied himself at the end of the row. He flicked the hood over his head, a movement so reflexive she wondered if he was even aware of it. Then a gentle exploratory step forward sent him tottering wildly to one side. His arm shot out, the bookcase on the opposite side just out of reach.

He would fall, his weapons would clang against the floor like alarm bells. The Guardians would hear it and find them. Would they think of her and of Daeron as hostages? No, they'd consider them accomplices. Even the best doctors wouldn't have been able to save the man Elise had stabbed. It would take too long to get him to a healing house. And the blood. So much blood.

Alora ducked under Askon's outstretched arm only just in time, stopping him from careening across the aisle and revealing their position. She could have trusted the Guardians, or her father hours ago, or Daeron, could have let him fall. Instead, Askon's body, surprisingly heavy for his size, collided with hers, and for a moment she thought he might topple them both over and to the ground, but she pushed hard against his momentum and her footing held. His hands, strong hands, gripped her upper arm and shoulder. With a second effort she managed to shift his weight into a balance between her shoulders and his own feet.

He smiled, almost sheepishly. "I came here to rescue you," he said, eyes glassy and unfocused. She wasn't sure which had taken the worst of the attack, body or mind.

"Maybe you still will," she said, trying to straighten and finding her hand pressed squarely into his chest. Had she felt a heartbeat? Pulling away, she helped him find purchase against the shelves. Warmth bloomed in her cheeks, from the effort of helping him stand, she told herself.

Líana appeared at the end of the row. "They've covered all the entrances," she said softly. Behind her came Daeron, followed by a wild-eyed Elise.

"Tell us how to get out," the pale woman growled, gripping Daeron's shirt with both hands and banging him against the bookcase. "I know you know!"

He struggled against her. "I will! I will!" he said. "Just—just let me go."

Elise released him but did not lower her hands.

"They're going to be after us now too," he whined. "You killed that officer!"

"And he would have killed Askon, and us!" Elise snapped back.

"No," Alora said. "At least, they wouldn't have if Askon hadn't drawn a weapon on them. They would have taken him, and the rest of us, into custody for questioning."

Daeron nodded. "And probably sentencing."

Elise took a step back. "For what crime?"

"Unlawful entry," Daeron said with a shrug. "They must have taken my access privileges after they came in harassing me about *The Book of the Tear* earlier."

"And now it will be murder," Líana finished. "Then Elise is right, Daeron. We have to get out. Tell us how. If not for us, then for Alora, and for yourself. Neither of you asked for a part in this."

Daeron looked off toward the sounds of their pursuers, then at each of them. When his eyes alighted on Alora, she knew he was seeing the thin distance between her and Askon. He stepped toward them, shouldering his way into the gap, and grabbed her hand. Looking back, he sighed. "Follow us," he said.

When he'd dragged her around the first corner, out of their sight for a moment, she yanked her hand back. "Stop doing that," she said, trying for a look that would tell him she was serious.

He only looked wounded. "Doing what? Saving you from those lunatics?!"

By then Elise and Líana had made their way around the corner, a slightly more sure-footed Askon propped up between them. Daeron reached for her hand, but she made sure he missed. "This way?" she asked, pointing down the aisle.

With a nod, and a flinch as the sound of boots drew nearer, Daeron hurried on. This time Alora knew that they were headed to the center, the big hardwood desk where Daeron and the other employees checked books in and out, answered questions, and recorded requests. He was fond of telling her stories of times past, stories he'd received second or third-hand himself, times when the requests page had been full every day and the halls were packed with voracious readers, each of them excited to find a long-sought tome of history, manual of technology, or just simple stories meant for leisure and contemplation.

After a series of sharp turns, they reached the innermost of the concentric rings, waiting just inside the last of the bookcase aisles. Daeron held up his hands to halt the group and peered out toward the big mahogany semicircle hunkering amid the building's central pillars.

Alora looked back to find Askon walking on his own ahead of Líana and Elise, unsteady but independent, reaching out to lean against the shelving once again as he stopped. He lifted his head and she glimpsed a flicker of green and blue before quickly turn-ing away. Had he seen her?

"What are you waiting for?" Elise said, giving Daeron a shove.

He stumbled forward then ducked back into the aisle. "I'm trying to be sure no one has beaten us to the desk."

"I know you're angry," Líana said to her pale friend. "I would be, too, but it isn't Daeron's fault." She turned to Daeron. "That's good thinking, to look out for them before we proceed. I'm just not sure we have time to wait. We'll have to deal with the trap from within if they've set it."

It was true. As much as Daeron knew about the library, there was simply no way to tell if someone, or several someones were hiding behind the massive desk. They had no choice but to risk it.

"Fine," Elise said under her breath, and pushed her way through Líana, Daeron, and Alora into the central circle. Daeron followed hastily alongside Líana, leaving Alora with Askon.

"Feeling…better?" she asked.

He smiled. "I will be, when we get out of here. I don't think I would fare very well in another encounter with those weapons."

They crossed the center of the chamber together, heading for the gap behind the desk. Behind them, the call of gruff voices rose. If the Guardians hadn't known their location before, they did now.

Askon slid into the gap between the large storage shelf and the desk itself, his cloak fluttering along the smooth floor as he ducked down and pressed his back against the wooden surface.

Alora slid in next to him, almost stepping on the cloak. He smelled like evergreens and dry sand and lonely campfires.

"Alora," Daeron whispered. "Help me with these!" He fumbled through a stack of books that had been scattered across the space behind the desk. "They must've come back looking for it after I left. We need to move these."

Líana and Elise had taken up positions at either end of the desk, waiting with weapons drawn for the Guardians to appear in the aisles. The officers had given up their efforts to surprise and now shouted loudly through the stacks. Calls of "This way!" and "They've made for the center!" volleyed around the chamber. Askon readied a long knife with a gently curving blade.

Alora rushed to the pile of books, following Daeron's lead as he tossed them out of the way. "Over there," he said pointing. "We have to clear the way, or it won't open."

With a clatter of pages, she worked as fast as she could.

"See?" Daeron said. "Right here." He pointed, tracing a rectangular outline in the floor. "Just a few more."

At the opening on Líana's side of the desk, two Guardians appeared, their glassy masks shielding their faces. They drew their weapons.

"There!" said Daeron, diving for the opposite side of the rectangle. He clicked a button rapidly, and she felt the floor begin to shift with a low grinding sound.

Behind her a *thunk* sounded as a cartridge buried itself in the desk only inches from Askon. Then a clang rang out as he parried a second one with the knife. The third would have taken him in the shoulder if not for Elise. With black eyes glittering behind a curtain of hair just as black, she leaned into the third shot. The force of it spun her slightly to one side, but she caught herself, taking a knee in the open.

Instantly a fourth, fifth, and sixth cartridge struck her, and Alora gasped.

Elise knelt there, motionless, the pulses flickering blue and white across her back. They popped and sizzled, and her hands drove hard into the stone floor, the blade of her sword ringing with a bitter clash.

Beside Alora, Daeron was shouting something, telling her to go, to turn and run. But her eyes were locked on the pale woman in the cold blue light.

A scream echoed through the chamber, louder, sharper than Alora thought possible, keening like rending metal, like death. It was Elise.

Then the cold dim blue winked into nothing, and the room was suddenly awash in red. The scream went on, higher, louder, filling the hall with sound and crimson light. Brighter and brighter it grew, and with it the scream sheared through the air, piercing Alora's ears until she was forced to cover them—anything to dampen the pain. Even then, she couldn't keep it out. She felt tears in her eyes. And when she thought the sound and pain and blinding red light would consume her senses, the scream stopped.

There was a brief silence, and darkness brought the entire building down upon them.

CHAPTER FOURTEEN

Sightseeing

Dansil splashed cold water over his face while the river chuckled along noisily through the rocks. So pure this time of year, and frigid. The afternoon had been warm, thankfully. Summer's days were long spent and autumn's nearly so. It had been, he thought, a day that ought to have been called winter but that had managed to convince itself otherwise. He imagined the slopes of the Southern Mountains, now well out of sight, covered in a white blanket that would remain even after spring's flowers had bloomed and wilted in other parts of the kingdom. It'd be cold in the Bones n' Stones, but Flarah would be keeping watch on the firewood supply, miserly about it as she was. Though, come to think of it, they never did run out.

He splashed again, working away the grit around his eyes and clearing the road dust from his arms. Next to him, Bird-dog, as he'd come to call the mare—though her proper name was Dawn—dipped her muzzle into the water and drank noisily. With a toss of her head, she made a slobbery mess of the work he'd just done, sending him back to the stream once more.

"That's about enougha that!" he said with a splutter. "We're not careful, you'll turn full into a hunting hound. You'll like carryin' me on your back even worse after that."

Bird-dog made no response that Dansil could readily interpret. She simply returned for another drink. This time, he thought, a bit more primly.

"I have got to find some actual people to talk to," he said drawing his wet fingers slowly down his cheeks. "You're not much of a conversationalist."

By the time evening had settled in, the day's unseasonable warmth had traveled to that place in memory that hides itself dependent upon its own convenience. Names of acquaintances whose company you didn't particularly enjoy, instructions for a tedious but infrequent chore, the way your belly feels the morning after a night of filling it to twice its capacity with good ale and then filling the night to twice its capacity with raucous carousal. Wherever all of those memories went, that's where the day's warmth had gone. The nighttime chill had seen to that. And try as he might, Dansil couldn't seem to recall even the faintest reminder of what the sun had felt like in the early afternoon.

He'd considered lighting a fire, but he was alone, save for Bird-dog and the crossbow belted to the saddlebags. It didn't seem wise to set a beacon for bandits, or strange Norill like those he'd seen at the Stones, or even simple passersby. So he double wrapped himself in blankets inside the little tent he'd brought along. Not so much a proper tent as a tarpaulin curtain affixed to the rocky hillside, but it kept off the chill till morning.

When the sun chased away the remaining stars, a chorus of birds urging it on, Dansil awoke. His fingers and elbows had grown stiff after a night of squeezing them tight to his chest, the blankets twisted up in his clenched fists. With a groan, he stretched and set to work breaking the camp, rolling the blankets, eating a bit from the rapidly dwindling packs, and otherwise readying himself for the ride ahead. By the time he was finished, the soreness had dissolved.

He looked west at the enormous rock formation towering above with a sigh. "The Æsten Ridge," he said to the horse. "Always wanted to take a look down from the top. Never got the chance, though."

Climbing into the saddle, he saw ahead of them the same figure that had been there every morning since they'd set out from Finnestre: the bird. After one of its long slow circles, it fanned its wings and landed a short way ahead. It bounced and bobbed, flapping idly a time or two, beady little eyes looking at him like he might make a decent bit of breakfast if the falcon's primary intentions didn't pan out. Then it launched back into the air.

"I'm about half tired of that thing following us—or us following it." He patted the mare on the neck three times, for luck, and nudged it into a trot toward the western slope of the Ridge. "One side-trail won't hurt. If there were anyone out here to stake a wager with, my money'd be on that falcon finding us just as easy after a little sightseeing as in a straight line to Tolarenz."

Some time later the falcon still circled above them. Dansil wasn't sure, but if a falcon could fly in an irritated circle, he thought this was what it would look like. About halfway down the slope of the Ridge, Bird-dog nibbled at the grass. After he'd spotted the standing stones, Dansil figured it wasn't respectful to have a horse tramping through, even if he had no idea which gods these particular stones stood for—or when they'd been stood.

Quietly, he made his way through the stones, with their indecipherable carved lettering and moss-covered sides. They cast long cold shadows as the sun hovered low in the eastern sky, so much so that he caught himself avoiding their shade. When he came to the last row, he reached out and ran his hand down the side of one whose rune-work covered nearly the entire surface. He followed the lines with his fingers and leaned experimentally against the immensity of it, laughing to himself, as if he might topple this ancient fixture that may as well have been the tooth of whatever creature a giant thought was giant.

As he stepped out into the open space at the peak of the Ridge, he saw something that caught his breath. Without hesitation, he ducked back behind the huge rock, the coarse indentations of its letters imprinting themselves into his back. His heart thundered in his chest, and he worked to slow his rapid breathing. When the initial fright subsided, he leaned around the stone, taking a quick peek at what had stopped him in his tracks. It was a Norill encampment.

After another careful glance over his shoulder, he determined that if they had set a watch, the watchers hadn't spotted him. Steeling himself, he ventured a more direct observation of the camp.

All along the ridgetop, the Norill toiled at their tasks. A group on the north side stacked stones of surprisingly precise shape and size, mortaring them together with as much skill as he'd seen on any masonry in King's City and certainly better than most. Whatever they were building, it'd be tall. A watchtower perhaps, or some other kind of guard post, he couldn't be sure. The south side showed a similar project, though slightly further along than the north. For a moment, he simply marveled at the quality of the craftsmanship and consistency of not only the structure itself but the process of its workers. One by one they carried in stones, mixed mortar, stacked, fitted, and finished layer after layer. It was almost hypnotic to watch as they worked in near silence save for the dead scrape of trowels, shovels, and other tools. They did not speak. And not a single Norill noticed Dansil.

Now, he stood openly in front of the stone, inching forward a step at a time to get a better view. Between the opposing tower foundations the creatures had built a wide circular platform. Its border was of stone, similar to the work on either side but buried in the ground so that each block sat flush with the earth. In the center lay another circle, a giant disk of burnished metal unlike anything he'd ever seen, larger than the Bones n' Stones, larger than the Ham Hock in King's City, large enough, in fact, to fit both taverns inside with room to spare. It shone like a freshly ground knife edge but somehow reflected very little sunlight, and all across its seamless surface, ornate tendrils snaked wild ways toward the center where the symbol of an open eye had been pressed.

He stared in wonder as a handful of Norill crawled over the metallic surface, brushing and polishing with various tools. They made no sound save for that of their work and none looked up from that work. There were no directors or what in a human project might have been dubbed a foreman. There was only the work. How they had crafted the disk defied every explanation Dansil considered. He was no smith, but the brewery required minor metalwork from time to time, and he'd have been lying if he said he'd never admired the musculature of a proper smith's arm while he waited for a commission to be finished. No forge could be so large. And faultless as their mortared stonework was, no tool could fuse metal to metal at this scale.

Where had the stone, the metal, come from? Dansil had seen no evidence of mining or excavating on his way up the western side of the Ridge. How were they doing this?

"Unbelievable," he said in almost unconscious astonishment, and immediately regretted it.

Every single Norill on the Ridge stopped and turned. They did not lower their tools or chatter amongst themselves. There was no hue and cry, no alarm, just eerie silence and utter stillness, like the cold of deepest winter had fallen upon them in an instant.

Then the tendrils upon the disk began to glow, pulsing with light, a wavering, rippling heartbeat of purple that brightened to white at the center, where the eye stared up from the ground.

He didn't know whether he should stay still or run. They all faced him, aiming their eyes down the western slope of the Æsten Ridge, but they didn't seem to *see* him. The Norill looked on, unmoving, unblinking. So too did Dansil.

The light grew brighter, and the creatures made no move to react to his presence. Dansil assumed they would return their attention to the huge metal disk, but they did not. He looked past them where brilliant white faded back to purple, and for the sparest of moments, shorter than it took even to recognize that the moment had passed, he thought he saw the shapes of tall, smooth buildings, dozens of them—a city's worth with another city to spare—each covered in lights of their own. Then it was gone. The light faded, but now, at the center of the metal platform, a dozen additional Norill stood around stacks upon stacks of identical building stones. What had been a wide empty metallic circle now held enough material and new workers to continue, if not finish, the construction of the towers positioned at either side of the ridgetop.

Dansil gaped, heart thundering again, still afraid to move. One of the newly arrived Norill stepped forward and addressed the nearest which stood, long gray arms dangling, staring down the slope toward Dansil.

"*Sors?*" the newcomer grunted. And Dansil remembered that word, remembered listening to John's friends recount their experiences with Norill like those that had attacked the inn.

The other Norill stared forward and did not respond.

Dansil took a step back.

"*Sors?*" said every Norill, all at once.

And for a moment as brief as his glimpse of buildings beyond a cloud of violet light, his heart stopped. Then he ran, through the standing stones, down the slope, tumbling over a tuft of grass, regaining his footing, all the way to the bottom where Bird-dog stood waiting, eyes alert, ready to bolt.

He slowed, and put up his hands.

"Easy now," he said as calmly as he could manage. "Don't take off just yet."

The mare pranced away as he approached, but he managed to get a hand on the saddle horn, hoisting himself up and slipping his boot into the stirrup.

"Alright!" he said. "Now run!"

And she ran. Until the Æsten Ridge dipped beneath the horizon, she ran.

CHAPTER FIFTEEN

Deep Storage

Alora's mouth felt dry, like she'd been running a length of dusty road with no water to drink along the way. Her eyes were open but, dark as it was all around her, they might as well have been closed. She felt rough stone under her hand and something sharp against her back. How could she be alive? Blinking hard, she lifted both hands to her face, rubbing with outspread palms. Maybe she *was* dead; what would that even be like? Who could know? Or tell?

Distant murmuring swelled around her. Voices. Women's voices.

Slowly, the world came into dim view. The sharp edge was a stair, the topmost of a whole staircase, and beyond, a long low tunnel leading into darkness. A few steps down from her Askon sat, his eyes fixed on some point at the opposite side of the hall, his hand held firmly against the center of his chest. When she stirred, he turned a thoughtful expression to her. Further down, Daeron lay splayed against the wall. He looked very still. She leaned forward, reaching out to him, and nearly tumbled down the stairs. Firm hands gripped her and held her in place.

Looking up, she expected to see the two-colored eyes there, along with the rest of him, steadying her before she fell, but Askon hadn't moved. The murmuring grew louder.

"…will only get yourself hurt…" said Líana's voice.

"And…do something like that…will you be to him?" Elise.

Alora pawed at the hands holding her shoulders, keeping her upright. "I have to go to him," she tried to say, but it came out garbled and confused. Even bleary as she was, she could tell that it hadn't made sense. "What if he's dead?"

She steadied herself as best she could and tried to rise. The hands held her in place.

"He isn't dead," Líana said softly. "Look."

At the base of the stairs, Daeron's legs shifted slowly, but he still lay awkwardly crumpled against the wall. Alora turned her head with a conscious effort to face Askon. "Will you help him?" she tried to ask.

The thoughtful look in Askon's eyes shifted to concern, and he glanced down the stairs.

"Please," Alora managed.

He nodded and, descending the stairs to where Daeron lay, gently set her friend upright, a position that looked more comfortable—as comfortable as a person half-consciously propped against a stone wall could be, at least. Askon held him there for a moment, said something to him, but the deep brown face and closed eyes did not respond. Daeron lay peaceful and still, relaxed as if in deepest sleep.

"Get them up," Elise said. "Both of them. I don't think we have much time."

Alora tried again to rise, now with Líana's careful assistance. The world spun a woozy quarter-turn, rocked hard in the opposite direction, then came to a treacherous, unsettled balance. She ventured another step and found her footing more stable. After half a dozen more, she'd nearly reached the bottom. Líana had drawn back to see if Alora could steady herself on her own. With the help of the solid stone wall, she made a slow way down the rest of the steps.

Elise had gone ahead, attempting to rouse Daeron and failing. He was clearly alive; Alora could see it in the rise and fall of his chest, the pained motion of his legs, the occasional flex of small muscles in his face. But he did not wake.

Elise turned to Askon. "Can you carry him?"

"For a while, maybe," Askon replied. "Help me lift him."

Líana joined them, she and Elise hoisting Daeron's limp body over Askon's shoulder. He took a step, then another, and stood shakily. "I—I can't," he stuttered. "It's like my arms and legs won't follow orders." He lowered Daeron back to floor. "I'm sorry."

Alora couldn't tell if he meant the apology to her or them, but it seemed to wound the strange, green-cloaked man even further. She watched as his head fell into his hands.

"Then we drag him," Elise said to Líana. "We at least have to get down this hallway, find somewhere to hide. I can barely see."

At this, a dim blue luminance rose along the edges of the hallway floor. It had been a resource preservation effort, Alora recalled, that had directed the library's builders to line the floor's corners with band lights instead of the brighter overhead globes that circled the main chamber. The lines accomplished their task; one might see just well enough to travel from the ground floor to the basement storage area, and since the hallway served no other purpose, neither did its illumination. Though she'd never been on this side of the desk, and certainly never downstairs where only authorized personnel were allowed, Daeron had described it to her.

"It's mostly just a lot more shelves. Can't even properly read by the light down there. Well, I'm sure you'd manage anyway, if you ever got the chance. There are some strange works down there. Old stuff. Weird stuff. You wouldn't be able to resist."

Liana took a turn trying to wake Daeron, to greater effect than the others, but when he showed no signs of being able to move on his own, she nodded and ducked under his left arm. Elise looped the right over her shoulders and lifted. Together they moved slowly forward, Daeron's feet dragging loosely, Askon in the lead, and Alora following with uncertain steps.

The thin strips of blue faded and glowed intermittently as the five of them made their way down. Before long, her feet more solidly beneath her, Alora understood why the hallway had so quickly given way to darkness. The path was round. She imagined a long downward spiral, and wondered how deep it went.

Where were the Guardians? The thought had crossed her mind several times as she followed the three strangers dragging her now semi-conscious friend. She dared not ask, however, not yet. Elise's face maintained that hard determination Alora recognized from the fight with the officers. If they were going to explain, they'd do it in their own time. So she kept following.

Before long they came to the basement storage chamber. Rows upon rows of books filled a rectangular cavern that would have spanned the library's main hall and reached half its height. Countless racks with volumes packed tight stretched from end to end. Hearing about it from Daeron had been one thing, but seeing it was entirely another. Of course, it couldn't rival the majesty of the concentric pillars and clever mirrored lighting of the library's publicly accessible floors, but this—to Alora at least—was somehow even better.

"You see, deep storage is much more utilitarian in design than the upper levels," Daeron had told her once. *"It's naturally colder, and due to the insulation provided by the surrounding bedrock, easier to maintain the proper temperature, humidity, and to seal out unwanted contaminants."*

With her hands on one of the tall metal racks, she smiled to herself, almost laughed. He'd cared so much about the building, its design, its purpose. She'd just wanted the stories—to sneak down into this forbidden place and read page after forgotten page herself.

"After the established sterilization process, we shelve them as densely as possible, to prevent errant infestations or other ill effects. Though, I've always

guessed that the real reason is simple laziness. Pack the books tight against one another in the frontmost shelves to avoid venturing further down, and thus a tradition is born. The explanation probably came along later, an apocryphal justification of a process for which no one knew the original impetus."

Alora let her hand fall from the rack and tracked along the shelf at eye level: *Electrostratum; Elements of Elegance; Elementum: Reduction and Redefinition; Elm, Zephyr, and Flame; Elixirs and their Ingredients…* By the time she'd read another half dozen titles to herself, her eyes had gone blurry and her fingers wandered back to the books' spines, a quiet *tap, tap, tap* vibrating beneath her fingertips in soft rhythm as she went. At the end of the row, she found the others huddled around Daeron, attempting again to wake him, this time with more success.

"Get up," Elise ordered, shaking Daeron by the shoulder. "We're trapped here without your help, and though I gave those guards something for further consideration, we can't count on an advantage like that again."

Líana knelt with her hand on his other shoulder. It lay firm but gentle, holding him there for a moment more of rest. On either side of his face, their pale skin reminded Alora of the city's highborn, though neither of them had the telltale elongated ears, ears with points that stood much taller than Alora's own. She watched Askon watching them, and noted his complexion, more olive and tanned, though it seemed largely due to long days spent under the sun. Given enough time indoors, she assumed, he would go nearly as white as his sister, though Elise was another thing entirely. Alora tapped over the last title, slipping from textured linen to cold metal. She compared the warm brown tones of her fingers to theirs and wondered what other strange differences their worlds—

She stopped herself at this. What was she even thinking? She'd let her imagination carry her away into the romance of a story-book. Who were these people, really? Her father would have been beside himself with suspicions, brimful with questions, and here she'd allowed herself to simply follow along wide-eyed in their wake. It couldn't go on anymore. She needed answers, before they escaped, not after. For the entirety of their journey down, they'd heard nothing of the Guardians. If they were capable of pursuit, they would have followed already. And if they weren't?

She gripped the metal rail of the book rack and drew herself up. "He's not getting up. He needs to rest, and we can wait here for a time. I don't hear any of those officers, do you?"

Elise's eyes grew harder, colder as she looked away from Daeron. But Askon stepped between them.

"She's right," he said softly. "It won't hurt us to stay here until Daeron has recovered a bit. He won't do us any good in this state. We need him clear-headed in order to lead us to whatever escape route he has in mind."

He turned and tried to put his hand on Elise's arm. She pulled away as if it might burn before leaning back against the wall and sliding down to sit next to Daeron. Wrapping her arms about her knees, she stared straight ahead.

Alora looked to Askon, his shoulders lowering ever so slightly as a coil of tension released. He had expected an argument, maybe even a fight, and was now glad to see Elise's sullen acceptance. Or, at least that is what Alora had imagined from only a small movement in his shoulders. Then he too slid down the wall on the other side, next to Líana.

Alora stood over them all, working up the courage to speak, to get the answers she really wanted.

"Spit it out," Elise said without looking up.

The words put Alora off balance, but she would not be deterred. "I know that we've been over this," she began. "I know you said you'd tell me everything when we were safe, or when we'd returned to my father, or when you knew how to find Elise's husband." She shook her head and bit her lip. "I just—you just—"

"We just killed that guard," Líana finished, her voice even and light against the weight of her words.

Alora nodded. "And then Elise…"

"And then I what?" Elise asked, still staring through her to some point far in the distance.

"You—you…"

Elise said nothing.

Askon looked up at Alora, an anxious expression tightening the line of his mouth, the corners of his eyes. "She has a right to know," he said without looking to the others. And then to her, "You might want to sit."

She eyed them all, seeing now just how tired each of them looked. It had been the middle of the night when Daeron had arrived at her door. If the morning hadn't come already somewhere above them, it would soon enough. She shook her head. "No. Not now. I've just begun to find my footing."

"Alright," Askon said gently. He rested his arms on his knees, kneading the center of his palm nervously, first the left then the right. "We've come here from Vladvir," he began, watching her expression, assessing her reactions. "But not by road or trail, at least not entirely. We climbed the slopes of what in our land are known as the Southern Mountains, looking for a lost ruin, the Cold Valley, Dalkaldur. Miraculously, and at great loss, we found it."

She gave him an incredulous look and began to form a response.

"Please," Líana interjected, "just let him explain."

Alora held back the words.

Askon continued. "There, it is not like it is here, this place you call Dalkaldur Park. Not entirely. The shape of it is the same, the village and the keep, the lake. But there is no library, no carriage line, no sign of life whatsoever, only snow and ice and deserted ruins."

"But why would you even go there to begin with?" Alora asked.

Elise made a sniffing sound and readjusted her sitting position.

Askon eyed her for a moment before turning back to Alora. "Two reasons. The first was the series of strange attacks our towns and cities have been experiencing. Norill, but not ordinary Norill. These creatures do not speak or even recognize speech, save one word: '*Sors*'. It is all they will say, and then they attack. The second reason is you. We saw you—and I know this will be difficult to accept—in a vision."

He was right. She didn't accept it. However, they'd found her somehow, found and followed Daeron, knew a great deal about her life, her comings and goings at the library. Thinking for a moment, she settled on, "How were you watching me?"

Askon sighed and, reaching into the neck of his armor, pulled forth a green gem that hung on a silver chain. "This," he said holding it up. "And those." He indicated similar gems on the hands and wrists of Líana and Elise. "These are the fragments of Alora's Tear."

For a moment, no one spoke. Alora took Askon's advice and slid to a seated position on the floor. "That's—that's not possible. Alora's Tear is a fairy tale, told to children, if it's told at all these days. I know the story, but only because I've read the *The Book of the Tear*. None of that ever existed. You know that, right?"

"Then what about the tattoos?" Líana asked. "Daeron mentioned teardrop tattoos on the guards who approached him."

Alora looked at Daeron, awake now but too groggy to respond. "They could mean anything. There are a thousand reasons why someone might tattoo themselves." She shook her head again. "So you're telling me that you've come here from a fictional place I can only find in one book in a library containing tens of thousands, that you're carrying the broken pieces of a magical teardrop that fell from the face of a goddess, and that those broken pieces showed you a vision of me needing to be rescued. Do you know how that sounds?"

To her surprise, they all nodded, though Elise's nod carried with it an expression which underlined that she *did indeed* understand that they sounded like fools.

A smirk appeared on Askon's face. "Yes. It sounds ridiculous, but the fact that we're here is all the proof I can give you. These fragments opened a door to this world. Your world."

"The Glittering World," Líana added.

"And these fragments are capable of other things as well. Time, Sight, Space, Life, and Death," he said pointing to each of the gems. "But that power is inaccessible while we're here, or so we thought, anyway."

"What do you mean?" Alora asked.

He considered this for a moment. "Reduce the passage of time, heal deep wounds, move from place to place, see what others see, the things each of us can do to…use…the fragments, or that we *were* able to do back in Vladvir, are unreachable here."

Alora turned to Elise. "Except for you," she said. "Whatever you did back there, the red light, that horrible darkness, bringing the building down!"

"I didn't bring down the building," Elise said, her tone suggesting that though she hadn't done it, she might have if she had wanted to. She looked up at Alora briefly before returning her gaze to the same nothing upon which she'd been focused since they had stopped.

"That's what it felt like," Alora said. "And then Daeron—"

"I didn't bring down the building!" Elise shouted.

And Alora thought she saw the light in the red gem shift, to grow dimmer.

"I used the fragment to push the guards into unconsciousness, most of them. Then we dragged you two to the stairs and jammed the door mechanism after it closed."

"Will they recover?" Alora asked.

"The guards? Yes. The ones that I didn't push too far."

Alora glanced again at Daeron, who seemed to be trying to say something. When the words didn't come, he lifted an unwieldy hand to his face.

"Is that what's wrong with Daeron? Is that what happened to me?!" said Alora.

Elise stared ahead, unmoving. "Most likely. He'll be fine. I did my best to avoid harming you two, but I don't know you like I know Askon and Líana. If anything I did to your friend was permanent, we'd know by now because he'd be dead."

Then something changed in Elise's expression, a subtle shift of the eyes. She shook loose her hair, letting it cover her face like a deep black curtain, and said no more.

"Well," said Askon, "now you know. And now you've seen for yourself. Whether you choose to believe it or not, we were shown a vision of you by the fragments of Alora's Tear. We knew, *I knew* for a certainty, that they were directing us here, to you. For what purpose, I can no longer say. We saw you with the fragments, or some of them at least. We saw you attacked by soldiers like the ones we fought upstairs. Watched you fall to the same weapons they used on me." He winced. "You were in so much pain."

"But that hasn't happened," Líana said. "Whatever the fragments were trying to show us isn't happening now and hasn't happened before." She turned a questioning eye to Alora.

"No," Alora replied. "It hasn't."

"But…" Daeron's voice said thickly, "that…doesn't…mean… it won't."

CHAPTER SIXTEEN

Sight Unseen

They followed a low circular tunnel, filmy bricks of finished stone stretching out slick and green in the light of the opening that lay still some way ahead. There, a grid of metal bars cast thin cross-hatched shadows toward them. Far away, over the lake, beyond the old village and ancient keep, the sun made its presence vaguely known on the other side of the mountains, pale silver against the looming black of night. Alora traced the shadows with her eyes and wondered if the stories were true, that the city's highborn could sense the oncoming sunrise as early as an hour after midnight, that they experienced darkness outdoors for only an hour or two in total depending on the season.

"This blasted dark," Elise complained for what felt like the thousandth time. "You'd think someone would light a torch, or a candle…"

Alora had come to ignore her grumbling. Neither Askon nor Líana had argued when Daeron led them into the drainage tunnel, and Elise herself hadn't said anything for the first hundred feet or so, but after that it had been incessant. Yes, the tunnel was in fact, quite dark; and yet, the rest of them had little trouble navigating its small hazards.

It had taken Alora until the waterway had grown from a trickle to a stream to realize that Elise simply couldn't see as well as the rest of them. And as they followed the subtly sloping stone cylinder, Alora wondered if Elise needed a circlet with the same attunements as her own. Now, standing at the tunnel's end, she lifted the circlet off her head, watched the bars of the grate smear into a smudgy haze, and quickly replaced it. After a moment, the opening slipped into focus once more. Perhaps not the *same* attunements, she thought. Elise's struggles seemed to be an issue of light quantity rather than focus quality. Either way, a properly wrought circlet would do her some good.

"We're almost there," Líana said patiently to her friend. They'd clearly traveled with one another a great deal, and this seemed to Alora just one among many unconscious adjustments they'd made for each other.

Alora and Daeron reached the outlet first, tedious as the journey had felt as they crept carefully along, heads ducking low to avoid irregularities in the stonework. The central stream, now as broad and noisy as a forest creek, flowed through the bars and down a gentle slope to the lake, where quiet ripples disturbed the reflection of the fading moon.

"This is it," Daeron said. "This is where the drainage system runs into the lake. The lock isn't linked to circlets or keys. It's barred from the inside, plain and simple. We open it, and you three can be on your way."

A scuffle sounded further down the tunnel. "Ow!" Elise yelped, then stumbled forward, her arms waving wildly ahead of her. With a growl her hands found purchase on the wall, pawed along its slickened surface, and landed on Daeron's shoulder. "*Our way?* You say that as if you think you can just stay behind. Wherever we're going, you're going too."

Líana and Askon emerged from the tunnel's depths. In contrast to the growing light beyond the gate, the shadow behind them deepened into impenetrable darkness. Líana shook her head. "We can't just leave you here. There's nothing that guarantees those guards won't find you. Or..." She hesitated, a pained wrinkle passing over her brow. "That you won't find them and direct them to us."

"They're called Guardians," Daeron corrected, his voice petty and small. "They're the safety force here in Basin City. You break a law, you answer to the Guardians. Small law, small punishment. Significant law, like, I don't know...murder—"

"Significant punishment," Askon finished. "We understand."

Elise tugged on Daeron's shirt. "All the more reason to keep you close," she said. "I know Alora trusts you, but I don't."

"Something tells me I'm not the first to be bestowed with this honor," Daeron said rolling his eyes, and Alora saw him regret it immediately.

Elise balled the stretch of shirt into a fist and drove Daeron back into the slime-coated wall. He yelped and lost his footing, bringing Elise down with him. But she recovered, kneeling over him, the red gem glowing at her wrist.

"Let him up," Alora commanded. Elise's dark eyes turned on her, but she didn't quail before them as she had thought she might, as she had earlier. Instead she glared back. "I know it's important we find your husband, but hurting my friend isn't going to help your case." Alora reached down and carefully lifted Daeron from where he had slipped on the stones. "I don't know Thomas, but—"

"No," Elise snapped. "You don't."

This time Alora did retreat a bit. Daeron steadied himself on her shoulder, an allowance she knew she'd come to regret. She could feel it in his fingers, squeezing as if in releasing it he might cease to breathe.

"So I'll be the one telling *you* about him. Until, that is, he can tell you himself," Elise finished, rising unsteadily.

"It doesn't matter," Daeron said, still holding Alora's shoulder gently—ever so gently. "The Guardians won't differentiate between us and you three. We'll all be considered involved until our names are cleared." He gestured to Alora and himself. "So you might as well drag us along. That way, at least we look like the hostages we are."

Elise leaned forward, flexing a fist in his direction, and Daeron, despite having Alora between him and the pale woman, flinched in response.

"Let's just get out of here," Askon said, reaching for the lever on the gate. Flecks of rust crackled away from the metal and flickered in the segmented light. He pulled, but the lever didn't budge. Another tug and it groaned as the latch moved, not even a quarter-turn. Askon sighed, pushing it back down to its original position.

What must've been a half hour later, everyone had taken their turn, up and down, up and down, slowly working the handle loose bit by agonizing bit, their hands growing discolored with rusty powder, using clothing or armor pieces to keep the rough metal from rubbing through the skin. Finally, with a last frustrating ef-fort, Líana wrenched the lever to the vertical where something inside the mechanism came free. Swinging loosely, it slammed against the bars with a brittle *clank!*

For a moment, they all held perfectly still. Alora tried to stop her breath, then to slow it, softening its sound while she tried to listen beyond—to the sounds of the park, to the sounds of any-one that might have followed them. But all she could hear was the rush of the stream. She watched as the others did the same, heads tilting, eyes steady, listening.

After nothing came, and the sound of metal banging against metal receded into memory, Líana gently pushed the gate open. Alora had expected a screech, or some other terrible sound threat-ening to draw unwanted attention, but the gate rotated smoothly, giving only a subtle groan before it thumped against the damp earth surrounding the tunnel's exit. Then they stepped through the opening into the rising light of early morning. Before them lay a second reflected sky, Dalkaldur Lake.

"There's not much cover," Líana said. "If they're still looking for us, we'll be easy to spot."

Daeron brushed his rust-covered hands against the front of his trousers. "We could always head back." He gestured to the tunnel.

"No," said Elise. "We might as well turn ourselves in if we do that. Someone must know about this exit besides you."

"Not to mention that they'll have sent more officers and possibly emergency assistance," Alora added.

Askon rubbed his hands together, kneading away the chill. "There's our best bet," he said, pointing across the lake to the small village and hunkering keep. "It's the only place other than the water where I haven't seen any lights. It must be deserted."

"The Dalkaldur historical site?" Daeron asked. "It's at best a half-crumbling collection of antique woodwork. No one goes there."

The others, Alora included, stared back at him for a moment as the dawning of the obvious flashed over his face. He turned away, mumbling something only he could hear.

Askon started down the slope, aiming for the nearest clump of high brush and trees. "We'll have to use what cover there is as well as we can. There must be somewhere in the village—"

"Historical site," Daeron corrected. "It's essentially an outdoor museum."

"The historical site," Askon continued, "where we can lay low while we make a plan to find Thomas."

And Alora found that she was already following him, Líana and Elise behind her, Daeron trailing reluctantly along behind them. With the sun nearing the edge of the horizon, they picked their way from stone to brush to grass to trees around the northern shore of Dalkaldur Lake. Further north, carriage after carriage buzzed along swiftly to the same destination.

They'd hit the wall of fog—or the wall of fog had hit them—well before they'd reached the site, at first a beautiful set of white coils extending itself over the eastern shore, then a damp haze that enveloped them entirely. Alora had looked back through it, past its feathery edges and over the water to the library's glowing blue ring. By the time they reached the sparse collection of barely-standing cottages, even the library had been shrouded in white.

Daeron had suggested the largest building, a mostly-intact tavern or community house, as a prospect for them to rest and remain out of sight, but Elise had waved off the idea in favor of a small hovel that seemed ready to surrender its form and return to dust. A large solid building, she'd said, would be the first place pursuers would look, while the hovel, fragile and decaying as it was, still had four opaque walls, plenty of cover against prying eyes.

They padded along through whorls of mist and vapor, their outlines shifting from silhouette to solid and back again as the sun began the slow work of burning away the fog. Askon led the way, approaching the hovel's door with caution, scanning all around them one last time for signs that they had been followed. A bird cawed somewhere far off along the shore, and he waved them inside. Across the water the lights of Basin City, visible only as dim positionless globes in a swirl of white, faded and winked out. The full light of day would be upon the valley soon.

The one-room shack was more spacious than it appeared from the outside. Each of them had an arm's length or two of space all around. None stood shoulder to shoulder unless they chose to. Daeron, of course, chose to. He hovered mere inches from Alora, while the others lined the opposite wall.

Askon smiled a curious smile. "This place has been tidied recently. I thought we might surprise a nest of mice, or at least have to clear away a handful of cobwebs. Someone tends to this building. It's been swept, dusted, furnished." He tapped the simple but sturdy stool upon which he'd taken a seat. Unlike much of the ruin, it and the other furniture looked to be years old rather than centuries.

"I told you," Daeron said, as if speaking to an inattentive toddler. "This village is—"

"An historical site," Askon interrupted. "Yes, but it wasn't clear that the place is still maintained."

Daeron shrugged. "Well it should have been clear. What else would be the point of establishing an exhibit if there were no plans for upkeep?"

"For one," said Líana, "where we come from, if a structure or location is of historical value, it simply *is*. There's no official declaration. Most such places declare themselves through the permanence of their construction. Otherwise progress simply builds its way over them."

Askon's eyes narrowed. "And again you leave out details that could get us caught, Daeron. If people still tend to this place…"

"Not peop—"

"Don't," Elise said, her voice like a hammer stroke. "Norill tend to it. Isn't that what you were about to say?"

Daeron managed a weak nod.

Elise's anger grew. "Norill like the ones we saw working in the gardens. Norill like the ones we saw in Tolarenz and atop the Æsten Ridge. Norill who know nothing other than tasks and labors, who say nothing but that single syllable…"

Her eyes seemed to darken, and the red gem darkened along with them. Whatever was angering her so, Alora could not guess. She glanced over to Daeron, searching for some sign, but his face showed the same confusion that she assumed stood just as plainly on her own.

"Elise, wait," Líana said, her voice gently dousing the other's fire. "Look at them. They don't understand."

"Norill?" Daeron asked.

Alora searched her mind, aware that she'd heard the word before, from somewhere other than the three strange travelers—and then she remembered. She hadn't heard it; she'd read it in the pages of *The Book of the Tear*.

"They were creatures of evil," she said, "in the book. Is that what they are where you come from?"

"No." Elise's voice was firm. "However, many people still believe so. But what you've reduced them to here is worse. At least if they were evil, they'd be able to make their own decisions, live their own lives. But here…"

"The gardeners and trash collectors? They're mindless," said Daeron as if he were telling them that the sky beyond the ancient roof were indeed, blue. "They don't speak. They clean and build and don't interact with anyone. Half the time, I don't even notice they're in a room. Have you ever been in the same room as a highborn? They treat us the same way. Especially those of us who 'look the part.'" He gestured to his dark face, arms, and hands. "Even those Guardians, the ones with the tattoos. They aren't highborn themselves, but they execute their laws. You saw what they thought of me. They'd have said the same for Alora."

It was true, she thought to herself. It was just how things were in Basin City. Highborn at the top, everyone else somewhere below, but people who looked like Daeron—or her mother—lower still. She hadn't even considered the creatures that Elise had called Norill, so invisible, so easy to simply overlook.

"Perhaps we can show you," Askon offered, "that there is more to these creatures than you know. Why they behave as they do here in the Glittering World, I cannot say, but maybe if you could see it for yourself, you'd better understand."

"What do you mean?" Alora asked.

"Elise," Askon said. "Can you open the clasp on the Sight fragment?"

Elise looked dubious. "Don't you remember what happened when you tried before with Time? You can barely carry the other fragments on your own. What makes you think you can use them?"

"Maybe I can't," Askon said. "But maybe together we can, as we did back in Tolarenz. It's worth trying at least."

Reluctantly, Elise raised her arm. Wrapped about the wrist was another bracelet, similar to the one with the red gem. This one, however, had a curious clockwork face that clicked and turned before popping open to present a sky blue gem of different shape but the same strange inner light.

"Put out your hand," Elise said, rotating the bracelet until the stone fell into Alora's outstretched palm. There, it grew brighter, its light solid and steady.

Alora watched the pale woman grow paler in the bluish light. At her wrist the red glow matched the now stable blue. On either hand, Líana's rings cast similar shades of deeper blue and purple. Askon drew out a silver chain, verdant green flashing through the fingers of his closed fist.

"Now what?" Alora asked.

Askon stood and, crossing the small room, knelt in front of her as he had done when they first met. This time he reached out and held his hand above hers, hovering there for a moment. "I'm hoping to show you something we've already seen," he said and lowered his head. And then his hand.

When his skin contacted hers, a reflexive smile quirked the corner of her mouth and warmth rushed to her cheeks. Her heart raced, and amid its fluttering beats she glimpsed Daeron's face, watching Askon's hand on hers. But then it was gone.

She stood atop a mountain, or a hill, or something between. Everything seemed to blur and waver like the morning fog in the village. All around, large stone slabs towered, their surfaces heavily marked. With what, she could not tell. She saw Líana there, and Elise, and others whom she'd never met. Three men stood side by side—one tall and black-bearded, another, curious of face and timid of step, and a third, handsome, regal—all with shimmering blades drawn. They were looking at the same thing. She turned to inspect it herself.

In the shifting ripples before her, a creature shook with fright. Its gray, mottled skin shone under the moon, and it held a dagger outstretched toward them.

"Sors?" it said weakly.

The line advanced: Líana and Elise, the three men, and from the place where she now stood, a fourth wearing a deep green cloak. She watched the six of them stalk slowly forward. As they did, the creature, so much like those who worked the library gardens and building sites, turned the knife on itself. No... Some outside force was turning it, against the creature's will. Its large eyes expanded with frantic terror and the dawning realization of what would come next.

It screamed and the fragile image shattered.

She opened her eyes. Askon lay sprawled on the ground before her, two men pinning him down. One of them yanked a black hood over Askon's head and cinched it tight with a gag. Not an arm's length away on the floor, the Time fragment lay glittering, its silver chain broken and hanging loosely in the dirt. Alora snapped it up—pocketing it along with the other that Elise had given her— and took a backward step away from the attackers. Across the hovel, Elise and Líana had both been similarly hooded, their hands tied at the wrists. Another man and a tall woman stood grimly on either side. But Daeron was free, his back pressed up into one corner of the hovel.

When Askon was bound, the man nearest Alora rose. His wiry black hair had been tied into a loose tail low on his neck. A short, beaded braid hung near his right eye which stared down at her as if she were very small. A runnel of sweat ran down his ebony forehead.

"Jhed?" she asked.

He drew a long finger to his lips, urging her to stay quiet.

"It's alright," whispered a familiar voice from somewhere behind her. "These three can't hurt you now."

She turned toward the voice. There in the doorway stood her father, Corwin.

CHAPTER SEVENTEEN

Top Level Clearance

The fabric of the sack they'd pulled over his head, soft and fine as any he'd seen in Edward's wardrobe, quickly grew musty, his breath dampening the inner layer and making his nose itch. When he'd fought back, before they'd dragged him and the others away, his words had been met only with a sharp prod in his ribs, and a gag which they'd tied around the outside of the hood. They wanted him quiet. They wanted all of them quiet.

Líana and Elise had resisted at first, but with Askon kneeling, concentrating on the memory of the Norill and the Æsten Ridge, he hadn't stood a chance when the two men dove on him from behind. They'd slammed the hood down before he contacted the ground, threatening his death to keep Líana and Elise from forcing a fight. That was when the other footsteps had sounded in the little hovel and, he assumed, the women had been bound, hooded, and silenced as well.

Then they'd been moved. Askon could hear whispers between a deep voice and a reedy one, but he caught none of the meaning.

After they'd been intentionally disoriented and tied back-to-back in a rough triangle of chairs, Alora—not among them—had tried to speak up once or twice, pleading for an explanation, but each time she had been hushed by their captors into silence.

Now Askon listened as the two men's voices murmured a conversation behind closed doors. He shifted abruptly, knocking the back of his chair against the one on his right. It responded gently. The chair on his left rattled and tipped, but did not overturn.

"That's enough of that!" hissed a woman's voice. "Just be still, and keep quiet. They'll be done deciding what to do with you soon enough."

The chair on his left stilled, and he felt its occupant go from rigid to slumped.

In the quiet that followed, he heard new voices beyond the partition, not loud enough to fully understand, though he caught the errant word here or there. They grew louder, more indignant, as conversation turned to argument, and Askon recognized Daeron and Alora's voices as the new additions. The pitch swelled, rising in volume and energy until he could almost piece together what they were saying. Then someone quieted them again. He listened as the now hushed debate played on, wondering who would win, and what price the winner would demand.

A door opened, and for a moment, the words became clear.

"I told you, those three are coming with us," said the reedy voice. "But the Guardians have eyes all across the shoreline. Moving them here may have bought us some time. Though, they'll be sure to sniff us out soon enough. And if what you say is true, that these people killed one—or more—of them, we'll have no choice but to turn them in."

So they'd decided.

The deep voice spoke next. "We need to get out of here before the officers arrive."

"You've done nothing wrong," Daeron protested. "The Guardians should be thanking you."

"They won't," the deep voice replied.

"Tell them they escaped," Alora said. "Or better yet, let them escape."

"No," said the deep voice. "We take the strangers to the safe house, blindfolded and bound, as agreed. Then *we* do the questioning. I didn't get into this only to get nothing out of it."

"Please," Alora begged.

A heavy knock sounded against brittle wood. Once, and then three times in succession. A moment of silence passed. Askon heard their captors moving, whispering. Two sets of strong hands gripped his shoulders and the chair, lifting, dragging him somewhere. The knock rattled the door again. He felt Líana and Elise's chairs take their places on either side of him, in a row this time. A door clicked softly and the knock sounded once more, quieter, muffled. They'd been moved to the side room.

+ + +

Alora stood at the doorway as Jhed and the others dragged Askon, Líana, and Elise away. Her eyes darted from them to Jhed to Daeron to her father and back again. As the last of the three strangers passed through the door, she hovered there, feeling oddly as if this decision were larger and even more permanent than her dive for the carriage car door. Her father's eyes narrowed, curious and confused. Jhed tilted his head slightly. If she didn't step through, he'd close it and she'd be stuck in the main chamber when the Guardians came through.

She hesitated. Daeron was right. What wrong had she even done? The three who claimed to have come from Vladvir—an unbelievable story that she somehow found herself believing—were killers. She'd seen it with her own eyes. But, she reminded herself, she'd had no hand in it. The Guardians weren't after her. Maybe they'd just take the strangers away, leave her and her father in peace. She turned from the doorway.

And then Daeron reached for her hand.

She shot him a glare and slipped free, ducking into the side room where Jhed gently pressed the door into place behind her, lifting a finger to his lips. He breathed a soft "shh..." and leaned against the ancient wooden panel. Closing his eyes, he listened. Alora heard the hinges shift and then nothing. A long moment passed and she used it, breath by breath, to step across the little room until she'd managed to position herself behind the row of chairs.

"Good morning!" she heard her father say, as he opened the door in the main chamber.

A scuffle of boots came in response, the Guardians pushing their way in. "The Dalkaldur Historical Site property is closed to the public," a low voice said to the room at large.

"We're here at sunrise for just that reason, my research team and I—"

"Shut up!" the voice commanded. "These premises are the subject of Guardian Search 05-12T6. Now get out of our way."

More footfalls entered the room. She couldn't have said how many, even if she'd had an hour to listen. Jhed remained still as stone, as did the prisoners in the three chairs.

"Now wait just a moment," her father said shakily. "If I'm under search, I have cause to know the reason."

A pause.

"Legal cause," he added more firmly. "Yes! We invoke—"

"Denied!" the Guardian shouted. "This case is top-level clearance, with orders direct from the High Spire."

Elise flinched at this, the cords around her arms and hands tightening. Orders from the High Spire?! Alora could hardly believe it. The strangers had been right. She used the moment to her advantage.

Looking down, she saw a glimmer of red at Elise's wrist and deep blue and purple on Líana's fingers. In her own pocket, she felt the sharp edges of the green gem she'd scooped up from the floor when her father had surprised them: the Time fragment. These were what they had been protecting, why the two women refused to share their purpose when they had first appeared at Alora's home. These were the reason she'd been forced to pack up and leave, *again*; the reason why they'd murdered those Guardians back at the library.

She knew what had to be done.

"Apologies, apologies…" her father was saying, stalling them.

"Hey!" another voice called. "*That one* fits the description. It's the librarian!"

"Grab him," barked the first Guardian.

It was now or never.

Had she paused to look up, Alora of Basin City might have seen Jhed's reaction, his slow realization and attempt to stop her, but she did not. Her mind was clear and focused. She slipped the rings from Líana's fingers and pocketed them.

Had she taken her attention away from the task, she might have heard the Guardians shouting, "Search the house!" but she did not. Instead, her hands moved to the intricate mechanism that held the Sight fragment, passed over it, and released the clasp on the bracelet instead, refastening it to her belt.

Had she paused for even a heartbeat, she might have heard Jhed's men and women spring into action on the other side of the door, heard their attempts to stop the Guardians from taking Daeron and her father, too. But her purpose did not falter. Her hands alighted on the final gem. Red light bloomed and Elise's fingers bit into Alora's wrist like knives until they drew blood. With a gasp of pain, Alora yanked her hand back.

Jhed was shaking his head, eyes wide and starkly white against his black skin as the door shuddered. She watched him blink, so slowly, his wiry shoulder muscles flexing beneath tight sleeves, the rest of his body turning to meet the threat at the door. He drew a baton like those the Guardians used, only his was lightless, its energy expended. Inch by inch he drew it. Her heart pounded. Why wasn't he hurrying? Her father was out there.

With a splintering sound, a cloud of dust erupted through the doorway, moving like lazy morning fog. She flinched, but the door itself swung as though it were a great slab of stone, bit by grinding bit. She looked down toward the backs of the three chairs and saw…

Blinking hard, she looked again.

Many things she saw, where the bound hands and chair backs should have been: a tired, intelligent face, bound and filthy, with one eye bruised and swollen; a towering waterfall, cascading past a stone bridge; a handsome, frowning man in a vast castle; a peak of rock standing sharp and cold over a wide field of gold, and in the distance, a falcon in flight above a harried rider. Lightning flashed, and for a moment her vision was washed in white. Then she saw what she could only guess was the other side of the wall, beyond the still-opening door; a fight, her father locked in a grapple with a Guardian Officer, Daeron being wrenched free by two women who'd come with Jhed, another of Jhed's men fallen and twitching with a spent cartridge lying nearby, and half a dozen additional Guardians—with teardrop tattoos between thumb and forefinger.

Lastly she was looking at strong hands, Askon's hands, alongside her own. A hairsbreadth away, so close to touching that she could already feel it. But the tingling energy didn't last. There, on her wrist, where Elise's nails had pierced like daggers and her own blood had run red was… Nothing. No wound, no scar, no trace, just brown unmarked skin.

There was no time to think. She had to give them a chance, even if she had already taken the jewels, even if she could still end it all by simply handing the stones over to the officers. Instead, she thrust her hands into the binding cords, loosening the knots. Askon first, then Líana. When she reached Elise, she paused. The other two hadn't moved at all. Why? And when they did spring into action, they would fight the Guardians. What would Elise do? Alora thought of the secret place, that peaceful place where she'd kept the capture of her mother, that place along the waterside that never moved even though she and her father never stayed. The cool grass, filled with white flowers in the springtime, the sound of wind in the pines around the park.

Alora never could remember closing her eyes in that moment, there with Elise still bound and the battle with the Guardians just beginning. But she always remembered opening them. When she did, she stood on the water's edge, a sliver of dawning sun glinting across its surface, no more than a hundred feet from the mound of grass that covered the little chest.

A voice called out from the historical site nearby. They'd seen her standing there, bewildered and panting.

Moments later she flung herself into the brush as the Guardians followed, gaining on her all the time. She ran as noisily—as clumsily—as she could, leading them away from the chest, the tuft of grass, and four fragments of Alora's Tear.

CHAPTER EIGHTEEN

A Fragment Remembered

He had heard her, at least he thought it was her, sidling behind them, pausing first at his chair, then at Líana's. It was there that he could sense something happening. Rustling. Shifting. Was she freeing his sister? Then came a pained, sharp intake of breath. Shouts, on the other side of the wall. A heavy slam as the door broke loose. A featherlight touch brushing his hand and vanishing like the wind. All of it happened very fast.

Askon's arms came free, his bonds loosened or cut. Whipping the mask off, he pulled a lungful of dusty air—a welcome change from the cloth bag's stifling interior. Líana had already done the same. Elise did not rise, and Askon recognized immediately that she had not been done the same favor as he and his sister. He spun to his left just in time to see the man with the low voice charge out of the little room where they were being held, knocking one of the helmeted soldiers aside, unaware that they'd been set free. In the room beyond, another Guardian (as Alora had called them) leveled an all-too-familiar weapon through the opening. Askon kicked the door shut and felt the cartridge bury itself into the brittle wood.

"Catch!" Líana called, almost too late.

Askon wrapped his arms around his sword belt and blades as the heavy bundle of leather and steel struck him in the chest. Unrolling it, he cinched the belt around his body and drew the long curved knife. Líana, sword in hand and already a step ahead of him, sliced the cords that tied Elise to the chair. Askon pulled the hood from Elise's head.

"She took the fragments!" Líana's voice was frantic as she shoved Elise's sword into her hand.

Elise gripped the hilt and laughed dryly. "Not all of them," she said, holding up the bracelet.

"Of course she didn't," Askon said. "I still have—" He felt for the familiar sharp edges hanging from the chain at his chest. "Wait... No," he began.

"It's gone," Elise finished. "Alora took all of them except mine. And she tried, just not hard enough."

Askon spun a full circle, scanning the room. No windows. No crawlspaces. No gaps in the brittle wooden walls. Just one door, and the chaos of battle clattering through from the other side.

"How did she escape?" he asked.

"Only one way out," Elise replied.

Líana gripped the door's handle. "Then we follow," she said and pulled it open.

The three of them burst into the room, blades gleaming. Thus far, the fight had not gone well for their would-be captors, although two men still stood back-to-back inside a ring of Guardians. One was a stranger, with skin darker than any Askon had encountered in all his travels. The other, Askon recognized from Thomas's description: light skin, glasses that sat low on his nose, and a shock of gray hair standing on end—Corwin, Alora's father. A woman, likely another member of the group who had brought them here, remained on her feet as well. Daeron cowered behind her. The others either lay on the ground, twitching to the pulses of the Glittering World's weapons or restrained by other means. Only two Guardians had been felled, but they seemed dazed rather than unconscious or dead.

Líana sprinted to the center, dropping to her knees and sliding across the dirt floor. Her sword sliced through the cords that bound one of the women the Guardians had restrained, the blade arcing over Líana's head to halt a baton strike. The freed woman rushed forward, tackling the officer, wrestling over his weapons.

Askon headed for Corwin and the man he presumed to be Jhed. Without them, they had no way of reliably navigating the Glittering World, or Basin City, or whatever it was. Before the others could react, he swung the flat of his blade against the helmet of the Guardian whose back faced him. Not expecting such a strike, the man stumbled, momentarily stunned. Askon reached for the officer's baton and ripped it free, burying the tip into the padded armor on the man's back.

Nothing happened.

"The switch!" Corwin shouted. "Press the swi—"

Askon felt around the handle of the baton, his fingers contacting a small upraised piece of metal, and pressed it.

The end of the weapon crackled with light and the dazed Guardian fell. Askon released the switch. Below the baton's tip, a row of dots glowed, smaller than the nail on his littlest finger and perfectly circular. The first was red, and the remaining two were blue-white. Then it was gone—struck from his hand. He met the next attack with his blade, sending sparks off to one side. Diverting another blow, he looked beyond his new opponent and saw Daeron pointing at Elise—shouting—not to her, or even to Jhed's companion who still stood between him and two menacing Guardians, but to alert the *officers* of Elise's presence. One of them turned to face her.

Askon parried again, and the baton came free of the Guardian's hand, clattering across the room. His sword reacted to the force and looped gracefully down for what would have been a kill, had he not considered Alora's reaction to how they'd dealt with the Guardians in the library. He halted the blade and instead aimed a kick at the man's knee. His boot landed with a crunch and a soft pop. The scream that followed drew the attention of the Guardian ring as their comrade crumpled to the ground. The dark-skinned man at the ring's center seized the opportunity to retrieve the baton Askon had dropped and lanced it toward one of the remaining soldiers. The second dot on the end of the weapon faded to red and Jhed's target fell. His eyes met Askon's with a nod before batting a cartridge weapon from the hands of the next Guardian.

But there were simply too many.

The ring turned on Jhed and Askon. Across from them, Líana had engaged two of the soldiers in an attempt to free another of the bound men, but she was being driven bit by bit into a corner. Daeron was screaming now, his eyes wild, arms flailing, the extended finger jabbing toward Elise.

She crouched low to the ground, her hair dangling over her face, pale flashes peaking through as she moved. A wicked grin appeared, whiter even than her skin. Her hands rifled through a collection of weapons gathered at her feet. She lifted a baton and drove its tip into her wrist. No, not the wrist itself, but the bracelet she wore around it, and the smile went from white to red.

A long, low laugh bubbled up from inside her small frame, her lip quivering. A Guardian dove for Askon, but he deflected the strike and shoved the man aside. Elise slammed the tip of the next weapon into the bracelet, pulled the trigger, and watched the red light glow. Then as the Guardians finally seemed to heed Daeron's screaming, she jammed the remaining baton into the Death fragment and pressed the switch. The corresponding dots changed with each flex of her hand, blue to red, all three charges.

Líana had retreated as far as she could, her back flat against the wall, the two Guardians beating her sides with spent batons. She managed to absorb several attacks with her blade before taking a blow across the cheek that spun her out of position. Askon rushed them, but only managed a single step.

Elise rose—sword now in hand, the grin flattening—and stabbed the blade through one of Líana's attackers, pinning him to the wall through the midsection. He clawed wildly at the gleaming metal, then weakly. Askon could only watch as silver was painted red.

Without even brushing the hair away from her face, Elise lifted the hand with the bracelet, fingers splayed, red gem pulsing with the energy of gods-knew how many Guardian weapons. For a moment, everything was still. Then she closed the fingers into a fist.

As if he had just remembered something terrible and urgent, the Guardian who had managed to strike Líana's face murmured half a panicked syllable and fell lifeless to the dirt floor. The other soldiers looked on in horror as Elise turned to them one by one. Splayed fingers, clenched fist. Each time, another gasped or whimpered, then buckled—like puppets cut free of their strings. And each time, her fingers opened and closed more slowly, the red light dimming closer and closer to black. When only two remained, Elise shrieked as if her hands had caught fire, but when the scream ended, they too were dead. The gem went dark. Elise fell to one knee. And for a moment, all was silent.

"Where…is…*Thomas*?!" she roared, her voice ragged and quaking. With a flick of the lank strands of hair in her face she stood, crossed the room, and gripped the hilt of her sword, still buried in the midsection of the Guardian and the wood plank wall beyond. With the other hand she ripped the helmet from the man's head, and with it struck him across the face.

"*WHERE IS HE?!*" she screamed again.

His head rolled to one side. "Top lev—ugh…" he gasped.

Elise pulled back the helmet and drove it forward.

"*WHERE?!*"

A third time. Askon heard the nose snap.

"*IS?!*"

The fourth blow struck and glanced wetly aside.

"*THOMAS?!*"

A sound escaped the dying man, but it was not an answer. Elise stared, her eyes looking not at him, but through him. She took a shuddering breath, and ripped the sword free in a gory arc that even John of Dalstone would have left to his listeners' imaginations. The body fell face down, and Askon thought that at least there it could retain a measure of its dignity.

Líana rushed to Elise's side, attempting to comfort her. "We'll find him."

Elise roared, a wail of rage and grief and helplessness, wild and terrifying. And before Askon could react, her sword flashed through the air at his sister's neck.

Where Líana's blade met it. "*Don't,*" said the voice like water.

The blades screeched against each other, shrill, ear-splitting for a moment, until Elise's fell loosely to her side. She turned, dragging the tip of her sword along behind her and took a faltering step toward the door, then another, and another. She continued, whether seeing the rest of them or not, Askon did not know. She passed him and Jhed and Corwin, then rested her palm on the door.

"Elise, no!" Líana said, her blade hovering steady and still. "There could be more of them out there. We can't fight that many again."

"Maybe…" Elise murmured, turning her wrist to gaze into the Death fragment. "Maybe I can." She opened the door and walked through the brittle beam of light that poured in.

They followed her into the square: Askon, Líana, and Corwin. Elise walked some several steps ahead of them, turning a slow arc, looking at the empty buildings, deserted paths, and gleaming lake. Jhed and the others remained inside, where the fight had taken place, tending wounds and binding the Guardians, and Daeron. When she had completed the semicircle, she gaped back at them. Her mouth opened slowly, poised to speak. "Th—"

Across a corner of the lake, so faint even Askon's sharp ears shouldn't have heard it, came the sound of rattling leaves. He put out a hand, staying whatever she might have said next. Looking across the water's edge, he saw the sound's source.

Three Guardians searched along the tree line as something came thrashing down through the underbrush. They readied themselves as it drew nearer, only a few feet from a thick hedge of roses, their weapons burning blue even in the bright morning sun. Suddenly a figure burst through in a shower of red petals, toppling one of the officers and rolling down toward the water. It was Alora. Behind her the Guardians turned and the rosebush exploded again in a cloud of dusty leaves. Her head tilted as if to look back, but she stumbled, turning her ankle on a loose stone and landing on her knees. For a moment, even so far away, Askon felt her lock eyes with him.

Then she shuddered and fell face down onto the grass, her body arcing with the energy of the Guardian's weapon. Beyond her at the tree line, the lead officer stood cradling his helmet with his other arm outstretched. Before Askon and the others could even reach the water, let alone follow the shoreline, they'd dragged her away, beyond sight, beyond reach.

Where they were taking her, he knew more certainly than he had known anything in the whole of his life. They were taking her to the High Spire.

CHAPTER NINETEEN

Trust

"Why would she do that? Steal the fragments from us, I mean."

Elise arched an eyebrow. "Because they're objects of unexplainable power and immeasurable value? Why does a thief steal anything?"

"Safety and security," Líana said softly. "I used to think the same as you, until I heard Edward mention it more than once with his advisors."

The trudge around the lake's eastern side had taken longer than Askon had wanted. They'd rushed at first, but exhausted from the fight and lack of sleep, they soon reached the end of their reserves. Alora's father, and the men he'd brought with him, made a show of keeping an eye on Askon, his sister, and most of all Elise. At least at first they had, until Elise proved it was nothing more than a show by raising her bracelet-clad fist in open threat. After that, and a few diplomatic words from Líana, they had backed off, a tense alliance settling around their shared goal to find and recover Alora.

Determined as he was to reach her, or even just the site where the Guardians had captured her, Askon found himself struggling to muster the energy for each step. All the while his sister and Elise bickered like no time he could recall, Líana giving Alora the benefit of the doubt and Elise suspicious to the brink of paranoia. He wondered, as they started around the endless circle again, how Alora had traversed so much of the landscape in so little time. Their fight with the Guardians, like so many battles before it, was begun and ended in only a few short moments. He thought of the Time fragment's dormant ability to lengthen a moment, slowing everything around him and bringing the world into a focus so clear that the subtlest of alterations seemed impossible to over-look.

As they approached the place where Alora's flight had burst through the roses, he wished for that power at his command once again. He dropped to one knee and lifted a petal from the flat-tened grass, unsure of what he hoped to see. But in the vision, and now, with the reality before him, the red was too vivid to ignore. Somewhere behind him, the continuous argument between Elise and Líana prattled away, rising and falling in intensity as they went. Askon stared at the flower petal.

"The grass might be a better sign to follow," said a rumbling voice. He knew to whom it belonged.

"Jhed," Askon said.

The dark-faced man gave a terse nod and peered across the slope, gesturing to the path the Guardians had taken. "We watched them go that way and disappear into the trees. Why stop here?"

"Just before she fell, I felt her look at me," Askon said. "Maybe she left something, dropped something for us to find."

Askon knew that no such sign would be found. There had been none in the vision, and the scene that had played out across the water from where he stood helplessly watching her fall was too similar to what the fragments had shown them, too similar for there to be anything he wouldn't have already seen. However, Jhed, Alora's father, and the rest of their people had only recently ceased being their captors, threatening to, or at the very least considering, giving them over to the Guardians. Standing shoulder to shoulder in battle had strengthened Askon's trust by a notable measure, but not enough to reveal the true reason he now knelt in the scattered flowers.

"Unlikely," Jhed's voice rumbled. "If she left something behind, the Guardians will have found it. Although, they *did* retreat without hesitation. So I imagine it's possible." He knelt and began combing through the grass. Askon did the same and hoped that his efforts looked convincingly earnest.

After a long moment's searching, Askon heard the rapid approach of footsteps. Looking up, he saw the spectacled eyes and gray hair of Alora's father.

"They're gone, Jhed," he said, his looks wild and fretful. "They've taken her. And I don't understand why. Unless…unless they finally know. They know who I am, who *we are* and—"

"Shh…" Jhed hushed gently, slowly rising from the ground. Askon did not follow. Instead he turned his face back to the grass, hiding half a smile at Alora's father's paranoia, and the irony that his new companions seemingly had plenty of secrets of their own.

Jhed placed a heavy hand on his friend's shoulder. "We'll find her. And, there's no telling what *these people*," he tilted his head toward Askon, "might be into or up to. Perhaps they will tell us more, given time. Our…history hasn't been more than a theoretical risk of danger to your daughter before. There's no reason for that to have changed."

The wind picked up, rattling the brush and grass all around them. At the tree line, Líana and Elise reappeared. Askon rose to meet them, his cloak rippling in the breeze.

"There's nothing here," he said.

Elise arched an eyebrow. "Of course there isn't. Why would you think that?"

Next to her, Líana narrowed her eyes. "What she means to say is that there's a more obvious place for us to look than here."

"Don't tell me what I mean to say!" Elise snapped.

"Enough," Jhed's voice boomed. "It's a strange occurrence to see the Guardians of Basin City simply disappear after only apprehending one suspect. They could be waiting for us somewhere, or gathering reinforcements after what your pale little companion here has done." He kept his hand firmly in place as Alora's father chewed a thumbnail and eyed points of interest along the hillside.

Gently, Líana rested a hand on the nervous man's other shoulder. "Askon, this is Corwin, Alora's father. Elise and I met him earlier. Then, after some ill-considered *choices* were made, we were separated, and now find ourselves reunited. It seems necessary at the least that you two be formally introduced."

Askon bowed his head, but did not lower his eyes. "Corwin."

"Askon," Corwin replied. "You must be the brother." He took a breath, a glare forming on his face. "If the three of you think—"

Elise pushed forward. "No. There's no time to discuss this now. Askon, come with us. Corwin, follow if you like, or wait for the others to return, or send Jhed. I don't care. We came for two things—two people—and now the second of them has been taken, probably to the same place as the first."

"What does that even mean, you came for two things!" Corwin spluttered.

"Askon, now!" Elise commanded. Líana nodded, and Askon followed. "My husband and your daughter, if they're still alive, are being held in the High Spire, or will be as soon as Alora arrives. Come with me or stay behind. Either way, Líana and I know where to go next."

The five of them climbed through the brush, some distance from where they had left Daeron under the careful watch of Jhed's men. Líana led, followed by Askon, Corwin—whom Elise refused to leave behind "to scheme with Daeron again" despite her assertions concerning whether or not she cared—and Jhed behind him because Corwin had protested "being taken by those three" without someone he trusted by his side. Elise stalked along in the rear, watchful, impatient, and for the moment, silent.

"It's not far now," said Líana.

"What isn't?" Corwin asked. "Where are you leading us? What are we looking for?"

Jhed grunted. Askon wasn't sure whether it was in agreement with Corwin or in spite of Corwin's questions; questions that all of them knew wouldn't receive direct answers, at least not for the time being.

"There!" Líana held out a hand. She scanned the space, turning a slow rotation that encompassed the shoreline ahead and tree line behind. A breath came in and she listened with closed eyes for any sound, any trace that they had been followed or that any Guardians remained, lying in wait. Askon used the moment to do the same, peering down over the tussocky grass and gnarled trees to the pointed green reeds along the water. All seemed quiet as he turned his gaze to the trees that hushed the better part of the wind.

Corwin stepped forward first. Askon expected Elise to stop him. She didn't. Instead Líana opened her eyes and held out her hand again. "You stay here, for now."

It wasn't a suggestion. Askon turned, prepared to reinforce the statement if necessary, but Corwin halted. Behind him and a few feet up the slope, Jhed, with his thick arms crossed over his chest, only smiled, seemingly pleased to let the situation play out in whatever way Líana intended.

"It's simple enough," Líana continued. "You need our help, whether you know it or not, in order to get Alora back. And we need you, whether Elise likes it or not, to find our friend Thomas."

"And?" Jhed offered.

Líana smiled back. "Partnerships like these have to be built on trust."

Corwin bristled. "How are we supposed to—"

"And," Líana interrupted, "after the lack of trust you demonstrated back on the carriage, Corwin, you owe us one."

"At least one," Elise added.

"Sounds fair enough to me," Jhed said grinning. Corwin nibbled at his thumbnail again, opened his mouth to speak, and thought better of it.

"Alright," Líana replied. "We'll only need a moment. We'll be right where you can see us. All I ask is you give us that moment to show Askon something. Once he's seen it, undisturbed, then we'll decide what you need to know."

Jhed laughed. "She's bold, I'll give her that."

"And pretty enough that you find that boldness amusing," Elise muttered.

"I see it in you, too. The boldness, that is," he said.

"Hmm…" was her only response.

Líana led the way with Elise marching up alongside her. Askon followed them.

"Fine," said Corwin. "But I'm keeping track of—"

The sentence ended abruptly as Jhed jabbed an elbow into his friend's ribs.

Askon and the others walked slowly down the hillside until they were perhaps a hundred feet away from Corwin and Jhed. Distance enough, he thought, to confer privately, but not so much that they could make any sort of meaningful attempt to escape. And, if Líana was considering an escape, where would they even go? He hadn't seen any carriages on this side of the lake, and Jhed and Corwin had a superior knowledge of the terrain. It could only mean that, unsurprisingly, Líana had been truthful about their purpose here. Then suddenly he recognized the place where they stood.

He looked down dumbly as Líana kicked open the lid of Alora's hidden chest. Only this time, alongside the several books, a faint glow lit the interior, the light of the four missing fragments of Alora's Tear: Life, Space, Sight, and Time.

With a heavy sigh, he dropped to both knees before the opened box. He reached down to remove the Time fragment, to place it back around his neck where it belonged. The relief at seeing it again was palpable. His hand stretched out.

"Wait," Líana said.

Askon tilted his head toward her. It was a near miracle that the gems hadn't been taken with Alora. That she'd had the presence of mind to realize she'd be captured regardless and that she could communicate her loyalties by leaving the fragments behind felt near impossible.

"Why?" he asked.

Líana bent down next to him, like a hunter on the trail, and he smiled to himself as he realized for perhaps the hundredth time that *that* was exactly what she was.

"What do you notice? What do you remember?" she said.

He thought back, through the battles and lost time in front of the library, to the very spot where they stood, to the opened box and its contents. "The books are there, but the keepsake portrait—"

"She called it a capture when we spoke," Líana said, "And you're right. It's gone."

Askon nodded. "Probably collected it when she left the fragments. She knew she would be caught and taken by the Guardians. Do you think she might have *let them*?"

"I'm not sure, but that's not even what I'd hoped you'd see." She gestured back down to the chest. "Look again. Think further back."

And so he did. Beyond the library, and the voiceless Norill, before the long march down from the ridgetop, before he opened the door and stepped from Vladvir into the Glittering World. He thought back to the first time he'd been here, in the vision granted by the fragments. The wonder of dropping down from the sky, into Dalkaldur, seeing her for the first time, harried and on the run. Her flight as the soldiers, who he now knew to be the Guardians, chased her along the waterside and through the trees. He remembered watching her kneel, as he now knelt, and place the Time fragment into the chest.

He looked up at Líana and Elise. "There were only three fragments here in the vision. And two were already in the chest before she arrived. The last was Time."

"Exactly," said Líana. "Elise and I noticed it first when we were listening to Corwin and Daeron's conversation about *The Book of the Tear* through the door, after following him to her house."

"Noticed what?" Askon said.

"We're reliving the visions, both ours and Thomas's: Daeron taking the book; Corwin meeting him in the night; Alora's capture." Her eyes grew intent, willing him to complete the list.

Askon rocked back on his heels. "The imprisonment, the white room and the dark. The torture."

"The dying man!" Elise screamed. But it was in exasperation, Askon saw, at him, at what he was missing. "What if that is Thomas?!" And she too fell to her knees, sobbing.

Shaking her head, Líana continued. "No. This is one of the things she and I have been over. Thomas would have recognized seeing *himself* in the vision. And more importantly, or at least what I've come to think of as our best hope, the events are similar but none have been the same."

Askon thought for a moment.

Líana did not wait for him to work it out. "*We* showed up at Alora's home in the night; in the vision we were never there. Alora appeared on the far side of the lake, not the village side like the fragments showed us."

"And it's not the same set of gems," Askon finished.

CHAPTER TWENTY

An Unwelcome Darkness

Hoofbeat thunder. His own hard breathing. The mare's energy flagging. Much farther and he'd push her past limits she'd never come back from. The wrappings that bound his chest had worked themselves loose someways back along the trail. His hands reminded him that they could feel pain after going senseless for miles, and a clear, distant sun peered down on them. They'd have to stop. There was just no other way. Somewhere beneath the hoofbeats, the sound of the river was waiting, while behind them, well, he dared not look behind. Couldn't chance it before, couldn't bear to try it now. Maybe after they'd had a rest. He pulled back on the reins and Bird-dog slowed, bit by bit, step by step, to a stop.

"Hell of a run there," Dansil said, realizing his feigned confidence fell upon no human ears other than his own. "Hell of a run," he repeated. "Hope I didn't push you too hard. We've come a long way. I won't be losin' you now, so close to the end."

He managed a chuckle to himself, despite the circumstances, at what lengths a person will go to just to have a conversation—even when there's nobody to converse with. Unfortunately, the ripple of mirth was short lived. After seeing to the horse's immediate needs, he mustered the courage to peer out over the golden grass of the Vladvir Plain proper, fearing he'd see signs of the Norill he'd imagined were pursuing them in their flight. He leveled a hand over his eyes and tried his best to think what a seasoned scout or far-sighted half-elf might look for in the distance. But there was nothing for miles, nothing all the way to the horizon. Even the Ridge itself had long since slipped from view.

"Well, it's no surprise they can't outrun you!" he called to Bird-dog, who he'd left by the river's edge.

A sweeping glance around to the north, toward their destination, yielded similar results. Nobody for as far as the eye could see. Nothing at all really, besides long golden stems of grass waiting to lie down for the winter. The emptiness was freeing in a way. No one out here to ask questions, with mouths or with eyes. There'd be plenty of those, he was sure, soon enough. Making his way down to the water, he untucked his shirt from his trousers and peeled it off, feeling the wrappings give up their last remaining grip and dangle loosely down to his hips.

"A pain in the ass is what it is!" he said to no one, not even to Bird-dog this time. And it was true, but even so, it was necessary as breathing. As he worked the shirt up over his head and arms, exposing his bare chest to the cool sun, he half expected to hear John making some flat-footed comment about being caught out alone down by the reeds.

Expected or imagined? Imagined or hoped? Or was it all of them at once? Whatever it was, the feeling passed and the chill reminded him that though it hadn't yet arrived, winter wasn't far away, even here up north in the Plain where spring and summer seemed to take up more than their fair share of the year. With practiced hands, Dansil re-wrapped the cloth, starting at the bottom and working upward, round and round, pulling tight, but not too tight, until he came to the end of the strap. Then, after checking and double checking that it had been made secure, he slipped the shirt back over his head and tucked it in.

A battering of wings buffeted him as he was making the finishing touches. What felt like only inches from his ears, a shadow whipped overhead, and there, perched on the saddle, was the falcon. Its head bobbed as it stretched its wings, picking absently through the sable gray feathers. If anything it seemed…pleased with the accelerated progress its charges had made over the course of the morning. However, it didn't take flight again.

"Aha," Dansil said to it. "So even *you* have your limits eventually. Good thing, too. Because I'm thinkin' Bird-dog's gonna need a good while before she's ready to go again. Might as well make ourselves at home for a bit."

Dansil stepped forward, but the bird didn't move, it only stared him down as though it disapproved of this break, of breaks in general. Ignoring it for the moment, Dansil focused on rifling through his packs, gathering and eating a good portion of what food remained. There would be enough, or so he guessed, if they had to sleep another night. But, with the memory of the Norill on the Æsten Ridge still haunting his every ragged breath, he resolved to reach their destination before nightfall. The risk of dreams composed of countless expressionless Norill faces, of that unison repetition, the chanting of that one word—no. He did not want to contend with that out here on the road alone, even if it *was* only in his mind. They'd make a final push for Tolarenz, and they'd be there before sunset.

At the very least, he thought, it'd make their somewhat temperamental guide happy.

He laughed at himself again. And it felt good to laugh, even a nervous one.

They did not reach Tolarenz before nightfall. Far off along the edge of the world—that is, before the edge of the world disappeared under a glowering cloud of dusty storm—the peaks surrounding the valley of Tolarenz had been visible. Not for very long, Dansil thought, as the wind and rain pounded down and Bird-dog plodded morosely along. Wherever their feathered friend had gone, there'd been no sign of his silently-judgmental presence for several hours. Meanwhile, the darkening of angry clouds had deepened into the dark of night. And in that darkness, where the wind howled, Dansil found no shelter, no hollow in the hills, not even a twisted tree too stubborn to know what was good for it growing tall anyway in the flat infinity of the Plain.

He tucked his chin, retreating deeper into his hood, and wrapped the cloak's flying edges closer to his body. Shivering and miserable, he urged the tired horse forward, the rush of the great river Estelle rising and subsiding as the wind rested briefly, only to return with vengeance on its voice. Beneath him, rhythmic hoofbeats had given way to the slick slop and pop of deepening mud. However long they might proceed, it seemed to Dansil that his plans would have to change. And if the storm kept up, the change would have to be fast. Another wind-whipped sheet of rain pelted him, and he shook off what he could, but the damp had finally succeeded in soaking through. His spirits fell, but the storm seemed not to very much care how he felt.

On and on they pressed, for what else could they do? It was too dark to see anything but the road beneath him, though at least he knew the road did eventually lead to the little gap in the mountains, and from there to Tolarenz, and from there to John. With nowhere to shelter for the night, they pressed on, until the wind at last gave up and moved on over the plain to harry some other ill-provisioned travelers. For that, he was certainly grateful, but the rain still misted down, and from time to time somewhere far off, thunder boomed. Then, a lull in the rain brought with it a lull in Dansil's will to keep himself awake. He caught himself nodding off more than once. He knew that his mount would be feeling all the more exhausted from the morning's run and from carrying him along with the provisions for their journey, scant as they might now have been. The world grew bleary, and the slow slap of muddy hooves became a comforting murmur that drifted far away. He remembered falling asleep.

"Halt there!" a voice shouted. "Halt, I said! You hear me?! Stop and identify yourself."

Dansil heard the voice, was slow to respond. Bird-dog stopped.

"What's yer name, and what brings ya here in the middle of the night?!" the voice barked. "I got orders, an' they say to hail any an' all travelers on the road into this valley."

Sitting up in the saddle, Dansil blinked through a wide yawn and tried to shake the sleep away. "I thought the Valley of To-larenz welcomed folk of all kinds? Is that no longer the case?"

A few feet distant, a man came into view under the red glare of a torch that struggled to keep its own light alive. Drenched from head to foot, the man raised the brand slowly, careful not to spook the horse, presumably angling for a better look at its rider. "Pretty dangerous, ridin' alone in the dark, and under the storm that just passed." The man screwed up his face against the cold, or the damp, or at Dansil himself. "Well, lonely rider—though I find that suspicious enough as it is—who are ya and what brings ya to Tolarenz?"

"I'd rather not say until I've had a warm meal and a cozier bed than Bird-dog here," Dansil said with the softest breath of a smile. It was a smile he knew could've won over any number of shift-addled guards back at the Bones n' Stones. The squinting, rain-soaked man before him, Dansil figured, likely couldn't see it in the smoke-smeared red of his torchlight, and was probably too thick to observe it even in broad daylight.

The reaction that followed said as much. The man raised his other hand, spreading his fingers wide. "Now," he began. "I'm not the only person out here with these orders." He drew in his thumb. "And though my eyes are about as good for seein' at this hour as a hammer is for eatin' a bowl o' soup, *theirs* are sharp as a tack. Half-elven, ya see? So…" And he drew in his smallest finger. "Welcoming as ya might've heard we are, you'll forgive us if we aren't so stupid as to assume that everyone in Vladvir feels the same way, especially people *not* ridin' under the light o' the sun." He drew in the third finger.

"Alright! There's no need for whatever unpleasantness might come at the end of that count," Dansil said, sliding down from the saddle. As he planted his feet on the wet ground, he held his hands in the air. "I'm looking for John of Dalstone."

The man choked out a wheezing laugh at this. He lowered the middle finger. Now only one remained. "You mean to tell me you've shown up on yer own, at night, and asking for none other than the Lord o' gods-damned Dalstone? Ya been drinkin' tonight, boy?"

With a gentle raise of an eyebrow, Dansil took the insult in stride. It was, he knew, better than the alternative. And then an idea occurred to him.

"Who's in charge around here?!" Dansil asked, calling not just to the man in front of him, whose arms he figured must be growing tired, but to whoever was out there in the dark, waiting for that last finger to drop.

A proud smirk drew itself across the man's features. "At this particular guard post, I am."

Dansil tilted his head ever so slightly. "Not out here. Of course that's you. I mean of Tolarenz. Who's in charge?"

The man looked at him as if he had slid out of the saddle and laid an egg in the road. "John of Dalstone is in charge of Tolarenz. Given at the command of Askon of Tolarenz by way of King Edward himself."

"That's what I was hoping you'd say," Dansil replied, and he gestured behind him toward Bird-dog's saddlebags. "If you'll permit me?"

Eyes narrowing even further, the man nodded but lifted the final finger as if to say that he wouldn't hesitate to give the order.

Reaching into the bags, Dansil searched for a moment before finding what he was looking for. He gripped it in his hand. "I'm turning around, slowly. We've been through enough already today, and my horse does not need the added trauma of seeing me shot dead in the road." He turned and held the letter from King Edward out in front of him, the blue wax seal still clinging to the envelope.

The man leaned forward, peering past his guttering torch. After a moment he spread his hand again and gave a wave. "You try anything funny, you might have time to send me to the maker, but my men'll make sure you and I walk that road together."

Dansil tried to hold still, but he began to shiver. First, his hand, and then the rest of him, whether from the cold or the threat, or both, he couldn't say.

"Well, least you're afraid," said the man as he looked closer at the outstretched envelope. "That's the seal of the king's house, clear enough, and the color he fancies. You tryin' to say Edward himself sent you?"

Dansil nodded, and quicker than he thought possible, the man whipped his hand forward and snapped the envelope away. A small wounded sound slipped past Dansil's lips as it went.

The guardsman stepped back and carefully leaned the torch against a stack of stones. Slowly he extracted the letter from inside the envelope.

"It's not intended to be read by just anyone!" Dansil said, hoping that he'd covered the worry in his voice, knowing that he hadn't.

"That so?" the man said with a chuckle in his throat. "I'll see about that… 'Dansil, as I find myself busy with the work at hand, marshaling forces, investigating the Norill threat' and on an' on… 'Norill disturbances.' Here we are, 'duty to inform that…John of Dalstone…' Ow!" The man yelped and drew his hand back. Dansil thought he saw a gash appear and grow red.

A flutter of wings beat in the blackness and passed over Dansil's shoulder.

When he looked up, a glare furrowed the man's face, followed by a sneer. Then wide-eyed surprise, or maybe even fear took the place of both. "Oh, you keep that gods-dammed bird away from me!" he snapped.

Dansil turned, looking back to his horse. There on the saddle, the sable gray falcon perched, with the letter and envelope in its beak. Dansil turned back to the guard and raised a confused eyebrow.

"Don't you mock me," the man stammered. "I been on duty near the mews when that blasted devil was around. An' it didn't agree with me. Not in the slightest." He shook his head. "Belongs to Askon, that one does, if it belongs to anyone. Trained in the old elvish way. Birds like that are unpredictable enough as it is, even with all the tools an ordinary human falconer carries. But that one? Makes me uneasy just lookin' at him. Free as can be an' does whatever he wants."

Dansil breathed a little easier as he watched the man go from dire threat to ridiculous farce in the space of that same breath. He cocked a hip and shrugged. "So it seems you two have a history."

"You're free to go," the man grumbled. "Just take that thing with ya!"

Raising his hands again and taking a backward step or two toward Bird-dog, Dansil smiled. "We have a history too," he said. "And like you, I've come to the same conclusion. This falcon has its own agenda it seems. I suppose it'll leave when it pleases, and not a moment before."

As Dansil turned from the guard to face the falcon, he saw that the moment had already passed. The envelope lay wedged between the saddle bags, and a flutter of wingbeats trailed off into the darkness, headed north. Climbing into the saddle, Dansil tipped a nod toward the guard and urged Bird-dog forward. With the storm now past, the sky opened up above him, speckled with stars and a bright moon. For a while he rode on, gazing up into that sky, while off to his right, a stream glinted in the new light, silver and rippling.

CHAPTER TWENTY-ONE

A City of Cities

"It'll take longer," Jhed told Corwin after the latter had suggested something called the Maintenance Line. Apparently, folk from Basin City—or what Askon had again called the Glittering World, only to be corrected by several of their new companions—used two sets of the mesmerizing suspended carriages: one for ordinary citizens, and one for what Corwin had called *auxiliary workers*. Elise seized the opportunity to once again remind him that the creatures who silently, almost invisibly, did the bidding of the Elves in Basin City were, in fact, called Norill. Corwin accepted that such a fact might have been true in Vladvir.

But, true as it was, and whether Alora's father actually accepted that truth or not, they had all climbed into the rust-encrusted but otherwise functional boxes that rode the line down from the Dalkaldur rim and into the city proper. Gone were the glass doors and polished brass of the carriages they'd ridden around the lake; maintenance, it seemed, made do with just a square opening that passengers could use to step on and off the carriage. It had been less stable, less smooth, and certainly to Askon's judgment, less safe. Everything about them was just that: less. As such, only six passengers could fit into each carriage, though Askon came to think of them more like featureless airborne crates than anything resembling a carriage back home. He, Líana, and Elise had ridden with Corwin and Jhed, the two now seemingly inseparable, along with another of Jhed's people, a massive figure whom Corwin had introduced as Tinley.

"It'll take longer," Jhed said again, when the first maintenance carriage had come to a stop and Corwin had suggested they take intentionally unintuitive lines in order to confuse the path to their destination. This plan had sent them all over the southern side of the city.

But to call it a city was beyond anything Askon might have considered understatement. Here in the Glittering World, the word *city* meant something entirely different in terms of scale. He was sure that Thomas would have been able to estimate its size, the number of its people, if Thomas had been with them. On his own, Askon could at first only manage *immense*. Perhaps a forest of structures, he thought, as he watched row after row of buildings taller than any he'd ever witnessed pass by unendingly beneath them. Between the rows, channels that contained rivers snaked along, here and there peeking out and glinting in the sun. And far off in the distance, towering above it all, the High Spire pierced the very sky, sparkling like a spearhead of clear glass. A city of cities had been the last of his attempts to wrap the enormity into words.

As they'd descended from the ridgeline of Dalkaldur Park, and the novelty of the city's breadth and scope had faded, the monotony of building after building lulled Askon into its steady flickering rhythm. Sleep crept up, ambushing him with its heaviness. He awoke, or might have loosely described it as such, when they changed lines, each time nodding back into fitful dreams only to be awoken again to trade carriages, crate after crate, the same as the ones before. Such was the proper rest he so desperately needed held at bay. Elise and Líana had done much the same, as far as he had been able to tell. How far the carriages traveled, he had no hope of guessing. Had he been awake and focused, had he been determined to estimate the distance of their journey, the repetitive passage of similar structures would have confounded his efforts all the same.

"It'll take longer," Jhed was saying once more, as they stepped off the last of the maintenance carriages that Corwin was willing to ride. Askon blinked back sleep again and disembarked. The sun bent bright bars of light down on them, harsh against his face. He shaded his eyes with a flattened hand.

"I know," Corwin said. "But I'm not the only one who can repeat himself around here. As I said before, we don't want our new friends having any idea where we're going, and certainly not enough for them to lead someone else there."

Jhed smiled and looked them over. "Either they're who they say they are, from where they say they're from, or they're the best actors I've ever had the pleasure to observe. In the case of the latter, I'd have no choice but to give credit where credit is due." He laughed to himself. "And if it's the former, they've been asleep for so much of the ride they'd have little hope of getting back to Dalkaldur Park without a guide."

Askon sighed. Before he had fallen asleep, Corwin was refusing to answer any of his questions. Tinley hadn't spoken at all, only glowered in a relatively obvious, if not altogether unsuccessful, attempt to look imposing. The silence did enhance the effect, but the dark face was soft and concerned at the edges. Jhed, unlike the others, had spoken when he seemed moved to, out of boredom or simple amusement, but his words were of no use. He might as well have been as silent as the other two, for whatever he did say revealed nothing.

Askon surveyed their surroundings, an empty platform flanked by high walls of ramshackle construction. It reminded him of the half-elven quarter in South City, with its mixed materials and chaotic aesthetic compared to the surrounding architecture. Only here, the materials were more uniform on their own, with straighter edges and more consistency from piece to piece, though the overall structures were still a haphazard composite of wood panels, stonework, and discolored metal plates. The people's faces, too, were different from South City. The distinct mottled gray skin and wide eyes of the Norill kind passed in and out of doors or appeared behind windows, all too similar to those they'd seen on the Æsten Ridge and at the Greyarc. They moved about, but idly, as though the impulse responsible for sparking attention or curiosity had simply vanished from their minds.

"Well," Corwin said. "I don't intend to give away the position of the one safe house we have left. I vote we walk the remaining way. And yes Jhed, I am aware that it will in fact, *take longer.*"

And so they walked, sticking to the streets and alleys where the buildings were either occupied by Norill or vacant for the moment while their residents were away at their daily tasks. The still-fractured party wended its way toward whatever destination their leaders had in mind. Askon assumed they were going to the location Corwin, Alora, and a handful of others had called "Jhed's Place" by the most circuitous route possible. Líana and Elise talked as they walked, though pointedly not to one another, occasionally comparing what they saw to what they had seen while pursuing Daeron to Alora's home. They spoke of the lights in Basin City, a sight that Askon too had seen when they first arrived on the rim of Dalkaldur. There were no such lights visible in this section of the city, or at least none he could detect in the light of day. Corwin assured them that, indeed, there would be many such lights come nightfall, but that they were also simply less plentiful, even rare, here in the Auxiliary District.

Hours went by in their winding crisscross of the city's less populated streets. They met face-to-vacant-face with several Norill who didn't even acknowledge their presence, let alone question or otherwise accost them. All around, the homes and workspaces had remained an assortment of patchwork design. Askon refrained from comment while Elise lamented the treatment and behavior

of these Norill. Corwin and the others remained generally unmoved by her lecturing.

Eventually they had come to an abrupt separation between the
Auxiliary and what Corwin called the Lowborn District. Askon
noted that the division was immediate and unfaltering. In King's
City, or any other population center in Vladvir, such transitions
were gradual, often bringing folk of different backgrounds together as their spaces overlapped. Sometimes this was to the general
benefit and led to a certain familiar understanding between two
groups, but most times it was cause for contention and conflict. In
Basin City, however, they simply crossed from one to the other by
walking from one building to the next. Askon found it almost unsettling how clean the shift had been.

The change had also been as drastic as it had been abrupt.
Gone were the various structural materials, replaced by precisely
fitted stonework, glass windows, and brass fixtures. Líana and
Elise recognized the style from their time spent following Daeron.
Roads and walkways were clean, the sheer walls composed entirely
of the same uniform stone, with only a few variations from building to building, all of which were very tall to Askon's reckoning.
Perhaps not every one would have rivaled the Great Wall of South
City, but many did, and many surpassed that height, in some cases
doubling it as far as he could tell. Askon could not understand
how such things could be built, how they remained standing without being subject to the winds, or even just how they avoided col-
lapsing under their own inconceivable weight.

In the Lowborn District, Corwin had grown more furtive as they moved through the streets. And yet, they had encountered several individuals and small groups of people as they made their inconspicuous way. Most of the city's Lowborn folk were dark of face and skin—like Jhed, Daeron, and to a lesser degree Alora—with pointed ears longer than any of Vladvir's half-elves. Most spoke some greeting as they passed, others simply kept walking, absorbed in conversation or focused on their own errands. Nearly all wore circlets of some kind, whether of silver or copper, brass or dull iron; one even looked to Askon like polished glass. Some were lighter of skin—as were Corwin, several of Jhed's followers, and of course Líana and Askon himself. Elise, by comparison, was ghostly white and the only person Askon had seen with rounded ears since they'd come to the Glittering World. He wondered if there were any humans here at all. He had always imagined this place as somewhere that all, or at least most, of the people looked like him. Now that he was here, though, he had to settle for sharing very little in common.

And then Corwin's maze-like path led them away from populated areas, down narrow streets, into yet narrower alleys until they came to a dead end.

Líana looked to Elise. "Well, this certainly seems familiar."

"It does," Elise replied, "though the door's on the left instead of the right. Lower buildings. No cats."

Jhed chuckled, his voice low and deep. "Not yet, anyway. If we're still around tonight, step outside and tell me about all the cats you *don't* hear."

Askon watched as Jhed strode past them, past where Corwin had stopped, past the last remaining doorway to the end of the alley. "Well? You coming or not?" he asked.

Corwin and the others followed, leaving Askon, Líana, and Elise confused.

With a smile, and a glint in his eye, Jhed turned and disappeared through the solid brickwork wall as if it were no more than a bank of morning fog. The others followed closely behind while Daeron gaped along beside them. Corwin waited, motioning Askon forward.

"H-how?" Askon stammered.

When Corwin gave no immediate answer, Elise pushed past and vanished through the wall. It rippled faintly for a moment, like a pool under a gentle rain, and then grew still. Líana followed her lead but lifted her hands just before contacting the brick. Her fingertips passed through. She gasped and pulled them back. The wall seemed undisturbed. Then she shouldered forward and was gone.

"Yes, yes, it's very incredible, but we need to move!" Corwin said, and ducked through.

Askon approached, raised his arm as Líana had done, outstretched his fingers. A tingle traveled along them, the briefest sensation that reminded him of—

Then a pale hand shot through the wall, a familiar bracelet around its wrist. The fingers clasped his forearm and yanked him through to the other side.

Askon had expected it to feel similar to passing through a cloud of fog or thick mist, something like how it had *looked* when Jhed passed through, but instead, the image was no thicker than fine linen. Maybe less.

He stumbled forward into an alley that seemed in every way identical to the dead end they had just observed. He expected it to be dark behind the wall, like going indoors, but the sun shone down, casting his shadow out in front of him. He turned, looking back the way they had come, expecting to see the same unbroken brick-wall-image behind him. But what he saw instead was the full length of the alley and the wider street beyond. There, a distracted elven couple passed in energetic conversation, utterly unaware that the alley held a dozen fugitive citizens of Basin City and three bewildered travelers from Vladvir.

Askon squinted, trying to bring the illusion back into focus. The best he could manage was a blur at the edges of the stonework walls.

"It leverages circlet tech!" an excited voice said, high and full. It was a voice that reminded Askon of a few heavyset grandmothers back in Tolarenz that he'd always made sure to greet in passing. That is, before Iramov and the Death fragment had come. There had been grandmothers amongst the travelers who made their way from South City, of course, but most of them were lean and wary, with thin voices full of warning.

"Made it myself," the jovial voice went on, "using donations from folk who didn't require theirs for assistive purposes. It's why some of us don't wear 'em. Me, for instance, and Corwin. But there's plenty who simply cast theirs happily aside, soon as we found out they've been used to gather information on folks."

Askon turned slowly away from the alley where the illusion of the wall had appeared and looked up into the face of Tinley, where two brilliant blue eyes sparkled against brown skin and a wide white grin. Askon wondered if he'd ever seen someone look so genuinely and unreservedly friendly.

"Oh, don't worry though, friend!" Tinley exclaimed, palms out in a placating gesture. "I've masked that element, the signature they use for tracking, on all the circlets around here, whether they're being used as intended or…repurposed as I did with the ones in the alleyway. Folk need them for this or that sometimes. Corwin's Alora, for example, can't see from me to you without hers. Could hardly make it down the very street she lives on."

Askon's mind reeled as Tinley loomed over him with that broad, overpowering smile. "Tech?" was all he could manage.

Tinley lifted one enormous palm and popped it against an equally enormous forehead. "What'm I even *thinking*! Of course you wouldn't know anything about it, being from where you say you're from and all. Prob'ly best if we get ourselves inside. Then, assuming you folk are judged to be who you say you are—and I figure you are, amazing as it might seem—I'll tell you anything you want to know." A deep laugh shook the huge chest and shoulders. "And I'm willing to bet you'll have a great deal of questions that'll want answers once we get started. C'mon!"

Following Tinley to the single door where Líana and Elise stood waiting, Askon left the alleyway and its mysterious wall image behind. The door, however, was no illusion, and the interior beyond was dimly lit. He took a breath, his mind still churning through possibilities: from rescuing Alora and Thomas, to the wonders of the Glittering world, to the abrupt turn from kidnappers to allies that Corwin, Jhed, and their followers had made. For now, he did the only thing he could, and stepped inside.

CHAPTER TWENTY-TWO

A Clean Slate

At Jhed's beckoning, Askon and Líana sat at a long low table. Elise did not sit.

"You'll want something to eat, I assume," Jhed began, placing his hands heavily on the opposite side of the table and resting his weight there, "followed perhaps—and I mean no offense—by a chance to wash, and then a full night's worth of sleep, whether during the night or not." He gave them a half-smile and tossed his head, a thin beaded braid swinging down in front of one eye. "Do I have it right?"

Askon nodded, the hood of his cloak fallen in a shapeless bundle across his shoulders. "You do. About what we need, any-way. I'm not sure what my companion here is prepared to allow, however." He tilted his head to indicate Elise, who now stalked up and down the table's length. At the far end, a few of Jhed's men and women took seats, eyeing the new arrivals with curiosity more than suspicion, and generally paying little heed to them beyond that.

Jhed tossed his head again and the half-smile grew full. "I know we didn't meet on the friendliest of terms, but I hope you'll understand our reasoning."

"You were protecting Alora," Líana said. "Especially for Corwin's part, I understand. Who wouldn't be motivated to find their own daughter, to use whatever resources they could muster to rescue her from danger. I'm just grateful—for all of our sakes—that you didn't turn us over to the Guardians immediately."

Elise stopped pacing. "And I'd like to know the reason why. The *real* reason. No more deceptions."

Jhed's smile leveled. "Remember that this is *my* house," he rumbled. "It may not look like much, but it has taken us a very long time to establish and maintain." He breathed deeply, his eyes softening a bit. "But you could have tried to escape when the Guardians arrived. You didn't have to fight alongside us. Yet, you did. And how you fought, what you did to them, I'm not sure I understand. So… Now that we've seen battle together, traveled together, and will soon break bread together, maybe the three of you and the many of us can have fewer secrets."

Askon nodded again. "I think so. Though, I can't speak for my companions."

"No, indeed," Jhed said, rising to his full height. He waved to one of the men at the end of the table and looked back at Askon and the others again. "It's mostly soup and bread around here these days. Will that do?"

"Yes," said Askon and Líana quickly.

Even Elise's "Mhm…" sounded eager, to Askon's ears anyway, much more so than he imagined she intended.

Jhed's wave ended with four fingers waggling to indicate that he would be eating as well. Askon found the gesture almost comically lighthearted, and so too it seemed, did Jhed. One of the men at the end of the table disappeared down the long rectangular room and into a door on the right. Jhed slid onto the bench across from them, leaning forward onto his elbows, his dark arms flexing, and rested his chin on his hands. "So I see you had the pleasure of meeting Tinley," he said. "They're an endlessly fascinating individual. They could be silent as a post for hours, only to have the dam suddenly burst at the first sign of interest in one of their areas of expertise."

"I'm sorry," Líana said, leaning across the table and lowering her voice. "You said 'they' and 'their' as if you're talking about more than one person. Are there two people in there, two Tinleys I mean?"

"The Norill have a word for this," Elise interrupted. "It's a condition of the mind in which two drastically different personalities appear to live inside one body."

Jhed shook his head and frowned. "No. No. Nothing at all like that. There's just the one Tinley. They're simply neither man nor woman, neither 'he' nor 'she,' I suppose, in this context. Or so they tell me anyway. And who better to do the telling?" He grunted a laugh.

A dispute began to form in Askon's mind, but as he thought back to his time in the carriage and the alleyway with the irrepressibly kind-faced Tinley, he honestly couldn't say for certain if he thought the proportions and voice and mannerisms and size seemed more like that of a man or more like that of a woman. In some cases it was one, and in some it was the other, and there was a third category for which he couldn't say with any certainty at all. But many things in the Glittering World seemed to him inexplicable and confusing. This, at least, he could understand on the face of it, even if the finer details eluded him.

"I've never met someone like that," was what Askon settled upon as the best thing to say.

Jhed smiled, and gave them all a slow nod. "Neither had I. But as the saying goes, 'Lowborn or High, Basin City makes room for all kinds.'"

"Not for Norill-kind," seethed Elise. "Who, by the way Askon, do have a similar practice, despite my earlier mistake. You saw for yourself in Vitæsta."

And so he had. Many of the Norill in Brâghda's village—the village that had harbored Elise when she had nowhere else to go, the village that had come to their aid in the battle of Dalstone— had appeared genderless, or at least visually so. They dressed the same, were of similar size and proportions. Perhaps, Askon thought, the idea was not so unique to the Glittering World after all.

"Well," Jhed said, "depending on how long you're around, you'll have plenty of time to get to know Tinley. They seem to have taken a liking to you already." Jhed looked up as the person carrying the soup arrived, placing bowls in front of them and a large cutting board with two round loaves of bread in the table's center. He finished by laying a serrated knife along the board.

"Anything else, *sir*?" the young man asked.

Jhed chuckled to himself. "What's this 'sir' nonsense?"

The young man grinned back. "You were just looking very *official* with these new arrivals."

"Oh, was I?" Jhed replied. "Well, my apologies then. Thanks for bringing the bowls over. It just seemed right to make these three feel a little more welcome. Why don't you go get some for yourself? It's been a long day."

"Yes, *sir*," the young man said with a wry laugh and walked away toward the same door into which he had disappeared before.

Jhed had already begun cutting the bread into slices. He gestured to Líana and to Elise, who sat down at the bench in front of her bowl. Jhed dunked his bread into the thick soup, which Askon, if he was being particular, would have called a stew. He took a bite. The sight of it alone was enough to rouse Askon's appetite. When the smell reached him, he tried to remember the last time they had eaten a hot meal. By the third bite of meat and potato and carrot, he decided it didn't matter.

The wash came next. Try as they might, their efforts in the Dalkaldur Park lake had only marginally improved their cleanliness. Since then they'd been at times left lying in the dirt, dragged through the air on carriage tops, led down a drainage tunnel, bound to chairs, and battered by the foliage along the water's edge. Not to mention their encounters with the Guardians. By comparison, Jhed and the others from the Glittering World looked markedly better off.

Jhed led them past the kitchen to the end of the main chamber. There, two small hallways flanked either side. They took the path to the left which split again in either direction.

"One on the left there and one on the right," Jhed said unceremoniously. Then with a chuckle, "And unless you're used to going tandem, the third will have to wait their turn." He spun on a heel and began to walk away. Then he stopped. "Towels inside. Just be sure they make it to the opposite end, back through the main hall, and onto the racks when you're finished." He gestured lazily ahead of him. "Can't remember who's on laundry this week, but someone will get to them."

When Jhed was gone, Líana deferred to Askon, choosing instead to wait on a small bench between the two hallways. He protested, but she insisted, so he rounded the corner, unsure of what to expect. Inside there was a mirror—perhaps the largest Askon had ever seen, at least the length of his arm in height and width—with a small shelf below. To the side, a ceramic bowl rose from the floor, a privy of some kind, he assumed. But somehow, ingeniously, inside was only water and none of the smell he would have expected if such a thing had been constructed in Vladvir. He resolved to ascertain its intended use before making a fool of himself, but the seat and cover were of familiar enough design that he remained reasonably confident in his guess.

Somewhere above him, he heard the faint sound of running water. Turning further to his left, there was another shelf with several soft towels rolled neatly and stacked together. Beyond that, the wood floor ended at a low rounded lip of marble only a couple of inches high that transitioned seamlessly to gently sloping rows of wide stone tiles, each one carefully mortared into the next until a long grate joined the floor and far wall.

Askon wondered how Jhed's people kept the mortar from cracking, as such a floor would immediately have done back home. On the wall, a long burnished brass handle gleamed. Looking up, Askon saw that the wall only reached about three quarters of the room's full height. There a lip of stone, under which even a person as tall as Tinley could stand, protruded by a handsbreadth. From there it sloped upward, a bit more steeply than the floor, for a few feet. Beyond that, the light of the sun came streaming in through some window yet further on that Askon could not see, the sound of running water emanating from the aperture.

After he had disrobed, leaving his armor and clothes stacked and hung on the various shelves and hooks, he stepped onto the cool tiles and pulled the lever. He heard the water draw nearer and braced himself for the chill, but it never came. Instead he was suddenly awash in soothing warmth as if somewhere above him someone had fetched and heated bucket upon bucket and was dutifully, unfalteringly pouring it down the sloping wall, where it leapt from the spout and fell down onto him.

How long he stood there, Askon didn't care to consider. He lathered the soap into his hair, careful to work his way through its length, avoiding any knots or tangles. Suddenly the water turned cold. He jumped back at the abrupt change, nearly slipping on the marble lip. But as quickly as the heat had disappeared, it returned. Hurriedly, Askon rinsed the remaining soap from his head, pulled the lever back to its original position, and toweled himself dry. When he was finished, he thought he might be cleaner than he ever had been. The regenerative relaxation of the continuous water flow made him feel altogether renewed. To bathe in a warm tub, even one that receives new water mid-soak, was not the same. He added this curious contraption to his list of questions.

Clean, dry, and back into shirt and trousers, Askon emerged from the bathing room to find the bench empty where he'd left Líana. With a shrug, he adjusted the bundle of weapons, armor pieces, and cloak around all, and made for the opposite hallway to leave his towel as instructed. When he returned, Líana stood with towel in hand, tousling her damp hair, and with a similar bundle to Askon's under the opposite arm. She approached from down the hall, depositing the towel into the room from which Askon had just done the same. As he waited for her, he tried to remember the last time he'd seen her hair loose of its ever-present braid.

She grinned at him. "Even the baths in King's City can't compare to that," she said. I could have stood there for hours, but it kept going cold."

"Mine did once as well," said Askon. "And it seems maybe I felt the same, considering I'm only just out, and you're here already."

"Seems so," she said. "Let's go sit, and see if we can't get Jhed or Corwin to tell us more about this place, about what they're up to here." She flipped a long tress over her shoulder and shook out the rest behind her. "I've got to comb through this. Besides, I'll wager that Elise has already begun the questioning."

Back in the main hall, Elise had indeed done just that. She, Corwin, and Jhed were already engaged in what John might've called a "one person discussion for three people." The two men were sitting, Jhed leaning back looking mostly unperturbed and Corwin upright and tight as if he were a spring waiting to fire himself straight into the ceiling. Elise stood over them with both hands pressed into the table. She lifted one to drive a pointed finger in Corwin's direction before all but slapping it back down onto the wooden surface. Though Askon could see only her back, he could tell she had dropped all sense of decorum or politeness long before he and Líana had arrived.

"And if you won't tell us," she was saying, "and you won't let us leave, then how have things changed at all since you had us bound and gagged back in Dalkaldur?"

Jhed arched an eyebrow. "Well—" he began.

But Corwin interrupted him. "What makes you think you can show up out of nowhere, cause my daughter to be—be abducted, jeopardize our operations here, and then simply ask us to trust you with the details?"

"I don't see how you have much of a choice," Askon said as he slid onto the bench, making room for Líana. "That is, if you want our help getting her back." He placed the bundle of weapons and armor onto the tabletop.

Líana did the same and, producing a wide wooden comb, began to slowly, deliberately run it through her hair. "It does make the most sense," she said, her one blue eye peering out at them. "Otherwise, both your people and the three of us will try in whatever ways we might to retrieve her."

"And Thomas," Elise said, her expression level as a sharpened blade. "I am here for him first, last, and only. I've followed along for Askon's obsession with that girl long enough."

And now the spring did fire. Corwin shot up, nearly toppling the bench upon which he and Jhed were seated. "I will not," he exploded, "allow you—or anyone else, for that matter—to call my daughter 'that girl' as if she were nothing more than an afterthought!"

Elise balled her hands into fists and pounded the table. "Until Thomas is back at my side, that is *exactly* what she is to me!" she snapped, and though Corwin, Jhed, and the room at large would hear the cold command of the wolf, Askon and Líana shared a knowing glance. Beneath the veneer, Elise's voice spoke of panic, fear, and a wild grasping for anything she could still control.

Corwin sucked in a breath, but Jhed placed his wide dark hand flat on his friend's chest, easing him back down into his seat. Elise stormed away toward the bathing rooms. Other eyes had turned to face the spectacle, around the room as well as at the far end of the long table. A few of them glanced meaningfully from Elise to Jhed. He shook his head and waved them off, the beaded braid twitching alongside his expressionless face.

A long moment passed, the room slowly returning to its normal bustle and thrum. Askon wondered where Elise would go, and for how long she'd stay away, before turning his attention back to Jhed and Corwin. "Listen," he said. "Líana is right that we need to work together if we stand any chance of getting our people back. We could each have perfect plans that when executed independently end up doing nothing more than confounding the other. And, though Elise has certainly taken the wrong tack, she's also right that we can't work together until both parties feel they can trust each other. What do you say to that?"

Corwin ran his hands through his thick shock of white hair. Jhed leaned forward, elbows on the table, and kneaded the muscle in his palm with the opposite thumb. He let out a long breath through his nose, and his nostrils flared. He turned to Corwin and the two exchanged a small nod.

"Only if we ask the questions first," Jhed rumbled.

Askon didn't move, he simply stared back into the dark eyes across the table.

"Yes," Líana said. "We'll answer your questions."

The light in the windows high above had shifted, casting shadows across the gray mortar lines and red bricks. Jhed had called for a round of drinks, what Askon's assessment would have called a passable ale, though he had heard neither Jhed nor Corwin name it as such, and their conversation had left no room to ask its proper name in the Glittering World. Regardless, the cups had gone dry for the second time before Askon and Líana had finished the telling of their tale.

At times leaping from point to point or looping back due to an exhausting litany of questions and follow-ups, mostly from Corwin, the story more or less recounted the entirety of their journey: the visions that began it, the strange Norill attacks across Vladvir, whatever they were doing atop the Æsten Ridge, Sehlín's attacks, Thomas's capture, and their discovery of Dalkaldur. All the while, both Askon and Líana had deftly avoided any mention of the fragments. But now, it came to it.

Corwin was shaking his head, again. "This just simply doesn't add up. In your…" he trailed off, searching for the right word, "…where you're from—"

"Vladvir," Askon and Líana said together.

"Right," Corwin said, nodding behind steepled fingers. "In Vladvir you saw what was happening here, in Basin City?"

Askon shook his head and, even though he'd been considering it for some time, decided to share his working theory openly now. "No. That's what we *thought* we were seeing in the visions. We thought that whatever the visions were showing us was occurring in the Glittering World at the same time as what was happening in Vladvir. However, that wasn't the case, at least not entirely. I wasn't sure until Alora was taken, but now, I think I am."

Líana leaned in toward Corwin. "It's why Elise and I were so surprised to find you, Alora, and Daeron discussing *The Book of the Tear*. We knew exactly what you would say, what you would do, because—"

"You'd seen it already," Corwin finished, tapping his fingers together rapidly and then lacing them into his hair. "But if that is indeed true, in Vladvir you were seeing things not only from a different world but from a different time."

Askon nodded and tipped back the cup, finding it dry. "Yes. Both of those at once. We saw into the Glittering World, what you call Basin City, *and* we saw ahead of the time when we would eventually arrive, by a matter of hours, perhaps a day at most. We'd seen Alora be captured by the Guardians and thought we could change it."

"But you didn't," Corwin snapped. "She's still gone, and you still haven't told us the most important part of your story. It's incomplete. Visions, and maintenance creatures appearing in your world. Something is missing. You're leaving something out. I know it!" His anger rose as he worked through the list.

"You are," Jhed agreed. "Implausible as all of it sounds, we still don't know how the visions came, and more importantly, how you got here. What is it? What's missing?"

"Alora's Tear," Elise said.

Askon gasped and wheeled around to face her. When she had approached, or for how long she had been listening, he did not know. Before he could speak, even attempt to stop her, she pressed forward.

"Once we have explained," she went on, "you're going to tell us what you're doing here and how you can help us get my husband back. Rest assured, Askon will retrieve Alora—or die in the attempt," Elise finished and took a seat next to Líana.

Jhed laughed, loud and long. "You certainly know how to make a re-entrance, don't you?"

Elise's face was still. Her black eyes unmoving.

"Right," Jhed said after no response was forthcoming, "then explain this 'Alora's Tear' you say will complete the story for us."

Still stunned, Askon looked to Líana and Elise, the latter still as stone and the former looking back with eyes that told him there was no use in hiding things any longer. He inclined his head toward Líana and reached for the silver chain around his neck.

"This," he said holding the glowing green gem in his palm, "is a piece of Alora's Tear; the Time fragment."

Líana placed her hands on the table. "The Life and Space fragments," she said calmly, tapping the ringed fingers against the tabletop respectively.

"Death," Elise said flatly, though even to Askon it sounded like a threat.

Gently, Líana took Elise's hand in hers. After a moment, Líana looked back up at Jhed and Corwin. "Thomas carried Sight." She squeezed Elise's hand. "But for now that burden falls to her as well."

"We used them to get here," Askon said. "Somehow, in that place, on the ridge above Dalkaldur, we were able to open a door, a bridge from Vladvir to the Glittering World. The mountains were the same. The valley was the same, but everywhere we looked there were lights, of kind and number which do not exist in Vladvir or any of the near or far kingdoms. The Glittering World was Basin City, and the events we had been shown by the fragments had yet to occur, though we did not know it yet. All I knew was that the fragments had shown us a person who needed our help, and in attempting to do so, we had lost our friend. We sit before you now with the same goal: to bring them back."

Corwin tapped Jhed on the shoulder, leaning in to whisper something that, try as he might, Askon could not hear. After a moment Jhed nodded, saying, "It seems only fair," louder now, so that all of the group could hear. "I'll let Corwin tell it."

At this Alora's father glanced around the room. Askon thought him lucky to be amongst friends and compatriots, as had he been amongst wary enemies, his efforts at concealment would have been as obvious as a pigeon in a falcon's mews. After he had thoroughly scanned their surroundings, Corwin slid his hands onto the table.

"There are times when coincidence means more than just the timely concurrence of significant events," he said and licked the end of his thumb. Pressing into the soft area below his index finger on the opposite hand, he worked the thumb back and forth until slowly a dark mark came into view—a small tattoo in the shape of a teardrop.

CHAPTER TWENTY-THREE

Respite

A pale moon rode high in the night sky, awash in a spray of twinkling stars smoked with clouds of purple and blue that floated far above the world. Feeling small and slow, Dansil stared up at that moon and into those stars as if he might find an answer written among them. Catching himself in the process, he snuffed a little laugh and lowered his eyes to the dozen or so dim candlelit windows along the outskirts of Tolarenz. They'd met no further guards or sentries on the way in, none that he had seen at least. Once or twice, the falcon had circled out ahead, impatient as ever, a feeling Dansil shared.

As Bird-dog clopped through the silent streets, Dansil made for the building with the brightest lights, in hopes that he'd find it a suitable place to stable the horse, pay for a room, and perhaps later, a hot meal. "The Fledgling" he read on the sign, which had been tacked alongside the front door. He tied Bird-dog to the post, slid down out of the saddle with a stretch that made his spine crack from below his ribs up to his neck, and tried the handle.

The latch moved freely, but the door resisted, wedged tight rather than locked. "They'd sand that down if they knew what's good for them. First thing your customers come into contact with, and it's poorly maintained." He rocked back and gave the door a solid shove with his shoulder. It popped open and swung free. Straightening up, brushing back his hood, and running his fingers through his hair, Dansil pulled in a lungful of air laced faintly with woodsmoke before surveying the common room of the Fledgling.

A fitting name, as the place wasn't much to take in at all. The Bones n' Stones was larger by nearly double, not including the stage and accompanying seating area. At the far wall of the room he had stepped into, a fire burned heartily. Here and there a number of oil lamps sat cold and unlit, while two glowed dimly at either side of a roughly crafted bench that faced a pair of equally rough looking chairs.

Word had made its way throughout Vladvir concerning the tragedy of Tolarenz. Some of the talk, of course, had been concerning how "those folk" had "probably brought it upon themselves." Dansil had even heard a table at the Stones musing on their desire to have been present for the massacre. But he'd made sure those particular patrons vacated that table and informed them that they wouldn't have one again.

He was, unsurprisingly, in the minority in his consideration for Vladvir's half-elves, and though he often wished the others in Finnestre had been similarly considerate, half-elves and whole towns'-worths of people disappearing was just too much and too far away for most folks. They had instead drawn a simple conclusion—that it had to have been something the people of Tolarenz had done wrong—and thought nothing more about it. Their confidence that their own way of life would protect them from such tragedy was their only armor, and they kept it laced tight.

"Can I help you, sir?" a soft voice asked from the stairway leading up alongside the fireplace. "It's very late. But we've got rooms left, and we're still accepting coin from those who have it, day or night."

A bit startled, and dead tired, Dansil looked up from the dimly glowing lamps, and his reverie, to see a small woman in her late middle age looking genially across at him. "Oh! Yes, please. I'm looking for a place to stay for the night, and somewhere to stable my horse if possible."

The woman smiled, the shadows shifting across a dress clearly made for a comfortable night's sleep rather than a day's work serving customers. "How long do you plan on staying?" she asked, making her way down the stairs to a bar that looked more like a wide kitchen counter and that was indeed backed by the kitchen itself.

"I'm not sure," said Dansil. "Could be just the one night. Could be a few nights. Maybe more." He slid a thick silver coin across the bar.

She snapped it up and eyed it in the half-light. "This will do for a few nights, though if it's going to be on the 'maybe more' side, I'll need to be a bother about it again."

"Of course!" said Dansil with the most charming smile he could still muster at this hour. "I'd be glad to pay ahead if it will set you more at ease. We can settle up when I go."

"Certainly not," the woman replied, smoothing the front of her dress. "We're not so penny-starved as to need that much in advance. Like I said, when the time comes, I'll be a bother about it then."

"Thank you," Dansil said, leaning on the bar and blinking slowly. "You wouldn't, by chance, have any of the night's meal still sitting out?"

She reached out and patted him on the hand. "Of course, dear," she said. "It's not much, and might be in need of a bit of warmth, but it should serve. Why don't you go tend to that horse you mentioned. Stable's around the side to the left. I'll have a bite ready for you, meagre as it may be at this hour, when you come back."

Meagre was definitely the word for it, but as Dansil made his way up to the room, bone tired, bleary, and blinking, he simply felt grateful for a warm bellyful of anything besides the tough dry provisions he'd packed for the road. With a half-smile that he barely registered, he figured that Bird-dog might be feeling the same way right about now, sheltering in the stable, getting the rest she deserved even more than Dansil himself.

He slid the key into the lock, turned until it clicked softly, and pressed against the door. When it didn't budge, he tried again. This time with a bit more effort. Still nothing. Then the thought occurred: of course his host had left it open for him. A long yawn forced his mouth open wide as he reversed the key's position and swung the door open, stumbling a bit at the threshold. Shaking it off as best he could, he surveyed the lodgings in the dim glow of a small oil lamp similar to those in the common room downstairs, another consideration provided by the Fledgling's congenial proprietor.

Without a glance backward, he thumbed the room-side of the lock into place. Then after only a few moments, with sleep pushing in around the edges of his consciousness, he unlaced his boots, kicked them off, and peeled away the now slightly less-damp layers of his traveling clothes. The waxing on the extra bags had held off the rain better than he guessed it would, leaving the rest of his clothing as dry as it had been when he rode away in a cloud of dust from Finnestre. He tossed a long lightweight shirt over head and shoulders and tumbled into bed.

Outside, the moon peered down, glimmering over the rippling waters of the lake. Off in the distance, the mews lay blanketed in shadow and silver. Here and there, above the water and reflected in its surface alongside the moon, the falcons of Tolarenz rode the wind in wide arcs, descended on nighttime prey, or perched in silhouetted silence. Back at the Fledgling, one such falcon found one such perch above the stable, only a few feet from a singular lighted window. It peered through the glass, sable gray wings burnished orange in the lamplight. And then, the light went out, the falcon unflinching, fixed in place as if chiseled in solid stone.

When the morning sun crept up in the east, steely and cold, behind the Fledgling's facade and Dansil's window, the stables greeted first its presence, but there the animals slept on, regardless of the new day's arrival. They'd be awoken when they were needed, and if not, might simply doze away whatever number of hours felt agreeable until their bodies urged them to eat or stretch.

Inside the Fledgling, Dansil fought the oncoming light as best he could, first closing the curtains which he'd regrettably left open before plunging into the deepest sleep he could recall having in ages. Then, when the sun had pierced the curtains, he'd sunk beneath the blanket, hoping to find that peaceful depth where an illogical or nonsensical dream was the least of one's worries. All to no avail. The room grew warm, and the smell of something much more appetizing than the remainders of last night's meal wafted up the stairs.

He was somewhat surprised that he hadn't heard them, the innkeepers. Usually a light sleeper, Dansil wondered how softly they'd had to make their way out of their own rooms, through the kitchen, stoking the fires, peeling, chopping, and otherwise preparing whatever it was they'd begun cooking. Perhaps the journey, the worry about his upcoming meeting with John, the less-than-welcoming encounter he'd experienced upon arriving in Tolarenz, and the memories of what he'd seen on the Æsten Ridge had simply taken their toll, leaving him no other option than to bury them under the freedom of exhausted sleep. With that in mind, he basked in the burden-less haze of morning, stretching out the time before he'd have no other choice than to make his way up the path to his destination.

Checking his bags and supplies, accounting what was left of his food and the condition of the other items he'd brought along, absently ascertaining whether anything had been disturbed—or removed—in the night, he sighed at their state. It was all there, all in place. Even the damp had gone from his traveling gear, giving the room a mustiness that he hadn't detected the night before. Another sigh built up behind his pursed lips before bursting forth in a rush accompanied by a fluttering sputter as he pulled back the curtains and slid open the window to allow the breeze to stir the humid air.

And there, on the ledge, sat the falcon. It stared back at him, impatient, as if there was not even a heartbeat to waste and simultaneously as if it had been waiting a thousand years for Dansil to appear on the other side of the sill.

"Have you been there all night?" Dansil found himself asking the bird.

Unmoving, unblinking, it waited, and Dansil shook his head in disbelief.

"I don't know why I even bother," he continued. "What do I expect, that you'll respond? Honestly, it wouldn't be the most bizarre thing you've done."

Leaving the window ajar, Dansil pulled on some trousers and adjusted the shirt over himself. Satisfied that he looked presentable, he headed for the common room and whatever smelled so delicious.

"Now, don't you go anywhere!" he called wryly before closing the door behind him.

A few steps before the bottom, Dansil stopped. Several voices murmured out a sleepy conversation off to his left, near the kitchen bar. There had been no sign of other patrons when he had arrived, but it had been in the middle of the night. Either that or perhaps these folk had simply stopped in to partake of the morning meal before going on with their day. Regardless, Dansil straightened his shoulders, stood a little taller, and arranged his face into the ever-present beguiling smile and sauntering nonchalance that served him so well back home. Turning the corner, he took the final steps into the common room.

"Mornin' young man!" the woman from the night before called from behind the bar. "Wondered if you'd even make it out of the room before noonday. Showin' up at my door as late as you did, it wouldn't have surprised me if we didn't see you until supper." She spun a round loaf of bread on a cutting board and sawed into the crust with a serrated knife. Without looking up from her work she called, "Sit down and introduce yourself before you make the locals here nervous. We welcome all kinds, of course —the famous hospitality of Tolarenz and all that—but we prefer to know who we're welcoming at least."

"Fair enough," Dansil said with a nod. "The name's Dansil. And odd as it may sound, I own a place not so different from this back where I come from."

A thick-necked man in soldier's attire craned his head in Dansil's direction, the sword at his hip glimmering. "And where might that be?" he asked.

"Oh, you probably wouldn't know it." Dansil waited a beat, running a hand through his hair, knowing exactly what would come next.

"Try m—"

"It's a little town right on the edge of the end of the world called Finnestre," Dansil interrupted.

The man hesitated, turning his head slowly back to the contents of his mug and plate.

With a wink to the proprietor, Dansil slid into a seat at the end of the bar. "Was I right?" he said to the room at large. "Have you heard of it?"

"Well," said another man, older and also in soldier's garb, seated next to the first, "Parlen here has a hard time finding King's City on a map of King's City, so it's not really a fair test, but I traveled through there once or twice in years past. Don't remember seeing you at any inn or tavern though."

Dansil nodded, feeling some of the tension start to recede as they fell into familiar conversation. "I suppose it hasn't been there all that long, in the grand scheme."

The second soldier grunted an assent through a mouthful. He gestured at the graying sides of his beard. "No older than you look, I'd wager my time there was well before your time anywhere." He laughed to himself.

"Now Cotts," said the woman behind the bar. "You and Parlen leave our new guest alone. You've got his story enough for polite company. There's no need to pry. I'm sure he'll share in good time if he feels like it. Won't you, dear?"

Dansil leaned back, allowing his smile to broaden from neutral to beaming. "I imagine I will, in good time. But right now I'd love it if I could trouble you for a plate of all that." He gestured to the sausages, eggs and brown bread on the other men's plates. "If you don't mind."

"Of course, of course!" she said happily. "No paying customer goes hungry at the Fledgling, or so my husband and I like to say." She eyed the soldiers. "And some people's tabs are due."

An hour later, full and fully bedecked in fresh clothes, Dansil strode away from the Fledgling. Bird-dog seemed happy enough to stay put in the stable, and so there she had stayed. As for the horse's namesake falcon, it currently gripped a bit of wrought iron fence that encircled one of Tolarenz's curious gardens of tiny trees, a half-elven custom, Dansil had heard at some time or another. He'd actually expected to see more of them after recognizing the first, but few and far between would have been an overstatement of their number. Something to do with the tragedy that had befallen the place, he assumed.

Meanwhile, he and the falcon continued their awkward walking-chase through the town. On one side of the road, a blacksmith's work produced the telltale filament of smoke and pinging of metal on metal. Further ahead, a sight he'd not expected drew up before him.

It was a massive garden flanked by two trees, thick grandfather oaks, and a third smaller one, little more than an overgrown shrub, making a sort of triangle at the entrance. Beyond it, a maze of trees, bushes, vines, and the spent stems of flowers beckoned him. Behind that, he knew, thanks to the innkeeper's explanation, lay the Tolarenz town hall. He walked slowly into the garden, admiring the work that had been done to maintain the curving paths and woven arches. The whole space felt like entering a series of living hallways, almost as if they had spontaneously grown this way without aid of hand or shears or shovel.

That was when he heard it. Unmistakable somewhere off to his right. Broad and booming, gruff and rugged and—he thought with a stifled little laugh—quickly approaching the ragged edge of agitation. John of Dalstone.

CHAPTER TWENTY-FOUR

An Abundance of Concurrence

"He's one of them," Elise's eyes darkened as she glared down the long table and growled out the words, "leading us on all this time." She gripped the hilt of her sword.

Jhed put out a broad hand. "Stop," he commanded. "Remember, again, this is my house. We will have no such violence here. Let him speak."

Corwin, eyes wide now, arms retracted in a protective gesture across his chest, drew back another inch. He watched Elise relax her fingers and place her hands palms down on the wooden surface. Askon could see that those fingers were the only part of her not tight with tension and wild intent.

A dry click emanated from Corwin's throat as he moved to speak, showing them again the tattoo between his thumb and forefinger. "As I was saying," he began with a harried breath, "there are times when coincidence means more than just the timely concurrence of significant events. I show you this mark not to reveal my allegiance with the High Spire. On that matter, my position is quite the opposite, as you well know. Instead it is our interconnectedness that compels me. That I would have a teardrop permanently inscribed upon my skin, and that you have been pursued by those who bear this mark, and in turn have become their pursuers." He paused, seemingly beside himself at the immensity of his conclusion. "That in your world there exists, in tangible, physical form, an object of such power whose likeness is none other than a tear, and that my daughter, with her outsized interest in long forgotten stories had in her possession the book which tells the story of this thing. That now you arrive by means of its power—"

"Yes," interrupted Elise, still staring with a hardened darkness that no idle gesture or errant movement could hope to escape. "But none of this explains the *reason* for the mark you bear, which matches that of our enemy."

Líana leaned forward. "Basin City is not the only place we've seen or heard of such markings. Morrowmen described a man with a teardrop tattoo when he told us of the Elves' first appearance in Vladvir."

"Which," Askon said, "I assume is where Sehlín and her followers adopted the idea. It must be in *The Book of the Tear*. It would, after all, explain their persistent interest in that particular tome."

"It would," repeated Corwin, "if what you say is true for the book in both of our…worlds, but it is not the reason I allowed myself to be branded as they are."

Jhed reached over and gently gripped his friend's shoulder. "Tell them," he said seriously.

Corwin shuddered and seemed to shrink, growing thinner, paler, and suddenly deeply sad. "It was over her mother, of course," he began softly. "Alora's mother. We were happy. Life was good. I spent my days working at the High Spire. 'Energy Systems Analyst' was the title they gave me, and I enjoyed the work. It appealed to my intellect, challenged me, provided a means for my family to thrive. Or, at least that is what I was led to believe until the infirmary told us she wouldn't recover.

"But I had *seen* people recover from the same illness, watched them fade, as she faded, and then return to the halls of the Spire, full of life and vitality as if nothing had happened. And worse, when the illness seemed far more severe, I'd seen folk recover in the same manner! Any number of things that friends and even just the passing acquaintance might have survived, gone as if they had suffered only a common fever. It didn't make sense.

"I grew suspicious, while she worsened. I grew distant when Alora needed me close. But I couldn't stop because my suspicion led to the only reasonable pursuit I could envision. I did what I do best. I analyzed the data. Using my position at the Spire, I gathered information, made tables and ledgers that cataloged anything I could find which might help indicate what I suspected."

"Which was?" Askon offered. But Corwin, lost in his reliving of the moment, did not respond, or even seem to register that Askon had spoken at all.

"Then it grew beyond my control. Suspicion became obsession. I lived it, breathed it, took greater risks to pull the thread, to unravel their carefully woven layers of protection. When she died, I should have stopped, should have let it go and turned my attentions to Alora, but I didn't. Of course I didn't. I couldn't! Not with what I knew—what I had found: You see, Basin City runs on powerful currents of energy, and the systems I had been assigned to monitor directed these currents for the middle ground and lowborn districts. They power everything from the lighting to the carriages to the ameliorations in our circlets! But these are details nearly all of us knew, of course. My obsessions, my risks, my neglect of my family uncovered something else.

"The energy is failing, and as it has faltered, the greatest share goes to the Spire itself and the areas around it. They mete it out to the rest of the city only as they see fit and only so long as they are already comfortable. Comfortable and safe. The discovery that drove me over the edge, that drove me here, was that not only are the basic mechanics of the city powered and controlled in this way. Our food supply, the weapons the Guardians use to control us, and the medical procedures to keep us alive, all are tied to the energy that flows through the High Spire."

At this, Corwin's head fell to his chest. Jhed's hand gripped him tighter, sliding around his shoulder to steady him. Corwin did not breathe. The next words came out toneless and almost inaudible.

"They chose to let her die."

Jhed held Corwin firmly, for a moment saying nothing. Then he looked up at the others, the little braid swinging in front of his face. Corwin nodded, and Jhed released him.

"He came to us," Jhed rumbled. "Wild around the edges, clearly too deep in his pursuit of this knowledge to see the cracks forming in himself. But he was not wrong to approach me, because we had long suspected the High Spire was hiding something significant. We had made the search for answers our business, and yet we had been unsuccessful in acquiring someone on the inside of the Spire's operation." Jhed smiled at Corwin, though Alora's father still stared at the floor.

Líana said what Askon had already been thinking. "And now, you had Corwin?"

"Yes," Jhed replied. "Now, we had Corwin. He did not disappoint, and we did not take him—and his daughter—under our wings lightly either. I personally made sure they were safe and had access to our modest resources. This kept Alora and Corwin in their own residences, even if that meant changing them frequently, sometimes due to my determination of necessity, sometimes due to Corwin's more…sensitive concerns. We helped with those as best we could, pulling the cracks back together where possible, but they will never be whole again, obviously."

Askon nodded. "You started to tell us how Corwin did not 'disappoint'?"

Jhed shifted his legs on the long bench and glanced a moment with upraised brow at Corwin, who showed no signs of speaking yet. "He did not," Jhed repeated after a long breath. "That is where the tattoo comes into the story. He managed to worm his way into the lower levels of their organization, not only as a worker in the Spire, of which there are many, but to become initiated, if only distantly, into Sehlín's service."

"And for that," Corwin said, looking up, his hands pressed onto either side of his pallid face, "I needed a teardrop tattoo. However, my remaining time there was short. I discovered the location of the lab within the Spire from which they control the rest of the city."

"And that was enough," Jhed said with finality, "for us to remove him from harm's way for the time being. For a long time, we here have been planning and waiting for the right moment to strike, to take back control of Basin City, for the people, not just the Highborn and their sniveling sycophants in the Spire."

A grim laugh sounded at Corwin's end of the table, his shoulders jostling up and down as he covered his face with his hands. Then he pulled them away, looked up, and smiled a disbelieving smile. "Sometimes coincidence is more than just timely concurrence."

Dimness had taken over the sky beyond the slanting ceiling windows—for as long as the lights of Basin City shone, it was never truly dark—and hours had passed when Askon stood with the rest of them over the collection of scattered sheets of paper laden with schematics, lists of requirements, catalogues of supplies, and all the documentation of Jhed's research totaling what must have been the work of years. Beside him, Elise and Líana stood thoughtfully trying to parse the information that lay before them. But, as they had encountered earlier in the Dalkaldur Library, sentences and paragraphs of words made little or no practical sense. The words were familiar, the letterforms largely the same, but anything more than an item in a list, a measurement, or an observation of a few words was as impenetrable as if it had been written in another language entirely.

True as that was, Askon and his companions, with the judicious assistance of Jhed and Corwin, now understood their host's intent. Half of the time needed to explain came from an endless barrage of questioning from Elise, directed mostly at Corwin, his ties to the High Spire, her lingering suspicions as to his loyalties, and at the various workings that Corwin had discovered while embedded in their ranks.

Askon found little to be gleaned from Corwin's responses, though Elise seemed content for the moment. Over the last quarter hour, Askon had watched her relax, each point and detail pulling her closer to acting upon her search for Thomas. Meanwhile, Líana had been quiet and deeply thoughtful since Jhed's people's purpose had been revealed. She gnawed at a thumbnail, and had several times threaded and unthreaded the long braid as Jhed laid out the entire scheme of infiltration, sabotage, and escape. A plan that hinged directly on Corwin, and the teardrop tattoo.

"You see," Corwin was saying, one hand on his hip and the other with fingers splayed through his wild gray hair, "the ink used in the induction ceremony is not what you would find in an artist's shop somewhere in the city. Of course any number of such shops abound. Many of our own people already have everything from spiritual markings to family crests to floral patches covering as little as a thumbnail in size, all the way to the entirety of an arm or leg." He gestured around the table, and the room at large, to various folk who indeed had permanently marked themselves in all the ways he had explained.

Then he shook his head. "But that's not enough," he said, resuming a tone of informative lecture. "If that were the case, we could simply draw these onto our hands, wave on the way through security, and be done with it. Unfortunately, or deviously depending on your perspective, the organization uses ink that reacts in a unique, traceable way with the internal layers of the skin."

"In other words," Elise concluded, "the tattoos have to be real."

Corwin tapped the rim of his glasses. "Correct!" he said, smirking a bit. "That particular piece of intelligence was extremely difficult to acquire, another sacrifice that I refuse to see go unleveraged. We're going to make use of it. The lower levels of the Spire are easy enough to gain access to as long as you have the proper registration. It's the upper levels, and most importantly, the areas that Sehlín and her forces control that need signs of our apparent…" He hesitated. "Commitment."

"And why is that?" asked Elise. "Why not the same level of security for all of the Spire if it's so important?"

"A good question, with a simple answer," Corwin replied. "Not everyone who works within the High Spire is allied with

Sehlín. Myself, for instance, and others all the way to the highest levels."

Jhed gestured to a list of names, split into columns. "It is our current speculation that except for perhaps the central lab itself, near the top of the Spire, all levels include a mixture of those loyal to Sehlín and those entirely unwitting in their participation. Those like Corwin, simply going about their daily employment, unaware of the corruption that has festered around them." He frowned, eyeing the list of names.

Pushing his glasses up his nose, Corwin sighed, his eyes also fixed upon the various documents spread before them. "I know it's not the timing you wanted."

"It isn't," Jhed said flatly. "But when would it have been? After we knew with certainty every person working for Sehlín? After we knew which innocent workers might share our cause?"

"It would never have been enough," Corwin said.

And with a gruff laugh and a shrug of his wide shoulders, Jhed echoed, "It would never have been enough."

A long shadow loomed across the loose papers on the table. "A bit more time couldn't have hurt," a new voice said. Askon turned to see Tinley, and a number of the others who had fought beside them in Dalkaldur gathered expectantly. "I think we have the tools to suffice, and enough of the most critical devices, even with our latest personnel additions," Tinley continued, with a wave indicating Askon, Líana, and Elise. "Though we'll have to use everything on hand, regardless of reliability." A grimace worked its way across the otherwise cheerful face. "You don't mean to move tonight, do you?"

Jhed shook his head. "No. I don't see how that would be possible."

Elise leaned back against the table, crossing her arms, surveying Tinley and the others momentarily. "Can you make it possible?"

Tinley's grimace rippled, eyebrows knitting together tightly, clearly cataloging whatever equipment might have been necessary, and making other various calculations and approximations. After a long moment, Tinley shrugged. "A week's worth of dry running the plan would be more to my liking, but yes."

Corwin pounded the table. "Then we have to get started. Right now. Fit these three immediately. The sooner we bring my daughter back, the better!"

"Agreed," said Askon. "For her part as well as for Thomas. And, I'm afraid Elise has seen enough here to have made the decision to act on her own had Tinley not answered in the affirmative."

Líana, still pensive and withdrawn, stepped away from the table, her eyes sweeping the room, searching for something that she did not find. Another pass back across the group standing before them resulted in the same perplexed expression. "Where is Daeron?" she asked finally.

Elise duplicated the scan of the room and of the people gathered in the otherwise empty space. Her eyes narrowed. "Yes," she said. Her voice low and dangerous. "Where *is* Daeron?"

A cursory search yielded no results, and a more thorough investigation, including questioning anyone who might have seen Daeron, changed nothing. Alora's friend from the Dalkaldur Library was gone, and the preparations that might have needed days, and had been thoughtfully constrained to a matter of hours, now came near to panic. All around them, the building's caches of weapons had been emptied, its supplies stashed, and any evidence that they had been there at all hidden away behind the same sorts of panels, false walls, and secret compartments that Líana and Elise had helped Corwin and Alora with back at their residence.

The moment he became certain that Daeron had disappeared, Jhed ordered the dismantling, his booming voice firing off instructions for the better part of an hour. He seemed almost certain that, given the opportunity, Daeron would lead the Guardians back, and their long work of planning would come to nothing. Askon helped in any way he could, moving boxes, wrapping bedding and clothing, covering furniture or moving it to the various sleeping quarters. The effort certainly wouldn't have survived a thorough inspection, but if the Guardians arrived and Jhed's people had gone, it was possible they would see only an empty building and turn their attentions on the informant.

The only element remaining was the long wooden table, now completely bare and unadorned, where Askon sat next to Líana and Elise with his hand outstretched. Across from them sat Corwin holding what to Askon looked like one of the Guardian weapons with a bundle of needles affixed to the end. He explained as he demonstrated on a strip of old leather.

"The ink is stored here, more than enough for a great many of these marks. The delivery mechanism is designed to enable much larger works, of course." He lowered the needles onto the leather. "Now, on each descent, the points apply ink beneath the surface. Then they retract, at which point they are coated again before descending once more. The process occurs many times very quickly, so quickly in fact that the points seem only to vibrate rather than extend and return. There is some pain, but it's a small surface and will be finished in very little time." He raised his eyebrows, as if to ask the three of them for any final questions.

"What about the harm done to the skin itself?" Líana asked. She rubbed the intended area with the opposite thumb. "Won't others notice ours are new? Hundreds of tiny punctures must require time to heal."

Corwin nodded, his glasses slipping minutely down his nose. "Under ordinary circumstances, yes. Not these, however. Tinley has seen to that." He tapped the end of the device, near the needlepoints, where the continuous black metal of the handle and barrel were interrupted by a band of dull silver. "Any evidence will be good as new before you've left your seat."

"We understand," said Elise. "Get on with it."

CHAPTER TWENTY-FIVE

The High Spire

Thick leaves rustled against Askon's cloak as he lay prone on the south side of the plateau that their new allies called Perishia Heights. Sweeping far above, in a glimmering arc that reminded him of the thorn on an enormous rose, the High Spire shone in the darkness over the whole of Basin City many hundreds of feet below. Nearby, Elise lay, both of them silently awaiting the signal. A few dozen feet from their covert, a narrow path ascended to an otherwise undetectable door somewhere in the Spire's smooth outer surface. Sharp as his eyes were, not even Askon would have been likely to spot it if Corwin had not briefed them. But it was there, if one knew where to look, ever so faintly outlined in the semi-glow of the city's ever-present lights.

By several different carriage groups on several different carriage lines, each with its own stops and transfers along the way, the various folk from Jhed's secret safe house arrived at points all across the Heights. When Askon and Elise reached their planned destination, he had stopped momentarily on the crest of a small rise before they descended into the trees. There, atop the plateau upon which the High Spire's foundations had been set, he looked out over the city and watched the lights as section after section began to flicker, much like those on the Dalkaldur Library had done. It was enough to reveal the truth of Corwin's discovery. At the furthest distances from the Spire, the lights came to life only intermittently, while the nearest rings rarely even dimmed. Now, peering up through the foliage into an ink-black sky, Askon heard the quiet patter of rain begin against the leaves.

He turned his gaze again to the pathway and the door. In their hasty preparations, the cloak, and the leather armor beneath became the topic of heated debate. Askon, Líana, and Elise had been fitted for the curious garments of the Glittering World, those they'd first seen on Alora in the earliest visions and now had come to know as almost entirely uniform across all of Basin City's residents, except of course for the Norill. But only a few moments in the thin, tightly clinging shirt and trousers left Askon feeling exposed and vulnerable. The women had expressed similar reservations, though to a somewhat lesser degree. It was Jhed, however, who put a stop to the process.

"We are wasting time," he had informed Corwin and the remaining contingent who insisted that Askon and the others dress to blend with—and thus vanish within—the general populace. "I understand their attire makes them instantly worthy of scrutiny, and our initial entry to the Spire requires that we go unnoticed. But just look at them!" The gesture that followed laid bare the obvious: if the three of them were to proceed in the provided clothing, they would wear it so awkwardly as to draw nearly as much attention as their cloaks and armor.

"We'll have to think of another way," Jhed had finished.

And so they had. First, Askon and Elise would enter with Tinley's contingent from a lesser-used service door on the southern side of the Spire. Though they would not escape scrutiny entirely, they would minimize it, assuming that the service corridors were empty or only populated by Norill tasked with maintenance. Second were the circlet devices. Tinley's presentation of these incredible works of artifice far exceeded Askon's understanding, but he knew for certain that Thomas would have instantly grasped their opaque intricacies.

"You see," Tinley had said, demonstrating breathlessly, "they must remain attached to your person at all times in order to remain effective." With that Tinley clipped the twist of metal to their belt. Askon winced at what came next. Ghoulishly and most unnaturally, Tinley's broad brown face elongated and the color drained away to the pale white visage and extended ears of a Basin City highborn. The portion of their body not covered in the telltale Basin City garb remained deep brown as ever, yet another unsettling detail, but the face itself was a flawless transformation.

A clear *ping* resounded as the twist of metal came free of its fastening and Tinley set it back on the long table. In another breath, the friendly beaming face had returned. Askon blinked wordlessly.

"Circlet tech," Tinley said, "to make it more difficult to track us *after* the…event."

Again, however, it had been Jhed who suggested the alterations for the pieces that Askon, Líana, and Elise now carried. Clipped solidly to each of their belts were the same curious twists of metal. Yet, in the unsteady glow of Basin City's lights under the gentle rain, Askon saw the familiar ghostly white face of Elise next to him beneath the branches of their hiding place. Had he been in her position, he would have seen his own true face peering back through the darkness. The important difference was in their garments. Though he knew it was there, felt its weight, and heard the sound of the few raindrops that pierced the canopy against it, his cloak was all but invisible. Likewise, Elise appeared as he did, wrapped in the nearly identical thin shirt and leggings that appeared to be all one piece.

"There's just one remaining issue," Tinley had said tentatively as they showed the altered devices' function to Jhed, extending a wide flat hand and hovering it slowly alongside Askon from shoulder to knee. "Power draw is too high."

Jhed had nodded slowly in reply. A low rumble sounded in his chest, then halted abruptly.

"You saw it," Tinley said, the words half question, half disappointed confirmation, "the ripple in the image."

Unfortunately, time had run out and, despite the unflagging efforts of Tinley, the issue remained. A particularly deep dip in the city's power drew the lights inward, all the way to the base of the plateau upon which the Spire stood. Askon watched the smooth fabric of Elise's Basin City attire vibrate like a puddle disturbed by an insect trapped and flailing on the surface. Beneath the ripple, her black leather armor was revealed. The same was true for the bracers at his wrists until the city's power surged outward and the illusion returned.

Tinley's hope had been that the closer they were to the Spire, the more energy would be available, keeping the devices functioning properly despite the increased power requirements. Askon took a deep breath now, the benefit seeming marginal at best. Turning to his opposite side, where Tinley and the handful of others comprising the lower-floor team also lay, Askon saw the unsettling highborn visage looking apologetically back.

In the hour or so they spent waiting, little changed, and little life appeared in or around the Spire. Waves of rain rolled in, intensified, and rolled out, but even so, they remained mostly untouched by the weather beneath the leaves of the covert. Twice, Askon had spotted Guardian patrols of the grounds, though on both occasions the duos, like the pair they'd encountered while bathing in the lake, were more concerned with the tedium of their work than any real threat that might arise.

On the inside, Askon knew, Corwin was making his way past the Spire's visitors' gate. As described, it reminded him of the immaculately maintained gardens spreading out before the castle in King's City. Both the visitors' gate and the gardens existed as a sort of buffer between the nobility on the inside and the general citizenry on the outside. Once Corwin had made his way past this staging area, he would be able to enter the Spire itself, the workings of which began in earnest on the second floor. The door Askon watched now, ground-level with the slope climbing up the plateau to the east, led to that very floor and would, with luck, open at any moment.

Elsewhere, a third group, Jhed's, the largest by far of the three, had the most dangerous approach of all. Two thirds of the height up the long sloping side of the High Spire, a narrow observatory ring extended from its otherwise smooth surface. Jhed and those following him were tasked with scaling the building and waiting for Corwin to arrive and grant them entry. On the lower floors, a group so large would be conspicuous moving together. The upper levels, however, housed the bulk of their real enemy. Above the platform, they would need the numbers if they had any hope of succeeding. Unsurprisingly, Corwin had requested that one of the Vladviri travelers go with Jhed's team, as an assurance that they wouldn't simply vanish after retrieving Thomas, Alora, or both. Líana, in an equally unsurprising decision, had volunteered, much to Askon's concern and against his vigorous argument.

While Corwin climbed the Spire, it would be Tinley's task, along with the rest of the lower-floor team, to delay and repel any unwanted arrivals from the main entrances on the ground. Delaying by way of stealth and remaining undetected was their first priority. After that, in the event that the operation were to be discovered, it would be up to their team to slow the Guardians' progress in whatever way possible.

Meanwhile, it would be Askon and Elise's task to find and retrieve Alora and Thomas while Corwin continued to his intended destination at the top of the tower. Between the detailed schematics, Corwin's own notes and experience, and the recollections of the visions in the Tear, there were very few areas within the High Spire that they had not been able to map. They knew the rooms to avoid, the least trafficked passages, and the likeliest places where their friends would be held; they even knew the approximate locations of the white room and the dark.

The third time a pair of Guardians made their bored and bickering way across his field of view, the nearly featureless surface of the Spire split open, and a thin line of white light fanned out over the surrounding greenery. Next to him, Elise hissed a curse and clashed her sword against a stone. The two shadowy forms spun toward the sound.

Askon rocked up onto his heels, feeling his legs cry out after lying so long in wait. On the other side of the leaves, he saw the familiar glowing dots of the batons they'd encountered back in Dalkaldur Village. Slowly, the two Guardians drew closer to the brush and farther from the path. Askon let his hand drop to his sword, the strap on the long-bladed knife already loose at his other hip.

Elise held out her arm, gesturing for him to leave his weapons sheathed. She pointed to the batons. Askon nodded, and they leapt forward, rushing out from the trees and colliding with the two guards. Despite their wary approach, neither target was ready for the attack. They hit the ground in a jumble of grunts, clattering gravel, and rush of air. In the dim glow, Askon wrenched free the baton, raised his hands and drove the weapon down.

He pressed the switch, Elise doing the same almost simultane-ously, and the Guardians' bodies arched uncontrollably before fall-ing still. Askon rose, baton still in hand. Elise stood, disentangling herself with an effort, and pressed the switch on her weapon again, lancing it down into her opponent's midsection. Then, with a flourish and a final click of the switch, she did the same to the guard at Askon's feet before casting the baton aside into the trees.

"To be sure they won't get up," she whispered levelly, and turned to face the trees. "Tinley! Help us."

As quietly as possible, they all carried the Guardians into the bracken, where they left them, bound to a thick tree trunk. When the last loops of the same fine cord that had been used to tie Askon and his friends back in Dalkaldur Village were secure, he turned again to eye the door. The sliver of light in the opening winked out and returned. Three times, one time, three times. The signal.

Softly as shadows, Askon, Elise, Tinley, and the others slipped inside the High Spire. Behind them, the glow of the city dimmed, faltering and failing at the edges far away, under gentle waves of rain.

Inside, Corwin snapped the door shut, a sharp click echoing down the corridor. Askon squinted in the light. Like the white room in the vision, the hallway before him was nearly blinding. Floors, ceiling, walls, metal railings, all of it cast in searing, pierc-ing, unwavering white. After an uncomfortable moment, his eyes began to adjust, and he saw before him Corwin's bespectacled face.

"Aren't you worried you'll be recognized?" Elise asked Corwin.

Corwin shook his head. "Not yet," he answered. "Part of my role in the plan is to risk being seen on the lower and middle levels, where I was known to both those unwitting of our cause and those in the service of Sehlín. Fewer people at night of course, but not zero. If they see me, the latter might report us to the upper floors. Unlikely, but possible. In such an event, we'll have to hope to provide a distraction for Jhed."

"And for Líana," Askon said.

"Yes, yes. For her, and all the others as well," Corwin went on. "The former, however, are likely to simply ignore my return, as my disappearance could easily be attributed to the pursuit of work at a different location, a leave of absence due to illness, or recovery from…" He stopped, momentarily reliving the grief.

"It's alright," Elise said, not unkindly. "We understand. But now, we need you to lead us up, so we can find your daughter and my husband."

With a shake of his head and another breath, Corwin cast aside his reverie. The highborn that was Tinley pointed down the hallway. "We'll make a right about halfway along this stretch. It'll take us around the furthest edge of the building's interior."

Askon frowned. "And if we were to continue straight—"

"We'd end back in the main visitors' chamber," Tinley said peering back through the unsettling highborn face. "We need to avoid that if we can. It would be faster to cross through the center, but there's too much chance we'll be seen. Corwin alone, or even a pair or foursome might go unnoticed, but there are ten of us, plus the three of you."

"The long way it is," Corwin said, heading down the hall.

For a time long enough that Askon began to lose track, they continued in similar fashion: wary caution and quiet footfalls in a tight group through the hallways and corridors, feigned nonchalance and scattered pairings or trios through the open chambers. Large and unrelentingly imposing, the building's outer structure asserted itself in their traversal. Askon felt the curvature of the outer perimeter in the gently turning path beneath their feet. Eventually they encountered a wide multitiered waiting area lined with indoor plants like those in the library, and long soft benches at intervals that felt at the same time randomly placed and powerfully intentional. A scant few workers crossed the floor, the lighting here dimmer but steady, as if to mimic the late hour outside. A pair of thin, dark-skinned personnel sat in quiet conversation over a stack of pages, their brass circlets glinting.

Reluctant to linger, the group turned sharply from these observations, moving away from the sitting chamber and the apex of the building's form—on the north side if Askon had kept his bearings. After a time, the hallway grew narrower and the lights grew brighter. Down one short branch, Askon glimpsed two Norill collecting cleaning equipment. They acknowledged neither Askon's group, nor each other as they went silently about their work.

Several such corridors came and went, while on the opposite side, a number of long rooms with equally long tables lined by rows of pristinely white chairs sat behind faultless panes of clear glass. Upon encountering the first of these, Askon couldn't help but consider how much Apopsé, Lord of South City, would have coveted such cleanliness and ascetic beauty. Had he the tools and ability, no doubt, some equally unblemished collection of features would grace halls and chambers throughout the lavish palace.

Askon found it all viscerally upsetting. Something about the lack of *any* evidence of people, their passing, their existence, made his stomach roil, as if the building itself were a solicitous acquaintance who did nothing but unceasingly lie to his face. And still, they had passed room after room which confirmed again and again that the High Spire, in all its spotless grandeur, really did exist. Upon losing count of the meeting rooms, and when Askon sensed they had covered half the distance to the Spire's south side, Corwin stopped them.

"Here's where we part ways," he said to Tinley. "Now, you'll recall that in the analysis room there's a set of locked drawers which—"

Tinley, still under the illusion that made their face appear as one of the highborn, a face Askon might have described as a true elf from the stories of his youth and the long remembrances of Morrowmen, nodded almost cheerfully and waved Corwin's explanations away. "I remember."

"Well," Corwin said, hesitant for a moment. "If I don't see you again, th—"

"You'll see me again," Tinley said. "All of us, if things go right." And with a quick inclination of their head, they signaled to the others and led the lower-floor team down a branch similar to the one in which they'd seen the Norill at work, leaving Askon and Elise standing alongside Corwin.

CHAPTER TWENTY-SIX

Empty

Breathing heavily, steadily, Askon strode step by measured step up yet another featureless staircase. Corwin had warned him and Elise to pace themselves, and Askon, for his own part at least, had heeded the advice. Nevertheless, even in the cool stairwell of the High Spire, his forehead had grown damp with sweat. Similarly winded and a few steps behind came Corwin, his brow also glistening under the brilliant white lights. Somewhere ahead, the stairs would reach a landing, and they had traveled enough identical staircases already to know, almost to the step, how far they needed to go before they could rest. Above him, Elise's dark form flashed between the guardrail bars, moving faster the higher she went. Over his own footfalls and labored breathing, Askon heard nothing.

In accordance with the plan, the three of them had parted ways with Tinley and the lower-level team whose task it was to repel or delay any incursion that might enter from the ground floor. Corwin, deeply familiar with the Spire's entirety, had then led Askon and Elise on a series of winding ways through what Jhed and the others deemed "the empty middle" of the Spire, for both its lack of importance to their goals as well as in critique of the citizens who worked on those levels.

"They believe themselves essential to the functioning of Basin City, when their positions exist almost entirely to take the blame when the upper floors demand more resources be diverted to powerful, highborn regions," Corwin had explained. "None of them know this, obviously, and so they instead accept the critique and internalize the belief that *their* failures cause the breaks in lighting, water, temperature control, and all the rest. Their purpose is to appear as if they have purpose, nothing more."

And in their goings from one white stairwell to the next, Askon had even witnessed several of these "empty middle" workers busy about their tasks: carrying sleeves of paper, sketching ideas on wide vertical slates, or conversing intensely. From outside earshot, and without the context of their daily lives, it felt an almost impossibly fragile lie. How these people, the mythical elves whom Vladvir's people either revered or reviled, could carry on day after day and remain none the wiser left him baffled. If such beings as these, who had by Morrowmen's account saved Vladvir from certain destruction, could become so complacent and easily fooled, what did it mean for his own people? His own world?

As they came to the top of the staircase, Askon and Corwin found Elise waiting, impatient as ever. Determination marked her features, but even her unflinching tenacity could not deny the simple reality of prolonged exertion. She too shone with sweat, and the dark curtain of hair that usually covered her face lay matted against her pale skin.

"You have to let—us rest." Corwin pulled himself up the last few steps, his hand gripping the railing for support.

Askon leaned against the opposite rail, looking down the shaft from which they had ascended. "This is the last one?" he asked, breathing deep and slow to even out the rhythm.

Corwin nodded. "This is the last before things become complicated, yes."

"Meaning that Thomas could be on this floor," Elise said, her voice quavering at the mention of his name. She brushed the hair from her face and, with an effort, turned to face Corwin.

Alora's father removed his glasses and polished the lenses, wiping the dampness below his hairline away with a sleeve. Shaking his head slowly, his mouth drew out into a tense flat line. "It is possible, I think."

A moment passed, one in which Askon expected Elise to challenge Corwin's uncertainty. When none came, he turned to her but she looked away.

"This is just the first of the high-security levels," Corwin continued. "We're only a few floors below the observation ring. The interrogations could have occurred anywhere from this level up to the very pinnacle of the spire."

Askon turned away from Elise, focusing on Corwin. "I thought you hadn't been all the way to the top?"

"I haven't," Corwin replied. "But some of the descriptions you gave from your 'visions' sound similar to the highest floors I've seen. It's possible, though not probable, that the rooms where Alora and Thomas are being kept are even farther up."

"There's no way to know other than to keep going," Elise said, her voice ragged with emotion. "And the spire narrows the higher we go. Each floor is smaller than the last. Fewer places to look."

"And all the more likelihood of being discovered by Sehlín's agents," Corwin finished.

Elise glared at him. "I've had about enough slinking around on their account."

Protestations on Elise's part or no, the three of them took another several minutes to rest and arrange themselves before making their way along the hallway toward the entrance gate. At a half circle desk sat a bored looking highborn with a narrow face and dark hair, not too dissimilar from the illusion Tinley had worn when they departed. In the steady orange lamplight, the guard looked up.

"Security clearance?"

"Top level," Corwin said, authority lacing his words. "And these are my…" he let the empty space draw out for a beat, "guests."

The highborn's eyebrows lifted ever so slightly. "That so? And do they have the same clearance level?"

Corwin chuckled. "Certainly not. Though…" He lifted his hand to push up his glasses, blatantly revealing the teardrop mark between his thumb and first finger. At least by Askon's estimation, it seemed a convincing performance.

"I see," the highborn sputtered quickly, his eyes growing a bit wider. "I didn't mean to stand in your way, brother."

Corwin smiled. "No worries, friend," he said with a nod, and stepped toward the gate.

"Apologies," the highborn said, now sounding almost embarrassed, "but, the test?"

With another laugh, Corwin turned again to face him. "Of course, of course!" he replied with an easy smile.

From behind the table, the highborn drew a baton similar to the one Askon had taken from the two Guardians he and Elise had subdued outside. The device the highborn produced was shorter, but a similar row of three lights glowed along its side. Holding it a handspan above the desk, he nodded impatiently to Corwin.

Without breaking stride, Corwin extended his hand and let it rest upon the tabletop. The highborn yawned, pressed the switch on the handle, and dropped it onto Corwin's hand.

Involuntarily, Askon tensed at the contact, attempting to hide the rigidity of his posture, but the highborn didn't even look up. He simply stared at the lights on the baton.

Red. Red. Green.

"Perfect," Corwin said. "I always worry that thing might malfunction."

The highborn let out a wheeze of a laugh. "I've seen it happen. Not frequently, but on occasion. It can be…unpleasant." He turned to face Askon and Elise. "Alright. Now you two," he said, and waved them forward.

Elise stepped up first, making minimal eye contact, her distant stare communicating none of the doubt Askon felt on her behalf. The baton dropped down, and once more, against his best efforts, Askon's body tensed.

Red. Red. Green.

With a glance that looked through the guard as if he were one of the transparent glass windows outside the meeting rooms far below, Elise continued forward. Askon followed her, placing his hand flat beneath the hovering baton. Taking a long slow breath that he hoped would not betray his anxiety, he nodded, and the baton fell. His hand twitched, drawing ever so slightly closer to his body.

Red. Red. *Blue.*

Askon's heart leapt into his chest, and his eyes snapped to Elise and Corwin.

Overhead, the lights dimmed, their blazing white shifting to dingy beige. To Askon's surprise and terror, the image of his Basin City clothing flittered in waves that revealed his true armor and cloak. "Ugh!" the guard barked. "Damn thing fails half the time these days, I swear." With his eyes fixed on the device, he shook the baton vigorously and beat it against the table. "It's worse since the lights started dipping like we're in some maintenance district hovel. Upper floors say they've got it under control. I'll believe it when I see it."

As the lights rose abruptly back to their original brightness, and the illusion around Askon solidified once again, the guard banged the baton against the table a final time, for good measure,

Askon could only assume. Then with a shrug, the guard hovered the device above the desk's surface once more.

"Try it again," he said. "Blue just means a bad reading."

Slowly, Askon slid his hand beneath the baton. It came down, cold and unforgiving against his skin.

Red. Red. Green.

"I was convinced you'd give us away," Elise grumbled as they finished combing the floor for anything that looked like either of the interrogation rooms. "You understand I would have kept going? Even if I had to run."

Askon sighed. "I do."

Extreme as it sounded, all three of them had agreed before leaving the safe house: with the odds as risky as they were, and separated from Líana entirely as Corwin had insisted, the likelihood that they would all escape unscathed, or even at all, was slim. If an opportunity remained for any of them to succeed, then so be it. Askon knew Líana would never leave even one of their newly acquainted allies behind if she could help it, and he himself could hardly imagine doing the same. It was, however, what Elise had needed to hear, what she had needed to tell herself, and was still telling herself as they made their way up to the next secure level.

When they had repeated the search on two additional floors, Elise's patience had worn thin. At any opportunity, she peppered Corwin with questions he had answered a dozen times already. Did he know of any interrogation rooms specifically? Had he heard anyone talk about a room that felt like a basement dungeon? Was there a way to acquire a more complete map of any of these floors using his security clearance? Until, in a relatively uncharacteristic moment, Corwin had hissed back his own frustrations. Askon expected an equally explosive response from Elise, a threat with the Death fragment, or both. And she had raised the gem as if to do just that, but despite her clear fury and exasperation, it remained black as night.

"There's one floor left before we reach the observation ring," Corwin said, his voice a whisper fraying at his own frustrations. "It does make the most sense for at least your dark room to be on that level. It requires heightened security but isn't on the upper tiers where workers with more specialized skills and education would be needed, regardless of their loyalty to Sehlín."

To Askon, Alora's father sounded less confident and more desperate than ever. Climbing the stairs with the same dogged persistence he had employed on countless military operations back in Vladvir, Askon watched as the level below the observation ring came into view. Above them was the ring itself, a platform extending several yards beyond the walls of the Spire into the open air, visible through huge windows that encircled the entirety of the ceiling. If the windows were made up of individual panes, Askon could not see where one began and another ended. He suddenly felt an overwhelming sense of having seen such windows before, of having been here, in this place before. He shrugged it off.

Much like the waiting room at the base of the Spire, this level consisted of three progressively descending concentric circles. On each of these were a number of doors proportional to the size of the ring. The first set seemed to Askon's eye to be small offices or reading rooms of some kind, the interiors and supposed purpose of which reminded him of the secret chamber at the back of the Tolarenz town hall. The second ring appeared to have only four doors that led to large meeting or discussion chambers set behind walls of glass. But unlike the similar rooms they had seen, these walls followed the curve of the ring, a true circle, unlike the top tier's oval, in solid panes that continued unbroken save for the seams between rooms.

Then he saw the lowest ring. Two doors of burnished metal, no glass, and a wide circular table at the center.

"That's it!" Elise said in hushed voice. She rushed forward, her footsteps audibly tapping down the narrow stairs.

Askon reached for her as she slipped by, unable to halt her before entering the chamber completely exposed. Corwin stepped up beside him, and a ripple of uncertainty ran along Askon's spine, the hairs on his neck rising. What was it about this place? He turned on Corwin.

The older man stared back curiously. "Is something wrong?" he asked. "You look like you've been woken from a nightmare."

Askon spun again, gripping the baton until it creaked against the tightness of his fingers. "There's no one here."

Corwin's face went pale.

"Where are the workers? The security?" Askon demanded.

"I—I don't know," Corwin stammered back. "We expected only a few. But none? Something's wrong."

"Obviously," Askon snapped, and plunged down the stairs after Elise and toward the center circle, catching a glimpse of her as she rounded the corner to the stairs that led to the lowest level.

By the time Askon had descended the first set of stairs himself, Elise was already trying the first door. A shearing sound of metal against metal resounded throughout the open space. Spinning at the sound, Askon noticed the same sort of pillars he had seen in the Dalkaldur Library dotting the outermost oval, reinforcing the structure above. A roar of effort turned his attention back to the center, and another metallic screech followed. Elise's shadow disappeared into the opening while Askon bounded down from the second tier to the bottom.

The circular table lay empty save for a number of metallic spheres resting at intervals around the tabletop. The rest of the vast surface, Askon guessed, had to be cleared at the end of each day, or populated with documents only as necessary. He swung around to face the door, and was met with Elise's face, harried and wild-eyed, instead.

"This is the place!" she said panting. "I couldn't see, but I could feel, and I could hear. He's not in any of these cells, but the other door."

Pushing past Askon and the table at the great room's center, Elise collided with the door on the opposite side. Heaving against its unwilling hinges as she had presumably done with its twin on the other side. Askon had nearly reached her when she looked back for help.

Gripping the cold metal, the two of them pulled the surprisingly heavy door open wide enough to enter. Without hesitation, Elise ducked inside. Askon followed.

As if they had crossed a threshold of polar opposites, the soulless white-that-was-almost-blue of the multileveled chamber shifted abruptly to near total darkness. Askon glanced behind, where the door still stood ajar. Light lay beyond it, but it was somehow stifled, muted, casting no illumination on the walls of the hallway at all.

"Close your eyes," Elise said, her voice low. "You'll adjust to the dark faster."

He did. Taking one slow breath, and then another, he waited. Then he heard it.

Ticka-ticka-tick. Ticka-tick.

His eyes snapped open. Tilting his head, he listened again.

Ticka-ticka-tick.

"Did you hear that?" he asked, but Elise had already turned, already followed the sound farther down into the dark.

Ticka-tick.

Askon hurried after her, lifting the baton, trying to aim the tiny lights to cast their rays on whatever lay ahead. At the end of the hall stood a door: wooden, and utterly unlike the one they had pried open to enter the darkened corridor. In the feeble light of the weapon Askon found the handle, above which was a lock.

"A lock on the outside," he said.

"Just like in the other hallway." Elise's voice came from the darkness where she was little more than an outline, even to

Askon's sensitive sight. He wondered how she had found her way without him. "Open it," she said.

The command was unnecessary, as Askon had already begun twisting the mechanism before she had spoken the words. It turned easily, and the door swung open with none of the resistance required to enter from the main chamber.

Suddenly they were awash in the smell. Thick and inescapable, it swirled around them, a blend of moldering damp, excrement, and death.

Ticka-ticka-tick. Ticka-tick.

"A little light?" asked a voice from somewhere behind them.

Askon whirled around to face the sound, stirring the stench, and braced himself against the door. They'd not be trapped here.

An orb of light floated toward them, drawing slowly closer until, in the deep darkness of the hallway, Corwin's face came into view.

"They've done something to these halls," he said, unable to check his innate curiosity. "It's not ordinary darkness." He reached out to Askon. "Here."

The orb hovered in front of him for a moment, before he reached out and grabbed the handle. It was a lantern, one of the metal spheres he had seen on the table as he pursued Elise. Holding it low, he turned to inspect the room. Inch by inch the floor grew visible. Askon squinted, stepped forward, and felt the soft grit of bare earth.

"A dirt floor?" Corwin said to himself. "And what is that smell?"

Another nauseating wave made Askon's eyes water. He lifted the lantern, casting light over a single wooden chair with battered leather restraints lying loosely about the arms and legs.

"This is the room," Elise said. "Where they were keeping Alora in the visions."

Ticka-tick.

The three of them twisted to face the noise, Askon swinging the lantern to illuminate the opposite wall. Under the unnaturally dim glow, two vacant eye sockets stared back from a face wrecked by the scavenging rats that went scurrying at the arrival of the light. Another pulse of the overbearing stench, and Askon gagged, the lamp falling lower, to a five-pointed star protruding from the destroyed and festering shoulder.

Elise crashed into Askon, driving past him toward the tormented body, frantic and pawing at the corpse.

"No. No, no, no!"

"Elise!" Askon snapped, as loud as he dared. Grabbing her shoulder, he pulled her away from the horror. And though her eyes turned on him in the dimness, full of murder and grief, he dragged her further. "It's not him!" he said, with more confidence than he felt. It couldn't be him. He had told them of the dark room and the tortures Alora had suffered, of the kind-spoken woman who was Sehlín and the man who had died, his body wracked by a cruel five-pointed star.

And then, the light went out.

The darkness was complete, and so too was the silence. Only their shuddering breath made any sound. Even the skittering rats had gone still. In the reek, they waited. One long moment. Another. And another. Askon could feel Elise, still in his grasp, though lightly now and without resistance. Corwin too, he could sense on his opposite side. Then he remembered the Time fragment.

Pulling the gem from beneath his clothes and armor, he raised it in front of him and saw…nothing. No glow, no heartbeat rhythm, not even a glimmer in the endless suffocating black where his nose and weeping eyes stung against the putrid air.

Speechless, he let the fragment of Alora's Tear fall to length on its chain. He blinked in the dark, unsure what to say, or what to do.

In the silence a whistle arose, high-pitched and squealing. Three pulses then two. Louder and louder it grew, until Askon lifted his hands to his ears to dull the impact of its piercing cry. Three pulses then two, three pulses then two.

Suddenly the room came to life in a rush of deep red light. He turned to Elise, expecting the Death fragment burning at her wrist but instead finding it no more than a well of lifeless black under the rhythmic ripples of red. All around, the room's purpose was laid bare. Windows lined the walls where onlookers could see what progressed inside. The floor, which seemed to be earthen when they had entered was only so for a small portion of the space. The rest looked to be polished stone, the like of which made up most of the floors in the Spire. A tray of sinister tools lay splayed across a table, and of course the hideous face of the dead man stared eyeless back at them.

"It's an alarm," Corwin said. "No. Not *an* alarm. *The* alarm."

Askon released Elise's shoulder, hardly remembering he still held it. The lamp flickered back to life in his opposite hand, then went out, then glowed dimly, then flamed bright as a burst of sunlight. He cast it down, and it rolled wildly across the floor.

As the beams flitted about the room, and the red glow rose and fell, Corwin waved them back toward the central chamber. The piping whistle of the alarm screamed its three and two rhythm, again and again.

"We have to get to the others!" Corwin shouted. He pointed above them amid the sensory chaos of light and sound and smell. "They're just above us! If we don't help them, none will survive the climb!"

CHAPTER TWENTY-SEVEN

Watchers on the Walls

Nils, Xel, Velara, Brastin, Balon, Strevan, Corlianna, Malwin, Cheeks…

Líana shook her head, names rattling inside her mind, bouncing off one another like unruly beads. The list had long ago grown too lengthy to recall. Not to mention, she'd had so little time. Yet, she tried again anyway. Strevan, Xel, and the one who called himself Cheeks had been there when Líana and the others were taken as Corwin's captives. They'd been there, too, when the Guardians arrived and the battle broke out. Now they knelt beside her in the trees and thick brush that climbed the slope on the north side of the High Spire. The complete list had begun to vanish the moment they had stepped onto the first carriage. From there to now, she remembered only a few.

In place of remembering, she had instead done her best to trust the team to which Corwin had insisted she be assigned; however, besides their names, she'd gathered painfully little of any real meaning. It pained her not to know the men and women she'd be fighting alongside, and the feeling made her wonder how Askon had trusted the countless soldiers fighting nameless at his side in skirmishes great and small. How many had died, unknown to him, and to how many had he been equally unknown in survival? Running the list again through her mind, she decided to turn her attention from such thoughts and to their goals instead.

As the soft patter of rain tapped across the broad-leafed branches above, the wind picked up, shifting and jostling their cover, sending a chaotic spray of sound down through the layers of foliage.

"They won't have the wind on the other side," Jhed's low voice rumbled from the shadows off to her left. "In some ways easier. In some, more difficult. We'll use it to our advantage while we can."

The dark-skinned elf, like always, made her feel as if he were speaking directly and exclusively to her, even though she knew well that the words were meant for all of them. It was one reason, she assumed, that so many had chosen to follow him and remain loyal to his cause.

Líana's part in all this had been, like so many things in her life, outside her control. Had Elise been more stable, or had Edward rather than Thomas been captured by Sehlín, the outcome would certainly have been different. Líana would have stayed at her brother's side, making their way together up the levels of the High Spire from the inside, searching for Alora and their captive friend. But Elise was not stable. In fact, her behavior had been so erratic, so desperate that Líana hardly recognized the level-headed if sometimes imperious friend she had set out with from Tolarenz.

The loss of Thomas, and the doubt surrounding his return, was eating that friend alive.

And so when the time had come, back in the safe house, to decide how to divide the Vladviri travelers, Líana knew no other choice would suffice. She had to be the one to join Jhed. Askon would have accepted the responsibility, she knew, but Corwin would want to keep him close, within sight, and though he would not say it, Askon too would have wanted to be inside where he could be of the most help to the woman they'd traveled across worlds to meet.

Now, under the quiet rhythm of the rain, nothing remained but to wait for the signal. Jhed would decide when to begin, but from there, the plan would proceed, sustained by its own momentum, energized by the disorder they intended to create. Líana looked down at her armor and weapons and considered whether the illusion Tinley's devices had given Askon and Elise would actually convince a person skeptical of their presence. Either way, she was glad that on her side of the Spire, they would have no need for such questions. Their way in would be quiet, invisible, until it very much was not.

Peering through the scrim of leaves, and listening to the wind, she watched as their targets moved periodically from corner to corner of the massive stonework block that housed the Spire's security forces. Their numbers, Jhed had explained, were not too great to overcome directly, but the losses from doing so would hamper their designs once they reached their ultimate goal, the pursuit of which would begin upon the Spire's observation ring.

Instead of attacking head-on, they would use stealth and surprise to remove the guards likely to alert the rest of the forces, and then with the help of Tinley's circlet tech, scale the sheer north side of the tower.

If all went according to plan, a half dozen or fewer guards would be involved before they reached the ring. If, upon breaching the building, the security forces somehow became alerted, Tinley and the lower-floor team would hold the position long enough that the others could find the room powering the city. From there, the plan belonged to Jhed and a few trusted lieutenants, Corwin among them. It was not an arrangement she entirely supported, but it was the one that led to Thomas, Alora, and she hoped inevitably, back home.

Another gust rattled the branches, bringing a spattering of droplets down upon their backs. At the edge of her sight, in the shadow-dappled half-light radiating from the Spire, she watched Jhed signal the approach. All down the line the gesture repeated until it reached Xel, who crouched like a living shadow at Líana's right. Then Líana herself duplicated it for Strevan, who signaled Cheeks, one of the few highborn in Jhed's operation, and all those that completed the line off to her left. A moment later, they moved as one, prowling forward slowly through the trees.

Soon they could hear the shuffling steps of the guards above them, now and then a voice murmuring something to itself or calling across to another who watched with the same boredom as the rest. No more than half a dozen in total, or so Jhed and his operatives had determined. Reaching them unseen and unheard would be the most difficult maneuver, the walls too high and too smooth to scale by any ordinary means.

Líana placed her hand against the rough-cut stone and peered up through the surrounding brush. Dim beams of light wavered as the guards above them sat, or paced, or adjusted their equipment, or roused themselves from sleep. She reached down to her belt, feeling the cold metallic curves of the device Tinley had trained them to use at the safe house. Composed of two interlocking pieces, each resembling the singular component that Askon and Elise carried, the tool they would use to scale the Spire rotated without a sound. A gentle vibration radiated through her fingers as she pulled the elements farther apart, revealing a ring attached at the center of the belt. When the pieces came free of each other, a thin line of shimmering blue light appeared, threading itself through the ring. This, Tinley had called the tether.

Beside her, Xel tossed the throwpiece up through the canopy where, with a surprisingly quiet *snick*, it adhered to the stone—strong enough to bear the weight of any four people, Tinley had confidently explained. With a near soundless hiss, Xel ascended as if attached to a pulley, branches whipping against her clothing. Off to the other side, a series of identical blue lines glimmered against the stone followed by a ripple of hisses and rising shadowy forms. Setting her shoulders, Líana tossed her own throwpiece as high as she could, listening for a breath before, with another *snick*, it snapped into place. A quick tap against the remaining half of the device pulled her skyward through the branches.

Breaking free of the cover, her companions looked like no more than a row of odd, formless shapes against the flat sides of the structure. To a passing observer, they might have been sculptures or simple tricks of the light. Then, in another ripple of thin blue strands, the throwpieces were cast upwards and the line ascended once more. Líana looked down at her waist where the first piece she had thrown now functioned as an anchor point, securing her to the building. Grabbing the second throwpiece, she tossed it up and rode the silent glide ever higher.

The third length would take them to the level where the guards stood watch. What portion of the Spire's total height they had climbed, Líana could not tell, but whatever amount, it was a mere fraction. A whispered count echoed down the line.

"Three, two, one," she repeated.

Streaks of blue sailed up the face of the wall, and she fixed her eyes on her own tether as it tugged her silently upward. The pull began slowly, then accelerated as she reached the end. All was dim gray stone until suddenly she was swinging over a fence of open bars that gave way to the stunned expression of a High Spire watchman. Using the tether's momentum to assist in flinging herself at the unsuspecting enemy, Líana tapped the anchor point, releasing its hold. Leaping from the rail, the circlet device coiled midair back into its interlocked position.

The guard raised his hands in surprise, but it was too little to stop Líana driving both her fists in a hammer blow down onto his head. He crumpled to the ground beneath her as she brought down another strike. Stunned, he moved only slowly as she bound him to the rails.

Looking up, and panting at the effort, similar shadowy tableaus played out all across the wall. When the scuffling had gone still, she saw faint sparks as each bound person received a charge from the debilitating batons used by Sehlín's forces and the Basin City Guardians. She winced at the sound when Strevan struck the man she'd tied, his body twitching weakly against the weapon's energy.

"Better if you don't look at it," Strevan said.

Líana shook her head. "I've felt that pain. It's hard to forget."

"As have I," he said. "Maybe after tonight, there'll be fewer memories like ours." Tossing the spent baton to the ground, he retrieved another from the unconscious watchman's belt and handed it to her. "And either way, it does less harm than that sword of yours."

She nodded and turned to follow him toward Jhed, who had in similar fashion collected weapons from the guards that the rest of the line had overcome and bound to their assigned posts. As the others approached, he handed the batons off to anyone who was still without one.

"Right. Easy enough for our first step," he said softly, the low tones vibrating deep in his chest. "Now the real test begins." He waved them along. "Come."

Keeping pace between Xel and Strevan, Líana followed Jhed along the edge of the wall. They stayed low, and moved as quietly as possible. All across the rooftop, glass domes glowed with the same light that emanated from the rest of the Spire. Líana could see people inside, a scant few at this hour, moving here and there, unaware that the assault had begun. Looking up at the sky, she felt again the soft chill of rain and wondered if the domes simply allowed light from the outside to enter the guard station during the day, or if they amplified it like she'd seen in the Dalkaldur Library.

The scuffle of boots on stone snapped her attention back to Jhed. They had come to the end of the wall. There, the High Spire itself rose impossibly above them into the night. Twin staircases at opposite sides of the structure led from where they stood up to a narrow second tier that overlooked the entirety of the guard station's rooftop. Careful to keep low, and with weapons at the ready, they made their way up, wary of any watchers that might have observed their initial attack.

At the top, a long glass capsule stretched across the rooftop floor, inside which an empty planning room of some sort sat quietly unoccupied. Jhed leaned out around the corner where the stone sides of the stair corridor came to an end. The group fell silent, and Líana wondered if they all had simultaneously and involuntarily held their breath. A string of long, slow heartbeats passed before Jhed rose and nodded to them, urging the group forward.

Their luck, it seemed, had held. No guards were positioned on the upper level. The entirety had been at the wall, and nothing stood in the way of what came next. They gathered against the vertical face of the Spire itself, each of them gazing up with wondering eyes. Somewhere above them, the observation ring awaited.

Off to either side, the sprawling lights of Basin City stretched into the distance, wavering and faltering at the farthest edges, now here, now there, the countless inhabitants altogether unaware of what Jhed and his followers were planning. She turned back to the gleaming tower and ran one final time through the instructions he had given at the safe house.

"Tossing won't be enough once we reach the Spire. The distance is far too great. Once more, Tinley has given us a solution. The base of the throwpieces functions in the same way as a Guardian stun cartridge. It uses the same circlet-derived force to propel the object at great speed, and for our purpose, great distance."

Across the gathered crowd, the speech had set a number of heads nodding. They'd seen it already, or heard it told by Tinley before Jhed's final instruction.

"But we'll need power sources. So, any weapons we have now, and any we find along the way need to come with us. Batons are best, as they hold multiple charges and can last any one of us the full height of the tower."

The surprised noises that swept across the room at Jhed's next words had turned a smile up at the corners of Líana's mouth.

"Connect. Brace. Aim. Press."

A burst of energy and light had sent the throwpiece up and through the glass skylight, raining bits of glass upon them.

Now, at the base of the Spire, Líana watched Xel, Strevan, and Cheeks walk through the motions again in the shimmering light. How far the throwpiece would travel, none of them knew for sure, but Jhed had assured them, as Tinley had assured him, that the tethers would hold at a much more extreme length than the firing mechanism could propel them.

"We'd better go now, before Cheeks loses his nerve," Strevan grunted.

Xel laughed, aiming the baton and the attached throwpiece skyward. She braced it against her hip, and pressed the switch.

Líana squinted at the flash of light, the accompanying sound reminding her of the slap that a bucket of water makes on contact when emptied from a high window. Moments later, far above, she heard the now familiar *snick* of the throwpiece attaching to the Spire's outer wall.

"For every baton charge, we should get several firings. By our calculations, that should get any of us to the observation ring with a few firings to spare."

As Líana pressed the butt of the baton into her hip and held it parallel to the Spire's outer wall, she hoped that whatever *calculations* had been made were made three times. Taking a slow breath, she closed her eyes, lifted her finger and pressed the switch. The flash was apparent, even on the other side of her eyelids, and she opened them to watch the throwpiece sail to its full height, hover for a breath and affix itself to the building.

Suddenly, all around her the night was awash in blood red.

The Spire wall, the rooftop guard station, and the wild gardens below all pulsed in tandem with sinister red light. Líana knew the color, recognized the Death fragment's glow. But it made no sense. How could it be so bright? How could it cover the entirety of the space? She did not have time to consider the answer, as a piercing whistle screeched out across the quiet plateau upon which the Spire stood, now lit redly from beneath. Three blasts, then two.

CHAPTER TWENTY-EIGHT

The Climb

"Gods damn it!" Jhed roared over the screaming pulses of the alarm. "We should have blocked the hatches!" At a dead sprint, he bounded across the rooftop and down the staircase on his right. "Velara! Get to the other side!"

Three pulses, then two.

But it was too late. Líana watched as Velara's tether engaged, catapulting her up the vertical face of the High Spire. Several others nearby did the same, their expressions of surprise cast in deep red before they vanished, yanked from their feet at speed and out of sight. Frantically, Líana reached for the anchor attached to her belt, but she too had reacted too slowly. With a violent jerk, the tether lifted her off the ground, the force of it snapping her arms back, spinning her into the wall and nearly dislodging the baton from her hand. Her sword clattered against the Spire's polished surface, and up the tether pulled.

When she reached the first throwpiece which now served as anchor, her head was reeling. She set her feet and did her best to observe what transpired below. Jhed had reached the hatch in time, jamming it with a spent baton and then piling anything he could find atop the opening. In Velara's absence, others had raced to the opposite staircase where the second hatch lay, but they clearly had not reached it in time. Twisting her neck as far as she dared, Líana saw a pair of Jhed's agents fallen and dazed by the weapons of the Glittering World. A swell of armored figures spilled from the hatch, and Jhed's people met them in full force, fighting and falling, as they struggled to drive the guards back. She watched Jhed and a few others leap back up the stairs and into position, screaming all the while as the rest fought to buy them the time they would need to ascend. Flashes of white light burst through the pulsing red, and she heard a series of *snick*s as the throwpieces became anchor points all around her.

"Higher!" Xel shouted from somewhere off to Líana's left. Another series of flashes lit the Spire's side, turning angry red to brilliant white.

Líana did not follow. Her eyes had moved past the brawl atop the guard station and down to the scene playing out below. At the ground level, row upon row of Guardians marched down the path toward the main entrance on the western side of the building. She strained to see, twisting herself against the tether, and counted at least thirty. At the furthest edge of her vision, a small dark form trailed along behind the soldiers. It moved furtively, awkwardly so, as if uncertain whether it might already have been seen, nothing at all like the determined march of those he followed. And she knew it was "he" because she had seen such flagrant, self-conscious sneaking before in the alleys of Basin city.

It was Daeron.

Another gust of wind spun Líana off balance, her foot slipping from the polished wall. Flailing against the side of the Spire, her boots squeaked and slid wildly before catching some imperfection in the stone and finding traction once again. With heart racing, she steadied herself. *Daeron.* That was how they had been discovered! He was the one who had triggered the alarm or signaled ahead to warn the security team inside.

"Líana!" Strevan called from off to her right. "We have to keep going!" He lifted the baton, attached the throwpiece, and with a flash, sent it flying. Then he was gone.

Beside and below her, Jhed and the few others who had escaped the attempt to seal the hatches rose in a rush, setting their feet solidly against the tension of tether and anchor.

Three pulses, then two.

"Brace for fire!" Jhed screamed.

Across the row of their companions, red turned to erratic blue as the guards fired dozens of the cartridge weapons at their position, a number of which found their marks. Líana watched Cheeks shudder against the painful arcing energy, but unlike those she had seen before, felt before, this one began blue then erupted in sparks of red. With a final spasm Cheeks tumbled backwards, limp and lifeless, his head striking the Spire wall with a crack and a streak of crimson.

Líana turned away from the sight, stomach churning at the sound, and another volley of cartridges ricocheted off the wall, clattering around and above her. She heard the clenched-jaw screams of men and women who would, to her, remain nameless even as they gave their lives, some left hanging there from the Spire, others cut free, landing broken upon the guard station rooftop.

"Up! Now!" came Jhed's roar again.

And this time she obeyed, anything to escape the fate of the others. She set the baton to her hip, fired the throwpiece and ascended like an arrow from the bowstring, the wind whistling in her ears, the now deadly weapons peppering the space she had only just occupied.

As the second stage ended, she planted her feet, this time prepared for the impact. Again, she craned her neck to look down upon the rooftop. The cacophony of the alarm and her shouting companions swirled with the gusts of wind and rattling of another volley from the guards. She braced herself and tried to become as small a target as she could. Then something thumped into her back. Flexing involuntarily at the contact, she readied herself for what would come next. When nothing did, she exhaled in relief, her leather armor turning the sharpened prongs that would have delivered the charge and its now lethal secondary effect.

But just beside her, Velara was not so lucky. Líana watched helplessly as a cartridge clipped into the woman's calf and sent her swinging upside down, her back crashing into the side of the Spire with a dull thump and scrape as she tore the object free with a feral scream. She flung it away just as it burst into a shower of red shards, some of which embedded themselves into the pristine surface of the wall before dissipating like icicles melting under a morning sun. Dangling for a moment, Velara attempted to regain her balance, but the leg that had taken the initial charge would not bear her weight. She slipped and scrabbled, eventually stabilizing herself for long enough to fire the throwpiece. A heartbeat later, she ascended, and Líana lost the lines of her shape in a blur of wind and redoubling of the rain they had felt when first scaling the guard station wall.

Before the guards could ready another assault, Líana did the same, feeling the forceful tug of the tether followed by the rush of wind that meant she would soon be free of the threat. At the third stage, the cartridge weapons could no longer reach them with enough force to be effective. And for a moment, she felt a sense of calm. From her vantage point, she could not be sure how many of Jhed's forces had reached this height, nor how many had been lost. Xel, Strevan, and Velara, now heavily favoring her left leg, were all within view. Jhed pulled up beside Líana an instant later, and she could hear and sense a good many others just below and outside of her peripheral vision. She hoped their numbers would be enough.

Whatever had produced the awful sound had also faded at this height. Somehow though, the rise and fall of red light against the muted three and two rhythm from inside the Spire felt even more ominous. The wind gusted, but rather than the wild loss of balance, she simply allowed her bodyweight to sway against the tether, which shimmered steady blue against the intermittent red. Somewhere far away, thunder grumbled.

"I think," Jhed said, his voice raspy now, "we've made it through the worst of things, at least for the time being." He twisted his head, attempting to see below them.

"And we've lost too many," Xel called.

Jhed sighed. "Losing one is losing too many. But you all knew—*we* all know—the price that might be paid."

With his eyes now turned skyward and a level expression that Líana could see for what it was, a mask to hide his grief, Jhed set the baton to his hip. "We still have a long way to go. And now they know we're here."

"Daeron," Líana said.

Jhed turned, his finger hovering above the baton's trigger. "What?"

"I think Alora's friend Daeron is the one who alerted the Guardians or the Spire, or both," she explained.

Jhed frowned but did not speak. Líana shielded her eyes as he jammed his finger down and rose with the device's blinding flash. Soon the others were firing their throwpieces and rising along after him. Without looking down, Líana did the same, the guard station rooftop growing smaller and smaller somewhere behind her.

A chilling rain misted across Líana's back as they rose in determined silence several cycles later. From time to time, she had attempted to look down to the ground below, but the height had grown far too alarming, and she no longer dared. Lightning scarred the sky, and the wind and rain buffeted them. The higher they went, the colder the rain and fog became. Footing too had become more difficult. Halfway to the destination, polished stone gave way to a mirror smooth substance that she guessed might be some sort of opaque glass. And that too gave way in regular intervals to glass so transparent that when her anchor had attached to it for the first time, she felt she would fall straight through and into the Spire's interior.

All the while, she kept her eyes trained on the observation ring, their target, their destination. Now it was, by her estimation, only a few cycles of anchor, set, fire, and rise in the distance. There was no telling if Askon, Elise, and Corwin would have reached the same level before them, no guarantee that they would make it past the security inside at all, especially with the unexpected alarm and arrival of the Guardians. They had to rely on trust, and hope, and Corwin's knowledge.

With thunder booming across the darkened plateau, she lifted the baton, seeing that only the last of its indicator lights still glowed blue. The other two, now a sullen red, served as reminder that Tinley's tether device too had its limits and requirement for trust. Pressing down on the switch, the throwpiece soared upward and *snicked* into place. With a tug, the tether pulled her ever closer to the observation ring.

When she landed, the rain relented, growing thin in the whipping wind, and another wild gash of lightning sliced through the sky. Líana looked out across the entirety of Basin City, a blue thread obstructing her view where Strevan's tether hung from its anchor point a dozen feet above her own. Over the course of their climb, the orderly line in which they had begun had slowly grown more scattered, with some of the team now nearly a full stage ahead of the others. Tilting her head a bit farther back, she watched the city lights grow dim at the edges, then dark.

Rapidly, the sea of stars below winked out, the inky blackness that took its place accelerating toward them. Almost without thinking she readied the baton, aimed, and fired. As the tether latched into place somewhere above, the darkness drew closer to the Spire than she'd ever seen it come, until no lights remained at all. Thunder roared in her ears, and the blue line before her eyes flickered and grew pale just as her own tether launched her upwards. Rising quickly, she watched in horror as the tether obscuring her vision flickered again. Only a moment later, she passed the anchor, which quavered, vibrated, and snapped free, losing its hold and tumbling silently into the abyss. She turned her eyes to her own tether and tried not to imagine Strevan's face, his fall.

When her feet contacted the wall on either side of her anchor point, Líana held as still as she could. On her left, a throwpiece rose up, hovered, and snapped into place. A heartbeat later the tether pulled tight, its blue light spreading out across the smooth surface. Beyond, the city lay dark, save for glimmers and flickers here and there that reminded her of the tremors an aging hand suffers as it struggles through work once effortless and familiar. While she watched, the anchor point beside her, now carrying the weight of one of the remaining members of Jhed's operation, began to quiver just the same.

Jhed himself Líana could see on the other side of the anchor. He seemed to know what would come next, to know the inevitable end and, when the anchor clipped free of the wall, to know that what he would do would be foolish. Yet, without hesitation, he flung himself across the narrow span and reached for the detached anchor with both hands.

Sympathetic pain spiked through her shoulders as she watched Jhed's arms shudder at the full bodyweight of the person attached below. Pulling with all his might, he wrenched the throwpiece into place at his belt. With surprising force, the two components twisted themselves together, linking the remaining force of the tethers. Up out of the darkness, Xel's face appeared, sweat beading her brow, panic in her eyes.

Líana was not sure if Jhed had been prepared for the impact when the tether brought the elven woman's full weight crashing into his own. They caught each other in what might have looked like an embrace to anyone watching from afar. To Líana it felt like the force of colliding shield walls at the onset of battle. The crash knocked Xel's baton from her grip and sent the two of them swinging back toward Jhed's anchor, Xel clutching him for dear life as they spun, skipping uncontrollably across the rain-slick wall.

But the anchor and tether held, its force increased by the coupling of the two devices. As they came to a stop, Xel tightened her grip, freeing one of Jhed's hands to reach for the baton attached to his hip. He eyed its three red lights with a grimace and pitched it out into the open air. A moment later, he took Xel's throwpiece in his hand and hurled it upwards. And so they continued.

Líana looked at her own baton, its single blue light still growing strongly, and breathed deep. She aimed, tilting the device ever so slightly to her left, and pressed the switch. Above, the observation ring loomed larger and larger. When her feet planted against the glass, she saw through to a room pulsing red, the faint three and two rhythm of the alarm muted behind the thick pane and muffled beneath the gathering winds. Inside, armed figures ran from one side of the building to the other.

Reminded of her purpose, Líana turned her head to try and locate Jhed and Xel below her. Unable to do so, she turned her gaze to the anchor point between her feet, closed her eyes, and twisted her body, pivoting around the attachment. The belt, though uncomfortable at this angle, held tightly at her waist. She gasped, seeing the truth of their climb.

Hundreds of feet below, past sheet after sheet of windblown rain, the guard station had become a tiny imperfection at the base of the Spire's sheer smooth sides. Líana's stomach reeled and her vision tilted dizzily. Clenching her eyelids tight again she breathed once, twice, and opened them, this time focusing on Jhed's wide-eyed face as he cast the throwpiece up once more, the strain of Xel's weight growing more apparent with each passing moment.

"Just get to me!" Líana called over the surging wind. "I have more charges left."

Jhed nodded, his thickly muscled arm flexing as he threw the device again.

With that, Líana set her jaw and twisted her body, flipping herself back into position. Inside the spire, the guards scrambled forward, meeting some unknown resistance or obstacle at their destination. They beat their fists and weapons against the door, which for the moment, did not budge.

A *snick* to Líana's immediate left startled her from her observations, and soon Jhed, with Xel wrapped tightly around him, rose into view. She could see both of them straining to support the other's weight. They wouldn't be able to continue for long.

"Can the two of you operate it?" she asked.

Jhed nodded.

"I think so," said Xel, her breathing ragged and uneven.

Another arc of lightning flashed, and Líana carefully handed the baton over to them, watching as they worked in tandem to steady the throwpiece, aim it at an angle dangerously far from the surface of the Spire, and fire. As the anchor clipped into place on the edge of the observation ring, Xel passed the baton back to Líana. Then in a wild swing, they soared out into open air. Xel's grip slipped from Jhed's shoulder, but he pulled her close just long enough for her to clasp her own arms together around his neck before the tether lifted them to the lip of the ring.

While Jhed and Xel clambered up and out of sight, Líana braced herself and fired the throwpiece, aiming as Jhed had done, for the outer edge of the observation ring. The anchor *snick*ed into place, and she swung out over the vast emptiness. A heartbeat passed, then another, and finally the tether engaged.

Suddenly, the lights went out.

The wide glass room turned from dim red to utter black. Líana dangled from the tether with nowhere to go but down. She wondered if the impact would be painful, or if it would be anything at all. She wondered, fast as their climb had been, if the return trip would be faster. She wondered if Askon would find her body there where it would land. Would he bring her back to Vladvir, to Edward? Looking up, she watched the anchor twitch and shudder, thinking that this slowness-of-all-that-was must be how Askon felt when the power of the Time fragment wrapped itself around him.

With a final shiver, the anchor came free. And then, Líana was falling.

CHAPTER TWENTY-NINE

The Atrium

Askon's feet pounded down the pitch-black hallway. Red light surged, and the thin rectangle of the door drew almost imperceptibly closer, or was it edging farther away? Had it been this far when they entered? Certainly not, but how could that be possible? Beside him, Corwin's labored breathing went on and Elise's quiet footsteps trailed behind.

When they finally reached the door, Askon slid through, involuntarily leaping back as if the door itself, or something inside, might reach out and drag him back. Watching their similar expressions, Askon assumed that both Elise and Corwin felt the same. All around them, the three-tiered room glowed red, then dimmed to black, then grew red again.

Between the piercing screams of the alarm, Askon heard a sharp crack and looked in the direction from which they had entered this floor initially, where heavy, booted footfalls sounded by the dozens.

"Run," he said to the others, and they bolted for the staircase leading to the middle tier.

As Askon took his first step, he heard the thump of a projectile cartridge strike the floor where they had only just stood. He did not look back, but swerved hard left, toward another of the stairways that would take him upward, away from where Elise and Corwin had run.

His back slammed against the cold stone, and another cartridge pinged off its smooth surface. For a moment Askon huddled there, taking cover as best he could before he'd be forced to try the open space that lay between his position, the next flight of stairs, and eventually the upper tier.

Elise and Corwin made the move first, or at least that was what Askon assumed when he heard another volley of weaponry clatter off the pristine walls in the direction they had gone. Making use of the opportunity himself, he raced across the second tier, doing what he could to stay low and, reaching for the hem of his cloak, using it to slow or dampen any incoming fire.

Then, as he shouldered into the cover of the stairs that would take him to the upper tier, he remembered. His cloak. It was no longer invisible and his own armor lay there upon his chest before his very eyes. Whatever magic or cleverness Tinley had woven for them had failed. He banged his fist against the device, trying to inspect it in the intermittent light. Nothing.

A cartridge clipped the stair just below his boot, flipping and spinning in the air, finally landing a few feet above where he stood. He bolted for the door to the next level of the Spire. Corwin and

Elise already stood there, the latter with her hands wrapped around the latch. Another set of projectiles whipped past his ears and rattled their metallic beat against the unmoving slab.

Ticka-ticka-tick. Ticka-tick.

The door came free, swinging inward and catching another errant cartridge. Askon dove through the opening, followed immediately by Elise and Corwin, and with their help slammed the door shut behind them. With wild, flailing strokes Askon grabbed the baton from his hip and beat the handles until they bent double on themselves, jamming the device between the twisted wreckage, barring for the moment their pursuers from entering.

In the silence, Askon realized that the alarm had stopped. Light, steady and clear, filled the room, the walls all around no longer white but cold featureless gray. He took a slow revolving step, taking in the enormous space while Elise and Corwin frantically dragged anything they could find to barricade the door. But beyond their efforts, the room was not silent. A voice was speaking.

"…lost your way," it said, smug and self-righteous. "Stay right where you are. Rest a bit. Sehlín will put you back where you belong."

But Askon did not turn toward the voice; he turned away from it, to his right.

Ticka-clack! went the furniture Elise and Corwin had secured against the door.

Suddenly, he knew where they were, *when* they were. He stood in the huge atrium of the High Spire just as the final vision from the fragments had shown them.

"Alora!" he shouted, before he saw her, limping and bleary-eyed against the largest panes of glass he had ever beheld, even here in the Glittering World. And she saw him too, an expression of surprise and wonder on her face for but a moment, then she stumbled, fell, and lay still.

"No!" Corwin cried.

The three of them ran to where she had fallen, her father reaching her first, scooping her up in his arms, tapping her cheeks with a gentle hand, saying her name again and again. She murmured, breathed, and Corwin held her, rocking back and forth on his knees. "The door," he said, to Askon. "Get to the door! Get to Jhed. Let them in!"

It wasn't just Jhed who needed him to open the way. Líana was out there, if she, or any of them, had survived the climb at all. For a moment, Askon's feet hesitated, hovering there above Alora, so close to the reason he had brought them all here. Then he was pelting toward the giant wall of pure glass. At the far right was a door, just as transparent as the rest of the wall, with a handle and latch also wrought of purest glass.

On the other side, dark shapes emerged from the lip of the observation ring. Vaulting the railing, one after another, Jhed's forces multiplied, drawing closer to the atrium wall until Askon could clearly see their faces. Rain poured down upon the ring and streamed down the glass. He flipped the latch and the door burst inward with a rush of wind and water. But Askon did not stop. He sprinted into the storm. A moment later, Elise had tripped the latch of the door on the wall's opposite corner, and Jhed's forces flooded in on either side.

Out on the ring, the storm swirled and thundered around Askon as he searched through the too-thin crowd for his sister. The others charged forward, disappearing from view into the room where he'd left Alora. Scanning the handrails frantically, he watched for Líana, but she did not appear. Rain whipped across his face, blinding him momentarily. He wiped it away with a sleeve just as a large dark shape clambered up onto the rail. It was huge, too large to be a person. He brushed away the water again, and a flash of lightning revealed not one person but two. Jhed tumbled over the rail and onto the ring's surface, the second form hit the hard stone and rolled onto her back. In the darkness and rain, dark skin glimmered on her forehead and exposed arms. Tired but whole, the two slowly arose.

"Where is Líana?!" Askon demanded over the wind. Somewhere behind them, the sounds of battle clattered, and he hoped the reinforcements would be enough.

"She was just behind u—" Jhed's words were cut short as a metallic glimmer flinked above the rail, hovered, and attached itself with a *snick*.

Inside, clatter became clash and a scream tore through the din. It was one word: *Sehlín*. The voice that brutalized itself in its rage belonged to Elise.

Again, the lights went out.

This was not as before, not flickering or faltering, nor dimming in rhythm to the alarm. Now the darkness was absolute. Askon saw then that not only had the Spire gone dark, all the lights in Basin City were gone. In the storm, no longer did this world glitter, it yawned with emptiness.

But it was for only a heartbeat.

As the light returned, he saw the glimmering anchor-point on the lip of the ring. It quivered, shook, snapped free.

Then he was diving at the rail, something warm filling his chest. All around him the raindrops slowed their descent until, if they moved at all, not even the sharp-eyed Askon of Tolarenz could detect it. The wind grew utterly still. The sounds of battle ceased. There was only silence. There was only stillness—and the anchor—free of its attachment to the stone of the High Spire, suspended in midair as if frozen, the thin blue strand bent like a striking snake. At the other end, one brilliant blue eye and one green gazed upward in a serene expression of peaceful release.

Líana.

With the familiar power of the Time fragment engulfing him as never he could recall, Askon collided with the rail and grasped the anchor, pulling the slack tight.

The warmth at his chest went cold and the rain pelted down in sheets, the wind howling, and the tether drew Líana up from the abyss, over the rail, where she landed and rolled onto her side, completing several rotations before coming to a stunned stop. She lifted her head and looked at him.

"So that *is* what it's like," she said, a mixture of wonder and disbelief coloring her words. Then her face went pale. "Oh, gods. No."

Askon turned to see what she saw. On the other side of the glass, a battle had been joined. Jhed's forces, upon entering the atrium, found immediate resistance from the forces employed on the upper levels. A rush of Guardians gathered where the makeshift barricade had given way. They streamed in, one after another until the last had entered the atrium. Behind them, timid and halting, came Daeron. Corwin had dragged Alora to the center of the glass wall, where he knelt over her protectively. Seeing the two of them, Daeron pointed and shouted something to the Guardians, but they did not heed his words, his voice drowning in the din.

On the opposite side of the cavernous room and up one level, a wild-haired highborn glared down at the proceedings. The Guardians and other security forces seemed caught by surprise at the number of Jhed's agents. But they were better geared, and for the most part, better trained. For now, the fight went in Jhed's favor, though Askon could see it would not remain there for long.

Next to the scowling highborn stood Sehlín. Her weathered face, like a ship's planking, peered down at the fray. And, struggling against her grasp, his hands bound, beaten and bleeding, was Thomas. His ragged hair, matted with sweat, ringed deep bruises around his eyes which rolled as Sehlín shook him. In her other hand she held a baton; at the opposite of the painfully charged end, the weapon tapered into a sloping sliver blade. It glinted in the light, all save for the tip, which was painted with bright crimson. She swiveled it back slowly toward Thomas who seemed neither to fear it nor sense it at all.

Two identical staircases wound upward on either side of the atrium. At the base of the right-hand staircase stood Elise, the Death fragment smoldering at her wrist, her breath rushing in and out through flaring nostrils beneath red-rimmed eyes. It was then that Askon understood the lights, or the complete lack of light he had felt before catching Líana's anchor. Elise had called upon the fragment. At her feet lay a spent baton. The blood on Sehlín's own weapon—Thomas's, Askon could only assume—had stopped Elise and lifted the fragment's suffocating darkness.

Líana had already raced inside through the rain, and Askon followed, trying to get to Elise, to Sehlín, to help the others. Doing what he could to assist Jhed's forces, even as Jhed drove back the force of Guardians entering from below and disappeared through the broken barricade around the doorway. Askon beat his way through the battle, trying desperately to reach Elise's side. She did not look at him or Líana. Her eyes were locked on Thomas, whose head was drawn back, his eyes open but unseeing.

Askon remembered his dream, remembered standing atop the waterfall, staring down into that face.

With a slow smile that tugged one corner of her mouth, Sehlín spun the blade and drove the charged end into Thomas's side. He hardly moved as she retracted it and brought it down again. The smile tugged a second time and she turned away, dragging Thomas's spasming form through the ornate wooden door that stood behind her and the wild-haired highborn. Askon watched it close with ominous finality and spun to catch a wild baton stroke from one of the Spire forces.

Elise screamed.

The sound rang out over the raging battle, growing louder, harsher and higher, until no other sound seemed to exist, until the world was only scream, bloodcurdling and raw and everywhere.

Askon knew what would come next, though he did not know what had changed to awaken the power of the fragments here in the Glittering World. He knew what Elise could do, what she was already doing. He breathed deep, flinging himself across the room to where Corwin knelt with his arms wrapped around Alora.

And darkness fell upon him like the weight of a universe.

CHAPTER THIRTY

Echoes

Alora blinked in the blackness. Where was she? Was she blinded? Was she dreaming? Was there anything? The featureless dark stretched out all around her to what felt like infinity. There was no sound, no movement. Experimentally, she reached out a hand. Had she heard her father's voice after the world had gone dark?

She felt her face, and found her eyes were not yet open. So she forced them open, forced them to see. But there was nothing. The world was completely empty, completely silent, completely light-less.

And yet she knew she was not alone. He was there. She had seen him, seen the dark green cloak and the kind face drawn with concern as he shouted her name. Not just him, though, the sister too was there, with her comforting voice and keen blade. The one who was both pale and dark was also there. Alora knew her shape and outline without question, like knowing that a leap from a rooftop would bring the ground up to meet her. They had come to save her, each of them in their own way. From what, she hadn't known when they arrived, but now she'd seen: the white room and the dark, the voice ragged with threat, and the kind-spoken woman who was Sehlín.

Alora planted her foot, flexed her legs and hips in an attempt to rise. Something sharp pressed itself against the inside of her closed fist. Then she felt the certainty gathered around the one who was both pale and dark falter and fade, scattering like ash in warm autumn wind. Another step and another brought her closer to him, to Askon, though he was but a flitting shadow next to the sister who now burned in Alora's blackened vision like a bonfire— if such light, such warmth could exist—a thousand bonfires all in no more space than a pinprick.

Somewhere the last of the ash whispered out of existence, and suddenly Alora could see.

The atrium's high ceilings stretched up overhead, while the sound of the rain beat its relentless cadence against the vast window wall. All around, the noise and motion of battle had ceased. A room teeming with Guardians, Sehlín's forces, and Jhed's agents only moments ago now stood as empty as a tomb.

Alora blinked in disbelief at what remained. Across the floor, from one side to the other, everywhere a person had once been, a stark-white powdery substance formed a small circle.

On the level above, Elise charged toward the ornate door from which Alora had only recently escaped. Líana called tearfully after her dark-haired friend, following up the stairs with uncharacteristically clumsy steps. Her two-colored eyes glanced back once, then again, to where Alora stood dazed and unmoving, before closing the distance between herself and Elise.

Alora revolved her gaze to the floor at her feet, feeling the vast empty room swell around her. She felt again the sharp object in her left hand and focused her eyes upon it, finding there a thin silver chain. Beyond the closed fist, almost brilliant against the dull gray, lay three powdered circles.

She knew what she held, and to whom these shapes almost certainly belonged. Somewhere above, Líana's footsteps echoed. Unable to explain what drove her, Alora reached out to the circle on her right, her hand splayed and shaking as it contacted the cold dusty surface.

✛ ✛ ✛

There's no getting out of this now. They'll bring it all down before we can escape. At least she's here. At least I haven't lost her too.

A thin fog had crept over Alora's vision. Everything was blurry and unfocused, but somehow very familiar. She felt her hand reach down, felt her arms encircling the person curled up on the cold stone floor. The person she found herself embracing was… herself.

It's all right. We'll be safe somehow. And if not us, then you. I'll make sure Sehlín doesn't hurt you again.

Battle raged all around. Jhed had fought brutally, his thick dark arms flexing with every stroke of the baton. She watched him and several others drive the invading force of Guardians back into the room which led back down to the Spire's lower floors, parrying incoming blows and twisting Guardian weapons away from their hands, turning one upon the attacker and expending the last of its charges.

She felt tears begin to spill over her face. As she reached up to brush them away, her fingers met glass instead. She pushed up the spectacles, wiped under her eyes, and let her hand travel up into the familiar thinning shock of hair that stood straight up from the scalp. Clutching tighter the shoulders, head, and neck of the one she embraced, Alora felt her eyes close.

I let Sehlín hurt your mother by not doing something sooner, and now she's hurt you. But never again.

Above, Sehlín appeared, peering down from her liar's mask, the very picture of politeness and propriety, until a wicked grin wriggled across her face. With arms tense but steady, she held before her a man beaten and bloodied who could only be Thomas.

"Sehlín!" Elise's voice roared over the clash of battle.

Darkness pressed in, stretching out toward eternity, then receding like a failing tide until she could see again.

Sehlín held her weapon, blade gleaming, at the man's throat. Effortlessly she spun it and delivered not one, but two charges into her captive. As he shuddered, Sehlín simply turned, and dragged him away toward the upper levels.

I'm sorry! For your mother. For our life after she was gone. If we manage to leave this place, please, do more than I did. Do more than dream of what once was. Do more than dream of vengeance. Do more than hide.

Tears flooded her eyes now, and she buried her face into the person her arms encircled, remembering the life she'd made this girl lead, remembering the life they'd had before.

I'm sorry. I love you.

Darkness descended again, only this time with the weight of all that had been and all that would ever be, and she knew that this time it would not roll back. All at once, there was nothing at all.

A rescue from a literal tower! If she doesn't understand the lengths I'd go to for her after this, then I don't know what's left to make her understand.

Behind her, she felt the marching steps of rank upon rank of Guardians. Somehow, in a burst of glorying eloquence, she'd compelled them this far. Drawn their attention to the hideout Corwin and Jhed had so foolishly revealed, gutted and burned the place, along with all their contraband. Basin City had laws, and these officers upheld those laws. Was Alora going to throw that all away because three crazed strangers showed up spouting stories from a fantasy version of history she fancied?

Mad or no, she's here because of those three, she's hurt because of those three. I can still stop them, save her from them, from herself.

As the Guardians fought in the fray against Jhed's forces, she felt herself smile as a baton stroke fell on the man in the deep green cloak. Then, the smile became wonder, and all her breath seemed to rush out as her eyes alighted upon the familiar face fringed with chestnut hair and deep almond eyes, the lips that might one day, when the time was just right, brush against—

The face was her own.

She'll see. Alora, can you see? Me? These officers will help you, help us! And then we can run. Like I said before. We'll disap—

A tidal wave of black tore the memory to shreds.

The film of fog had not lifted, and Alora felt the deep green cloak swirl about her shoulders as she caught a Guardian's stroke, parried, and smashed her own baton into the man's curious glass-visored helm, sending him spinning to the ground. On the stairway, Elise seethed as Sehlín struck Thomas with the painful weapon of the Glittering World.

Not Thomas! Don't. Harm. Thomas. None of us will walk away from this. Elise is too fragile, too close to breaking, already too broken.

She felt her eyes turn through the fog toward the window wall. There on the polished gray floor, Corwin knelt with his arms around his daughter, around Alora herself. They were beautiful, the two of them together there, worth protecting even if visions and fragments and a journey between worlds meant nothing else. A few steps away, a person scrambled wildly across the open space, flailing to reach them. Daeron.

Back on the stairs, red light painted the wall, suffused the air, tinged every surface of the cavernous space.

Elise, no! The fragment can't bring him back. It can only take. It's going to take us all!

But the thoughts never became words, or if they did, they were drowned. A scream arose, high and piercing, like nothing she'd ever heard before in all her life. On and on it went, for too long, impossibly long, and then the darkness began to descend.

Amid the world of scream, she felt her chest rise and fall, felt her eyes affix themselves to the kneeling, bespectacled form and the one he pulled closer and tighter than ever. A warmth surrounded her then, all the world seeming to stretch as if the moment itself had stopped to look on, had forgotten that moments should pass.

And the void drew closer.

She felt her boots strike the floor as she sprinted, felt her cloak rippling, heard the unending scream continue in its torment, saw her sister reach out toward the source of the sound, toward Elise's shrieking form.

When the darkness finally crashed down, she watched an island of light bloom around Líana while the absolute absence of light enshrouded Elise. Only a few steps remained and she'd be there. She knew what she would have to do. She grabbed the Time fragment and pulled it free of her neck. She saw father and daughter clinging to one another— and the encroaching darkness grew still.

The Tear called me to the Glittering World, called me to you. And when I arrived, you knew our stories in a world where they had been forgotten. When you took the fragments from us, down by the waterside, I wondered how you escaped. But now I know.

Through the film of memory, she felt the sharp edges of the Time fragment as she reached past the father and placed the gem firmly into the daughter's hand, her own hand, and curled the semi-conscious fingers tight around it.

Alora, take care of them for me. If you have to, save them from them-selves.

The whirling mass of nothing came down in a final crushing burst, and far away a white light grew until her eyes were blind. It seemed to Alora that his voice drifted quietly through the emptiness.

But Askon of Tolarenz was gone.

Alora blinked away the last wisps of fog obscuring her vision and found her hand pressed hard against a backdrop of pure white. It ached with the pressure, and the fingertips, absent of their color, seemed eager to blend with the circle that lay upon the gray tile. Thin and gentle she heard the scrape of metal against the floor. Vanishingly quiet, the sound traveled out far into emptiness and its minute echo brought into focus the enormous atrium's full height, width, depth.

Outside, the storm rolled on.

She pivoted on her heel, reluctant to let the circles leave her gaze. If they did… no. No thinking of that now. Instinctively her hand went to her injured foot, remembering the pain, reliving the moment that Sehlín had struck, scolding herself for not thinking of it before. But she felt nothing.

Strong as ever it had been, her foot and ankle flexed against her weight. Running her fingers along it, she found it unmarred, unmarked, entirely healed. The Tear had done it, of course, one of the fragments had set things right. Líana's fragment, Life. Now, it was Alora's turn to help.

She stood, eyes still locked on the three powdery white circles upon the floor. A slow deep breath filled her chest, and a shudder of grief shook her frame. Closing her eyes, tears streaked down her face and tapped lightly against her clothes, their sound eerily amplified in the wide open space. Another spasm came, and a sad, frightened-animal sound lurched out of her mouth. A stutter. A whimper. She forced it out.

"I love you too."

Then came the flood. And Alora was running.

CHAPTER THIRTY-ONE

The Pinnacle

Flight after flight of stairs twisted dizzily below as Líana pumped her knees and forced herself upward, refusing to lose a single step to the maniacal energy that now drove Elise. Long ago hard breathing had given way to panting and that to gasps that came in arhythmic exhausted heaves. Now she hoped for just one more breath, and one more after that, as her muscles screamed.

When they had burst through the door and hit the first set of stairs, Sehlín, the wild-haired highborn, and presumably Thomas were already many levels above them, their footsteps audible but distant. It was a trap, of course. Líana knew it. And Elise knew it. Líana was just as certain of that. However, her friend ran like a woman possessed. Flight after flight after flight. But now, there were no more stairs to climb.

"Elise! Wait," Líana managed. "Don't just—" And she vomited onto the floor of the final landing.

Elise did not wait. She burst through a door just as ornate as the one they'd used in the atrium, and stepped through in cold silence.

Líana retched again and, fighting down another wave, wiped her mouth with her sleeve. With a growl she rose, and staggered through the door.

The room they entered was all but empty. A wide curved pane of glass wrapped the entirety of the High Spire's pinnacle. An all too familiar circle of pure white floor spread out faultlessly from end to end, interrupted only by a streak of red that smeared and faded, swerving crazily here and there toward the center of the room.

There stood Sehlín, her bladed baton in hand, her breathing unsettlingly level, her arm holding Thomas's semiconscious form as if he weighed no more than a child. The wild-haired highborn stood in front of her. Beside her shone a brilliant point of multifaceted light, glimmering in myriad colors somehow separately and somehow all at once. It hovered between two plinths or altars, one rising up from the floor and one descending from the wide white ceiling.

"Let. Him. Go," Elise snarled. At her wrist, the Death fragment flared.

"Did you tire on the way up?" Sehlín asked neither of them in particular. The lilt and serene propriety of her voice made Líana's skin crawl, a voice like so many of the blithering women in Edward's court. Chittering and puling over the half-elf girl who now sat alongside their handsome, once-eligible prince. "Well, it seems at least one of you did."

Líana squeezed her hand into a tight fist and felt there the warmth of the Life fragment. Inside, she smiled the wide, gleeful smile of a child who has been given leave from the washing and the cooking, leave from the sewing and mending, leave from Mother's tedious lectures, to run, run as fast as she can to the glade where the wooden stick-sword she carved herself leans against a tree battered by ten thousand sword strokes, an infinite history's worth of wars, fought until hands were bloodied and the splintered bits of stick-swords littered the surrounding battlefield.

On the outside, the two-colored eyes, one blue and one green stared ahead unblinking. The Life fragment glowed at her finger and her breathing slowed, her muscles and mind as fresh as if she'd taken no more than a single step after a long deep sleep. She gripped the leather of her sword's hilt and felt steel slide from the scabbard. Unbidden, the smile found its way to her face.

Sehlín sneered back. "Makes you feel stronger, doesn't it? Elise knows," she said, her voice obsequious in its feigned civility. The glowing point of prismatic color dimmed beside her, and outside, beyond the glass, Basin City's lights faltered.

"Educate them," Sehlín commanded with a shrug, tossing the bladed baton to the wild-haired highborn, who advanced with steady steps and a practiced grip on the weapon.

But Elise did not draw her sword, nor did she move at all. Absolutely every element of her being was bent on the form of her fallen husband. Had Líana not followed, the highborn's first blow would have landed cleanly on its target. Instead, the sloping sliver blade of Líana of Tolarenz met the highborn's first strike before it fell. The contact sent a shock through her arms, far stronger than she had anticipated, yet the sword had done its work in deflecting the opposing weapon. Another cut she met on the opposite side of her body, and felt Elise move toward Sehlín, Thomas, and the strange dais with its glowing orb of light.

Like lightning amid the storm outside, the highborn slashed across with his full strength. Her brother, or any other man she'd ever met, would surely have pushed back, attempted to meet the highborn's force with equal force, driving the baton against the opponent's strength. She knew this, had used it herself against Askon—and others—and so with no more effort than a leaf turned by a passing stride, she released her wrists, and felt the sharpened tip of the baton slide with the majority of its momentum toward the floor.

Breathing slowly, she pulled her foot back and reset her stance, lunging with her sword in her left hand, an easy mark. But the highborn did not loop his stroke around or pivot to reestablish distance before a counterattack. He fell to one knee, Líana's sword point sliding harmlessly past his torso into open air, and the brutal charge of the Glittering World's weapons struck her between the bones of hips and ribs. The energy rocketed through her, doubling her over, and bringing her to her knees. A scream tore from her throat and her back arched.

The highborn spun the blade, set his feet, and stopped dead. Across his neck whipped a sliver-thin line of red, then another, and another, until it welled into flowing rivulets of blood. The handle of a long-bladed hunting knife flashed into his side and hung there, where his clothes darkened around the blade. It disappeared, and he fell with a writhing gurgle and was still.

Knowing the fragments were again awake, Líana felt the warmth of it coursing through her again, and the pain of the baton charge faded until it was no more. She looked around to see from where the help had come.

Only a moment had passed since Líana had engaged with Sehlín's highborn guard, yet now Elise stood in front of the glowing light, mere feet from Sehlín, the Death fragment shining red at her wrist. To the side lay the battered form of Thomas, beaten, but clearly still alive.

Sehlín backed away, eyes wide, with her hands in the air. The air between Líana and the scene that played out before her shimmered, and she shielded her eyes against the brilliance of the orb. Then Sehlín's hand fell, and several things happened at once.

A flicker of green sliced across the room, and a figure skidded to the ground in a clumsy tangle of limbs just a few feet from where Elise stood. For a moment, she hoped against what her eyes had told her back in the atrium: the powdered circle and to whom it belonged. But as the tangle unwound itself, Líana knew. It was Alora.

At the same time, glints of purple and blue sparked toward the orb.

Then there was the telltale flare of red and looming darkness that welled up from Elise's wrist as she drove her outspread hands down toward Sehlín's exposed neck.

Líana watched as the darkness swirled around the circular room, coalesced around Elise's arms and coursed like a snake's venom into Sehlín.

And last of all, the sickly smile that spread across Sehlín's face as she squeezed the glowing orb, flexing her bony orange fingers until its light dimmed, dimmed enough for Líana to see, to understand what they'd done.

✢ ✢ ✢

Alora's feet, bare against the stone floor, flew back the way she had come. On the first flight of stairs the tears had blinded her, but her steps had known the way. A few flights more, and she'd felt the weight of the blade between the loops of her belt. With the hilt in hand, she ran on, her footsteps light as if she might be lifted from them at any moment. When she passed the floor that led to the white room, she gave it no more than a glance as lightness pulled her up, ever up.

Then she was standing at the top, facing a door just as elaborate as the one that led to the atrium. She opened it, and saw the truth.

Elise stalked across a wide circular room with a ceiling and floor of pure white, ringed with curved glass. At the center Sehlín loomed over Thomas and beside a brilliant glowing light.

"*You're here!*" it said.

And Alora knew it had pulled her up the stairs.

"Help them first."

She looked to the other side of the room, where Líana had fallen to both knees, her back arched and her face a grimace of pain and terror. The wild-haired highborn stood in front of her, both hands on the bladed baton, muscles driving its point forward, only inches from Líana's chest.

On the same weightless feet, Alora raced to her aid, slashing the man's exposed throat. When nothing happened she slashed again, and a third time, before stabbing him in the side with Askon's knife.

"He's gone," said the orb. *"Now, her. Quickly!"*

Alora knew the voice was right. The highborn's eyes were already lifeless, though he stood unmoved from the position in which she had first observed him. Turning, she dashed toward Elise, and felt the Time fragment rip free from her grasp. And she heard the voice once more.

"It's not too la—" it said, suddenly silenced.

Alora stumbled and fell, all the weightless grace gone from her steps. She careened into the lip of the circular floor's raised center. As she lifted her eyes, she saw Sehlín grip the glowing orb as Elise turned all the power of the Death fragment on her. But Sehlín was smiling. Why was she smiling?

The orb dimmed, flickered, faded, and in the glow of the Death fragment Alora saw it for what it truly was. There, hovering poised between the upper and lower plinths was a gem, teardrop in shape, with its light nearly extinguished, without color. Beside it floated its very obvious twin, multicolored and long ago shattered by means and hands unknown to any of those present. But, this second teardrop gem was not entirely complete. A single piece was missing, and it burned both bright and dark upon the wrist of the woman who had crossed space and time to bring her husband back, for her son, and for herself.

Sehlín's smile curdled and her brow furrowed as Elise bore down, but it wasn't enough; the gem that was whole dimmed again, and the woman who had crossed space and time hit the hard white floor with a gut-wrenching crack, as though something falling from a great height had dropped upon her.

The Death fragment snapped into place.

Sehlín released her grip and straightened the front of her uniform, then turned her placid gaze toward Thomas. The orb's light rose once again.

"*It's not too late!*" Alora heard it say.

Sky blue enveloped the room, and she saw herself quiver at the pulse of a stun cartridge, trip and fall amongst the rose petals, run through the trees and bracken along the lakeside, dig, dig for her secret place and see there her mother's image smiling up.

Somewhere else, Sehlín was reaching for the orb again, staring down at the helpless man she'd already beaten within a hairsbreadth of life.

Alora fought to know what was there, what she had left behind, what she needed. The blue intensified and she was there, by the waterside, and in the box were the fragments of Alora's Tear.

"I understand!" *she shouted, and the lake vanished.*

With feet light as a bird's wing she leapt before the lake was even gone. Leapt as he had leapt toward her.

"Take care of them for me."

And now her hands were clasped around it, a brittle broken thing, fragile and somehow sad. She remembered what had taken her to the lakeside, what had healed the scratches where Elise had drawn blood, what had given her the time to escape at all, and what had shown it all to her now.

Sehlín's hand was on the gem that was whole and her face was grim. She pulled against the forces that held it in place, and Alora watched as lights grew bright and burst into showers of flame all across Basin City. Sehlín pulled again and the gem dimmed. The multipart Tear began to slip from Alora's grasp, moving toward its twin. The light grew in the gem that was whole, struggling to shine in Sehlín's grip.

"It's time to let me go."

The gem that was whole succumbed to Sehlín's command and another flare erupted across the city. Alora's hands grew warm, then hot, then searing, but she held on.

Light of colors multivariate, heat that was icy cold, forces that pushed and pulled and crushed and stretched, exploded from the thing in her outstretched arms. She closed her eyes, and saw them, felt them, took them, one by one into her arms: Líana, Elise, Thomas. For she could now see there was more than enough space, enough time, enough life. And there had already been too much death.

CHAPTER THIRTY-TWO

Unanswered

"Now gods damn it, Leltan!" Dansil heard John of Dalstone erupt. "Reports have half o' the kingdom sidewise if I've heard a word. I can't be here waitin' on Thomas's princeling babe with Norill runnin' up and down, from hell to breakfast!"

"Be that as it may," a second voice began, "he *has* a wet nurse, and I'm not entirely without charges of my own. Askon left me with essentially the entirety of Tolarenz to care for, monitor—"

"Gods. Damn. It. Leltan!" John repeated, and Dansil found himself smiling and shaking at the same time. "You think I don't know that already? That we haven't been over it a dozen times more than either of us cares to?"

With a trembling step Dansil willed himself forward, and John's next words, as well as Leltan's reply, were lost in the rustle of his movements through vine and hedge, tree and grass and fading flower. He made his slow way through the living maze of the Tolarenz town hall garden, going now left, now right, toward the sound of the bickering. Above him, and above the arches of the garden itself, a rapid flutter of wings rippled off in the direction Dansil was headed. He checked again that his fresh clothes had remained so. Around the next corner, the corridor widened and stretched out to what seemed like an ending. Approaching the exit, Dansil swallowed hard, and heard John's voice again.

"Oh! By the king's codpiece, as if my day couldn't get any worse! Now *you're* here?!"

Stunned and still shaking uncontrollably, Dansil stopped a dozen steps from the mouth of the tunnel's end. How had John seen? How had he known?

"Curdles the blood, it does," John went on. "Always starin' down, lookin' at me like I'm his next meal. Got half a mind to lob a rock at him when he starts that. See what I mean, Leltan? Look at him! I'd rather sleep in a boneyard than suffer those eyes."

"Sir," the other voice said, Leltan, Dansil presumed. "Marten is nothing more than an ordinary bird following its training. With Askon gone, it's not surprising to see that he's returned home."

A deep breath that Dansil hadn't known he was holding, rushed out of him all at once.

"Who's there?" John asked. And this time there was no doubting where the question was directed.

Dansil took one step, then another, and emerged from the hallway of vines and leaves into the cool morning sun. At a small table spread with the remnants of a breakfast, John sat sprawling over his chair, a look borne of too much tedium imprinted upon his face. Leltan sat in a chair opposite him, sipping at a teacup. Behind them, one corner of the Tolarenz town hall filled the remainder of the space, its carefully crafted woodwork transitioning to rough-hewn stone. As Dansil emerged into the light, the look vanished, replaced with an open-mouthed amalgam of wonder and indignation, a sweet sight indeed, if Dansil was any judge.

"Dansil," John said as if he'd forgotten the name and only just remembered it. "What in the—"

The side of the Tolarenz town hall exploded in a shower of broken stone, splintered wood, and a rain of shattered shards of glass. The last thing Dansil saw was the debris colliding with John and Leltan, overturning their table, scattering its contents and sending them both to the ground in a cloud of dust. Then he felt himself swept up in the chaos, overturned by its force and sent tumbling into the garden vines. His head hit something solid, and for a moment there was nothing.

Ears ringing and eyes unfocused, Dansil awoke in the rubble of the Tolarenz town hall. A swift wind blew away the dusty clouds while a wild, sideways rain spattered his face and the surrounding destruction, mixing earth and stone dust into a gritty paste. He blinked and coughed and tried to wipe his hands clean, but the more effort he gave, the more the stuff clung to him.

A dizzy wave rolled over him and the wind and rain went suddenly silent. Far above, a falcon circled and the sun shone down. Pain lanced along his spine and jaw. Squinting through the pangs, he brought his eyes into focus. The town hall lay sundered, its northern side in ruins. The twisted wreckage of the little metal table where he'd last seen John lay smoking at the center of the larger scene.

All around, the clearing was blanketed with an uncountable sea of broken bits of glass. Dansil looked down and saw the toll it had taken on his own hands, which were slashed and scratched up to his elbows. Like a sparkling layer of hoarfrost, the glass covered everything. At its center John writhed next to Leltan and three additional prone forms.

Before them, with her back to the others, stood a woman with brown skin and wide almond eyes, standing as if nothing at all had happened, untouched and clean in strange tight-fitting garb. A circlet of copper glinted upon her forehead, pinning her chestnut hair down to where it curled past pointed ears and fell to her shoulders.

In her outstretched hands she held something white-knuckled in their grip. The hands trembled, released, and a stone fell with a brittle sound into the shattered glass. Prismatic colors rippled across the clearing for a moment in rings like waves in a pond. For a heartbeat that stretched beyond reason, the world glittered.

The woman stared down at the place where the stone had fallen. Then she looked up, directly into Dansil's eyes.

"Did I protect them?" she asked.

Acknowledgements

This one has been a bear, a battle, a lost cause, a white-knuckle ride that threatened to break loose at any moment. It has seen the end of a nightmare, a pandemic, a breath of hope, and a new nightmare, same as the old. There were times when I was convinced it would never be done, times when the threads had drifted so distant that I couldn't say if I would ever be able to pull them back together again.

But Askon's voice never left me; Elise soldiered on despite her brutal treatment of herself, a feeling not too unfamiliar; Líana grounded the narrative; and Dansil, Dansil made me smile when there was *only* inside, *only* social distancing, and *only* pixellated faces in grids, hinting at the life on the other side of cheap webcams. So, as weird as it might seem, I thank them: these imaginary, invented, very *very* real characters who live, as they say, rent free, in my head.

My appreciation goes out to Zoë, my editor, who always knows just the right way to tell me I'm wrong; to James (and Richie) for helping with Dansil and with Tinley; and to Isis, who came out of book cover retirement eight years after the fact to paint a perfectly battered Elise and wonderful realization of Basin City beyond.

I thank my family and friends: my kids, Derek, and the real Alora who has now read the books that bear her name and her mother's name; Bryan and Rayce and Chris and *Chris* and Joe, whose antics at the DnD table kept the fires of fantasy worlds burning when Vladvir's boundaries had grown vague and insubstantial in my mind; to Kel, of course, because *of course*, always, every single minute; and to Darliss, a colleague and friend who taught me to find patience, kindness, perspective. If I regret anything about the length of time it has taken to get this book right, it is that she will sadly never get to see it. I thank her for reading, as I thank anyone who has read even a single chapter of this series.

Your eyes on these pages make it all real, another tale that we humans share, another small story in the long story of us— and I am so grateful to be your storyteller.

About the Author

Nathan spends most of his working days with the students of Genesee Junior-Senior High School in Genesee, Idaho. Whether it's essay structure, a classic literary work, an invisible ball of energy and deep breathing on stage, or the occasional impromptu dance routine, he strives to keep students interested in the fun and the fundamentals of the English language.

When he's not teaching, he wears a number of hats, though the one that says "Dad" is the most careworn and cherished (it says "Husband" on the back). It hangs on a hook in a house where music is a constant and *computers* means both the object and the language. Most of them say "Apple" somewhere on their *aluminium* facades. Nearby, the family gathers for a favorite show or an hour of Zelda, and from time to time it is said that he ventures into the mysterious realm called *outside*, though the occasion is less rare these days. Afterall, outdoor walks count as exercise, and why not when you are lucky enough to live in such a beautiful place as Moscow.

Sign up for Nathan's newsletter:
www.barhamink.com/subscribe

Connect with Nathan:
Website: barhamink.com
       natebarham.com